PETER MARABELL

THE FINAL ACT OF CONRAD NORTH

A MICHAEL RUSSO MYSTERY

for Justin, Jillian, Maren, and Simon

"Fate was working its ass off when it got us all together."
— Elmore Leonard

"Justice is never given; it is extracted."
— A. Philip Randolph

1

I could have said no when Sandy answered the office phone. I heard her say, "Yes, I remember you." I looked up from the file I was reading and Sandy silently mouthed, "Patricia Geary," then gave me a look that asked "Yea or nay?"

I nodded and took the call. Three hours later, I pulled off U.S. 31 in Traverse City and slowed for the traffic on Front Street.

I'd first met Geary almost two years ago, when she was a key figure in the murder investigation of a Mackinac Island woman who was my client. Geary called to hire me, she said, for a "personal matter." She wanted to talk about Annie North, her lover who'd disappeared without a trace some years before. But that meant, eventually, we'd have to deal with Annie's ex-husband Conrad North, who happened to be suspect number one in the death of my client back then.

Geary was Senior Vice President of Boardman Bank & Trust. The bank building, on Front Street in the center of town, didn't look any more appealing on this crisp October afternoon than it had the last time I saw it. It was short on style and long on glass and chrome. It felt like 1970s suburbia had invaded northern Michigan a half-century late.

Patricia Geary met me outside her third floor office after the receptionist told her I'd arrived. I said hello as we shook hands. Geary was stocky, about five-seven, with clear blue eyes and salt-and-pepper hair pulled into a long ponytail. She wore a conservative two-piece business suit, black, over an ecru silk shirt.

"Good to see you again," she said, but it didn't sound that way. Geary pointed down the hallway.

Her office was a large, square room with wood floors, Oriental rugs and a huge mahogany desk that sat in front of a wall of windows overlooking West Bay. It was a pleasant contrast to the sharp angles in the rest of the building.

"Have a seat," she said.

"Thank you," I said and sat down.

Geary fingered a manila folder on the desk, then handed it over.

"What is it?" I asked.

"Everything I know about Annie."

"About her disappearance, you mean?"

"About her murder, Mr. Russo," she said, a sharp edge to her voice. "I didn't get you down here ..." Geary pulled back her next words. She folded her hands, like a church steeple, in front of her mouth. Tears dotted the corners of her blue eyes.

"I'm sorry, Mr. Russo," she said.

"It's all right. We've been here before."

"Yes, we have, but Annie was murdered. I loved her, you know that." I nodded. "You talk to the cops lately?"

Geary gestured at the file in my lap. "It's all there. The police said she disappeared. They still say that."

I glanced at the folder. "Police reports?"

She nodded.

"They're usually not that accommodating."

Geary smiled. "It was their way to shut me up."

"Uh-huh," I said.

"No new leads, or witnesses, or information. Nothing. The cops have given up."

"But you haven't."

"No," Geary said as she shook her head.

"If you think Annie's dead, Ms. Geary, how can I help you?"

"I have to know what happened to her. You know all the players, Mr. Russo. I need closure, resolution. Call it what you like, but I have to know."

"One thing," I said, "what if Annie's not dead ..."

"She's dead, Mr. Russo. Conrad killed her. You prove that, the cops will reopen the case."

"The police couldn't prove it," I said. "What makes you think I can?"

"You can do things," she said. "I called because you have ways to get things done." I saw a small grin, barely noticeable. "The police are, what's the word, more constrained?"

I thought about that, but let it go.

"You know where Conrad is now?"

She shook her head. "I kept track of him after he left Mackinac Island, but I had to stop. I was obsessing about the man."

I leaned forward and considered Patricia Geary for a moment. She was thoughtful and sincere. But, she fell in love with a woman caught in an ugly drama directed by a very bad man.

"What if Annie really went missing," I said, "really wanted to disappear? Are you ready for that?"

Geary straightened her shoulders and stared at me for a moment.

"I want closure, Mr. Russo, whatever that means."

"It won't be enough," I said.

"I need closure."

"All right," I said.

"How much will your services cost?" she said, taking a small checkbook from a desk drawer. "Fees and expenses?"

I told her.

Geary wrote a check and handed it to me.

We shook hands. "I'll call when I have something."

I took the file and went for the door.

"Mr. Russo."

I turned around. Tears slowly streamed down Geary's face.

"You're right," she said, angry now. "Closure is not enough. Conrad North murdered Annie, goddamn it. Get him for it."

2

I stopped in the lobby, at one of those high-top tables people use to fill out deposit slips, and opened the file. The first page read: "Detective Vincente Diaz. TVC police." Geary knew where I'd go first. I leafed through the other sheets. She said they were detective reports. Plenty of time for those later.

I left downtown, got in line with the traffic on 8th Street and caught Woodmere going south. The Traverse City Police shared a nondescript two-story building with the Sheriff's Department. Neither organization particularly liked the arrangement, but small-town politics seldom respected what people liked.

I stopped at the desk just inside the main door.

"I'm here to see Detective Diaz."

"And you are?" said a middle-aged woman who'd repeated the question once too often over the years.

"Michael Russo, private investigator from Petoskey."

"Is the Detective expecting you?" she said, staring off someplace.

"No," I said. "But tell him it's about Annie North."

The woman sighed, picked up the desk phone and punched some numbers.

"There's a PI here to see you. Wait, I'll ask. What's your name again?"

I told her. She repeated it into the phone.

"What case did you say?"

She'd heard so many answers she didn't listen anymore. I told her again, remaining polite, just to be nice.

"Yes, sir," she said, and put the phone down. She handed me a tag that read "visitor" to hang around my neck.

"Through that door," she said, pointing over my shoulder.

"Thanks."

I heard an obnoxious buzz and pushed the heavy door open. Four small, glass-walled cubicles lined a short hallway with worn gray carpet. The hall opened into a large room filled with desks, noisy machines and cops.

Out of an office on the right came a man who had to be Detective Vincente Diaz. He was big, six-two at least, and 215 soft pounds. His black hair was thin and combed straight back with a touch of gray at the temples. He had the long arms and big hands of guy who'd played competitive basketball at some point in his life. But not recently.

"Detective Diaz?" I said.

Diaz nodded and reached out. As we shook hands I noticed a tattoo on the back of his hand. A Bowie knife, the huge, heavy knife made famous at the battle of the Alamo.

"This way." He turned on his heels and went back into his office. I followed.

The office décor, if that's the right word, was a faded institutional green. The Detective's desk was mostly dented metal with a Formica top, covered with several stacks of manila file folders. He never offered, so I took one of the two chairs in front of the desk. A five-drawer file cabinet leaned against the wall to my left. Nothing decorative adorned the walls or his desk. No artwork, no pictures of the grandkids. Nothing. Either he had no interests outside the office or he was on the edge of retirement. Or both.

Diaz's face was dark and heavy with experience. His eyes were small and tired, his nose wide and mashed-looking, owing to repeated breaks. The man had worn out a long time ago.

"You have something on the North case?"

"No," I said, shaking my head.

"Then what're bothering me for?" Diaz said. "That case went cold a long time ago. I told her …" He paused, let out a lot of air and smiled a most insincere smile. "I've told Ms. Geary several times there's nothing new on the disappearance of Annora North."

That was too polite even for a cop on the edge of retirement.

"Patricia Geary hired me to find out what happened to Annie North. It was your case," I said, "so you're the best place to start."

"Did you tell her she's wasting her money? Did you? What the hell you going to do that I didn't do?"

Years ago, Diaz knew a fresh pair of eyes was exactly what a dead case needed. Not anymore.

I took a breath and pushed on.

"Do you think Conrad North killed his wife?"

"Think I'd be sitting here if I knew that?"

"Do you know where Conrad is now?"

Diaz shook his head. "No idea," he said. "Kept track of the prick for a while. A waste of my time."

A waste of time for a cop? Following a murder suspect? I was getting annoyed.

Speaking of wasting time … "How about this? Tell me what you know, what you think happened, I quit bothering you. I'm out of here."

Diaz climbed out of his chair and went to the file cabinet. He opened the second drawer, pulled out a thick file and dropped it in front of me.

"It's all there," he said, gesturing at the file. It was almost two inches thick, more than twice the size of Geary's file. The cops took something out of her copy.

"You want I should read it here?" I said. "Make notes? That kind of thing?"

"You out of your fucking mind?" Diaz said.

Now I was getting someplace. I pushed some more.

"Shouldn't take me more than a couple of hours, Detective. I need to learn all I can, after all."

Diaz rubbed his forehead. "Take the damn thing. It's back here in a week or I'll toss your ass behind bars. Understood?"

Cops didn't hand over files, not easily. He really did not want to deal with Geary or the case. I stared at the file.

"Go on. Get out of here. I don't like guys coming down here, telling me I'm not doing my job. One week."

I picked up the file, but I didn't get out of the chair.

"One more thing," I said.

"Jesus," Diaz said.

"I'll read the file, but I want to hear it from you."

"Yeah?"

"What do you think happened to Annie North?"

Diaz pointed at the folder. "It's in the file."

I ignored him. "Did Conrad North kill Annie North or didn't he?"

Diaz took in air and let it out slowly.

"What's the question again?"

This man needed to retire. Soon.

"Did Conrad North kill his spouse or not? There it is, in plain English. Did he kill Annie North?"

Diaz smirked. "Damn right he killed her."

For a moment I was taken aback. Not sure why. Patricia Geary certainly believed that.

"Then why isn't he in jail?"

I was frustrated.

"Because we couldn't prove it."

"You ever tell Patricia Geary you believed North was guilty?"

Diaz shook his head.

"Why not?" I said. My irritation with this guy wasn't going away any time soon.

"Look," Diaz said, glancing to his left like someone was listening. "We weren't sure about her."

"What? You weren't sure about what?"

Diaz shrugged. "We didn't … they were …"

I sat forward. "You telling me because the two women were lovers, Geary was unreliable?"

Diaz sat, stone-faced then shook his head. "Geary wouldn't accept that the woman might have run out on her. You know, just up and left. Made her unreliable. I don't like dealing with people like that."

"You let a murder case go cold because you didn't like the woman who filed the complaint? Is that what you're telling me?"

Diaz stood. "The file's back in a week, now get out of here."

I tucked the file beneath my arm and left.

I waved at the receptionist on my way out. She glanced up but didn't smile.

I found my car in the lot and beeped the locks. I sat there with the two folders on the passenger seat.

So Diaz didn't like Patricia Geary. He believed Conrad North was a killer, but he didn't want to deal with a lesbian? Seriously? Couldn't have been the first person, gay or straight, he didn't like. Got to believe he ran a good case. Giving up after all the leads were dead was one thing, but not running a good case? I didn't accept that.

I looked down at the folders. I was more curious why Geary's file was thinner.

I hit the start button and the BMW's twin-turbo growled to life. Got to love performance cars. I always have. Putting them through their paces smoothly and quickly was something I understood and did well every time. Which was more than I could say for the way this case had taken off.

3

"**W**ait," Sandy said. "The cop in charge of the case doesn't know where suspect number one is? Is that what you just said?"

The trip home from Traverse City took longer than usual. There was more traffic traveling 131 than I would have expected on an early October afternoon.

I had a date with Sandy and AJ at a four-top near the front window of City Park Grill. Sandy had a draft, AJ a Chardonnay and me an Oban. We shared an appetizer, coddled ostrich eggs with hollandaise.

"I hope you went back at him," AJ said, always reacting like the tough, experienced reporter she was. "The case might be cold, but it's still a big case in a small town."

I shrugged with my palms up.

"Don't shrug at me," she said, loud enough that two women at the next table glanced our way. "Cops don't get off the hook that easily."

"You're beautiful when you're mad. Have I ever told you that?"

"Don't change the subject."

"He can tell me I'm beautiful," Sandy said.

"You be quiet," she said to Sandy. Then, back at me, "Answer my question."

"I think I need another drink."

"How 'bout you take your scotch to Hemingway's end of the bar and drink it there?" According to local legend, the Nobel laureate thought up his best story ideas at the far end of the heavy mahogany bar.

"Maybe he'll inspire you to act like a real investigator," AJ said.

"Come on, AJ," Sandy said, smiling, "give the poor guy a break. Let him talk."

AJ shook her head slowly and said, "All right, all right. Let's hear it."

I sipped my scotch and leaned on the table. "The annoying conversation with Detective Diaz went nowhere fast." I offered details. "I'll have another shot at him," I said. "By that time, I should know more."

I looked over at AJ. She took a deep breath.

"Okay for now," she said. "How about you, Sandy?"

Sandy nodded. "Sure, it's okay. But we do need more information."

The waiter stopped by and we ordered dinner.

"I'll have the wedge salad," Sandy said. AJ chose the salmon BLT, and I took the whitefish sandwich.

The waiter picked up our menus and left.

AJ put her hand on my arm and smiled. "Sorry I barked, Michael. So what do you think Diaz is up to?"

"Could be anything," I said, and sipped some scotch. "Only one thing's for sure: he got pissed off when I started asking questions."

"Cops like to ask the questions," AJ said, "not the other way around. This is an unsolved case, and it's his unsolved case."

"Maybe that's all there is to it," I said.

"Where're the case files?" Sandy asked.

"In the car."

"Obviously the first order of business is to figure out why the cop's file is fatter than Geary's copy."

The waiter arrived and put down our dinners. "Enjoy," he said.

"Could be she has a summary of the reports," AJ said. "I've seen cops do that before."

"Probably all it is," I said.

"I can't understand why Diaz gave you his file," AJ said. "That's hardly police procedure." She picked up her glass but didn't take a drink. "Either Diaz is up to something, or he's as burned out as you say."

"Only one way to find out," I said. "Read the files."

"I'll start first thing in the morning," Sandy said. "Right now, this salad has my attention."

AJ raised her glass. "A toast."

"To what?" I said, and we clicked glasses.

"To us. Crime fighters back on the trail."

I laughed. "A little over the top, don't you think?"

"I like the sound of it anyway," Sandy said, and dug into her salad.

We sat quietly for a few minutes, enjoying dinner and each other's company. The three of us often spent time together, but it was usually in the office. The restaurant offered a pleasant change. Our visit also marked something of a milestone: the first time AJ did not remind everyone within earshot that the City Park Grill began life in the 1880s as a men's-only bar.

Our waiter stopped by. "Is everything prepared to your satisfaction?"

We gave him three thumbs-up, and AJ ordered another Chardonnay.

"Assume for a minute," AJ said, "that the files hold no surprises."

"Okay," I said.

"What's next?"

"Being the crack private eye that I am, we take information from the files, add it to what little we remember from two years ago, and put the puzzle together."

"What puzzle is that?" AJ asked.

"What happened to Annie North," I said. "Is she alive or dead? That's where we start."

"No, it's not," Sandy said.

"It's not?" I said.

"Nope. First we find Conrad North."

"Why first?"

"Because we'll get to him eventually," she said. "Let's track him for a while, see what he's up to, who he hangs out with. That kind of thing. Before he knows we're interested."

"You'd make a good reporter," AJ said. "You have the instincts for it."

Sandy smiled and raised her glass as a thank you.

"You want me on that, boss?"

"Well," I said, "you know how to find people, but I'd rather you start with those files."

"I'll get Henri then," she said, always thinking one step ahead.

Henri LaCroix was a friend to us all and a landlord on Mackinac Island. He often dropped by when his particular skills, skills finely tuned in Army Ranger School, the Middle East, and Blackwater, proved useful. Or necessary.

"Do we know where he is?"

"Probably on the island," Sandy said. "I'll find him."

The waiter cleared the table, and AJ asked for a dessert menu.

"Dessert?" Sandy said. "Time for me to go home."

"Ah, come on," AJ said, smiling. "Be a sport. We'll have something sweet and gooey."

"You have something sweet and gooey. I don't need the calories."

Sandy got up from the table. "Remember, boss, I'm stopping at the courthouse in the morning."

I nodded. "Coffee will be ready when you get there."

The waiter returned after Sandy was gone.

"I changed my mind," AJ said to the waiter. "I'll just finish my wine."

He nodded and left the table.

"Sure you don't want dessert?" I said.

"Next time. Are you coming home with me tonight?"

"I'd like that," I said. "You have something sweet and gooey in mind?"

AJ rolled her eyes and took my hand.

"I always have you in mind, dear," she said.

"Uh-huh."

"Okay if we sit for a minute?"

"Sure."

She hesitated, then said, "It's just, well, I want to talk about Patricia Geary."

"What about her?"

AJ sipped some wine. "This won't be easy."

"You mean finding Annie North?"

AJ nodded. "It won't be easy learning what happened."

I sat back, not sure where AJ was going with this.

"You could be bogged down for a long time," she said.

"Maybe," I said, then waited a moment.

"AJ, you're beating around the bush."

She glanced off, into the middle of the restaurant like she'd seen a familiar face.

"What're you worried about, AJ?"

She took a deep breath. "I'm worried about Camille North."

Camille North was Conrad's second wife, married long after Annie had disappeared.

"Camille North's dead, AJ. Patricia Geary is my client."

"But Camille was your client when Conrad had her killed."

"A fact I've never forgotten, thank you very much."

"Don't get short with me, Michael."

"What's your point, AJ?"

"My point?" She leaned in close and almost whispered, "Patricia Geary just gave you a chance to get even. That's the point."

"Yes," I said, "she did. Conrad needs to answer for Camille."

"The cops didn't put him away for killing Camille, the prosecutors didn't make the case. But somehow you think you're responsible for a killer on the loose?"

"Yes."

"Conrad's smart, Michael. He beat everybody." She sat back and put her hand on mine. "I know it's personal for you. What if he beats you this time, too?"

I shook my head. "Won't happen."

"You'll put him away?"

"Yes."

We sat quietly for a few moments, holding hands.

"Come on," AJ said. "Let's go."

It was a crisp, clear night. The last slivers of light cut through the trees from the west, highlighting clusters of red and gold leaves. Only a few people moved on the sidewalks near Lake and Howard.

"My car's over there," AJ said, pointing at the parking lot across the street.

"You have to be out early?"

"Yeah," she said. "Meeting first thing."

"I'm going to run in the morning, so I'll leave early, too."

She put her arms around my waist and pulled me close. "You feel good, darling," she said. "Get in the car."

AJ hit the SUV's start button, then reached over and put a hand on my cheek.

"Conrad's a dangerous man, Michael. Don't forget that."

4

"**W**here're you going?" AJ said, easing the covers away from her face. So much for trying to slip out of bed quietly.

"Have to go to work."

"Me, too," she said and sat up, holding the sheet across her chest.

I found my clothes scattered on the floor.

"Or you could do that thing to my nipples like last night," she said, letting the sheet fall to her lap.

I smiled. "How about a rain check for tonight?"

"Okay," she said, and fell back on the bed, pulling the covers over her head. I heard a muffled "Good-bye" from somewhere under there.

I dressed quietly and went out the back door. A dull, gray light in the eastern sky tried to break through the thick October clouds. The morning air was heavy and spit rain. I tugged at the collar of my jacket and stuffed my hands in the pockets.

AJ's renovated two-story Victorian sat above the ravine on Bay Street, an easy four-block walk to my apartment. Wet leaves littered the ground, red and yellow and green and brown, glistening in the light of the streetlamps.

I lived in a two-bedroom on the second floor of a small building at the end of Howard Street. From the living room it had a decent view of Harbor Springs across Little Traverse Bay, and it was a mere seven-minute walk from my Lake Street office.

I changed into running gear and took the rear stairs outside. The wind had picked up off the bay. I wore a Gore-Tex jacket over a T-shirt in case the rain let go.

I loosened my leg muscles on the curvy, tree-lined streets of Bay View, a nineteenth-century collection of Victorian cottages on the edge of Petoskey. Most of the buildings were closed for the winter, water lines drained, shutters latched, vulnerable shrubs wrapped tightly in burlap. Off-season remodeling had begun with the arrival of construction crews around the neighborhood.

Annie North had disappeared a long time ago: if she'd wanted to vanish, she would have needed help. It would be worth talking to old friends and co-workers.

Once Sandy finished reading the two files, we'd know what the police cut out of Geary's copy. I doubted that Detective Diaz missed anything during his investigation, but if he did, we'd find it.

Fifty-eight minutes later, I clicked off my watch and walked the last two blocks home. The light rain was steady now, but it felt good and cooled my face.

I finished a hot shower while the coffee cooked in the kitchen. I put on a freshly ironed pair of khakis, a red-and-white striped button-down shirt and a navy cotton crewneck. The perfect attire for October sleuthing in northern Michigan.

I was at the small table in the kitchen with coffee and my iPad reading the *New York Times* when my phone lit up. A one-word text from Sandy: "Johan's." Our favorite bakery would be supplying breakfast this morning.

I put the dishes in the dishwasher, grabbed my brief bag and a parka. The rain hadn't let up. I pulled up the hood, walked up Howard and took a shortcut through the parking lot. *Michael Russo Investigations* occupied a two-room office on the second floor of a Lake Street building I'd bought in 1998. Fran Warren's Mackinac Sandal Company rented the retail space at street level.

I was at my desk reading Steve Rattner on the *Times'* op-ed page when Sandy arrived.

"Breakfast is here," she said. "Keep your mitts off the cinnamon donuts."

I went to the front office and opened the box from Johan's.

"Geez, Sandy, how many people you expecting?"

"At least three."

"Three?"

"Henri took the first boat off the island. Something about a Home Depot run."

"Should we wait for him to eat?"

"We only wait if it's National Peanut Butter Day."

"That's in February."

"Then I'll have a donut."

"You skipped dessert last night, but you need a donut now?"

Sandy rolled her eyes, put a cinnamon donut on a napkin and filled a mug with coffee. I took a J-bun and coffee to a chair by the tall windows that overlooked Lake Street. The rain was steady and only a few people moved on the sidewalk, sticking close to the storefronts. Red and gold maple leaves gusted by on the wind.

"You read the files last night?"

"Most of them before I fell asleep," she said, and drank some coffee.

"Anything?"

"Besides the awful writing, you mean?"

"It's a police report, Sandy. What'd you expect, Scott Fitzgerald?"

"At least Hemingway."

"Give it a rest," I said.

"The cops added enough macho posturing to give Papa a run for his money."

I let that go and ate a large chunk of cinnamon roll instead.

"One thing, boss, the files? Patricia Geary's copy?"

"Yeah?"

"Summaries, rewrites. That's all."

"Not copies?"

Sandy shook her head. "No. That's what I meant about the macho language. Some cop rewrote the original report, the important interviews anyway, threw in a few diagrams and a couple of charts. So a ten-page report in the original file ends up being one page in Geary's copy."

"How about the Diaz file?"

"Standard police work. No surprises. Same boring stuff I've read before."

Sandy picked up her donut, smiled and took a big bite.

"So they gave Geary a doctored police report," I said. "Geary thought they were trying to shut her up ... guess she wasn't being paranoid."

"Sounds about right," Sandy said, "but it didn't work."

"Nope."

We heard someone on the stairs. The door opened and in came Henri LaCroix. He was six-three, 230 trained pounds with the angular good looks of a movie hero. He was smart, articulate and intuitive. His handgun, in a shoulder holster hung on his left side, was as much a part of his wardrobe as jeans and a Carhartt jacket. He was occasionally underestimated but never overmatched.

"Morning," he said, and looked at the open Johan's box. Henri hung his jacket on the hall tree and filled a mug with coffee. He picked up a cheese Danish and took the chair next to me.

"Been to Home Depot yet?" I said.

Henri shook his head. "This afternoon. Figured I'd see what you two were up to first."

"Not much," Sandy said.

Henri looked over at me.

"We've just started. Don't know a lot."

"In other words, you're off to your usual slow start."

"Bingo," Sandy said. "Fill him in, boss. I need more coffee."

I gave Henri the details. It didn't take long.

"So Geary's file is basically useless."

"Pretty much," Sandy said as she sat back down.

"But there's nothing nefarious going on, right?"

"Not unless you count the cops pulling a fast one on her."

Henri shrugged. "Routine cop bullshit."

"On the other hand," Sandy said, "the Diaz file is full of names, full of people who knew Annie North."

"Make a list of the names," I said. "Ask Geary for names, too. See if the two lists match."

"I already started a list," Sandy said, "but some of the names will be old. People move all the time. Or die."

"Still a good place to start," Henri said. "We'll sort the names out."

"What do we do about Conrad North?" Sandy said.

Henri laughed. "Now there's a familiar name."

"He should be at the top of our list," Sandy said.

"Agreed," Henri said.

"Thank you," Sandy said, leaning forward for a fist-bump.

"Of course, the minute North knows we're interested," Henri said, "he'll start being careful. I'd like to find out what he does and who he does it with first."

"Good idea," I said.

"Think he's still in northern Michigan?" Henri said.

"Well, he's not in Lake Forest any longer," Sandy said. "He sold the house. I checked."

"The tax rolls list a new owner?" I said.

Sandy nodded.

"Anybody we know?"

"Not a familiar name."

"He sell it recently?"

"A year ago, I think. I'd have to check my notes."

"What about those two sons of his?" Henri said. "Don't remember their names."

"Ah, Wolfgang and Wilhelm," I said.

"How could I forget? Didn't they work at a family plant outside Chicago?"

"Mostly they trailed after daddy," I said, "and tried to be tough guys."

"Anything on them, Sandy?" Henri said.

"Didn't check."

"Might be a better idea to look for them first," Henri said. "They're a lot dumber than their father. Certainly not as careful."

Sandy raised an index finger and pointed at Henri. "Which might lead us straight to daddy."

Henri smiled.

"That assumes the boys still tag along," I said.

"Want to bet good money they don't?" Sandy said.

I shook my head.

"All right then," Sandy said, "Wolfgang and Wilhelm move to the top of our list."

I stood up and leaned on the window frame. The rain was coming down harder now, the sidewalks empty. "Nobody's on the street."

"It's October, boss."

"And it's raining," Henri said.

I turned around. "You two are no fun. I was just noticing the difference ... oh, never mind. If you don't like my observations about rain, let's get to work."

"Now you're talking," Henri said. "Do we have a plan?"

I shook my head. "No."

"No?"

"If you two would shut up for a minute," Sandy said.

Henri and I fell silent, not an easy task most of the time.

"While you were playing at vaudeville, I've been hard at work."

"On what?" I said.

"On Google," Sandy said. "Facebook, too."

"This better be good."

"Wolfgang North popped on both sites."

"He have a page?" Henri said.

Sandy shook her head. "No, not his own, but that's what makes it interesting. He has a girlfriend. She works for a company just north of town named Bristol Garden and Yard."

"They cut grass?" Henri said.

Sandy shook her head. "Things for the yard, benches, cement animals, birdbaths. They sell throughout the Midwest. Wolfgang and the woman appeared in photos. She has her own Facebook page, too. The usual romantic postings, top of the Empire State Building, Lincoln Park Zoo in Chicago, restaurants having dinner."

"This woman have a name?"

Sandy glanced back at her notes. "Doreen Masie."

"Know anything about her? Is she connected to the Norths?"

"You mean other than a romantic interest in Wolfgang?"

I nodded.

"Hard to tell, but I don't think so. She's assistant manager in Bristol's office. That comes from the company website."

"Was Conrad in any of the pictures?"

"Nope. Just the happy couple. Want me to find out more?"

"Yeah," I said. "I could follow her around, might lead us to Wolfgang. See what you can dig up on brother Wilhelm while you're at it."

"Okay," Sandy said. "I'll email Geary about Annie North's old friends when I finish up the names from the Diaz file."

"Put it on my desk when you're done. I'll take a look when I get back."

"Where're you going?"

"Thought I'd talk to Don Hendricks." Donald Hendricks was the twice-elected Emmet County Prosecutor. We'd worked together before, sometimes easy, sometimes not.

"About a missing person in Traverse City?" Sandy said.

"He knows a lot of people down there."

"Want me to call his office?"

I nodded.

"Henri?"

"Yeah?"

"You want to look for Conrad?"

"Be my pleasure."

"All right," I said, "let's get to it."

Henri took his jacket and went for the door.

"Henri."

"Yeah?"

"Stay under the radar as long as you can. When Conrad finds out you're on him, he'll call in a shooter."

Henri smiled. "Hope so."

5

"The prosecutor has a few minutes right now," Sandy said. "He's gone the rest of the day."

I dropped my feet to the floor and pushed back from the desk. "Guess I'd better hustle up there."

"So you're coming back here after Hendricks?"

"Plan to, why?"

"I'll make sure the Diaz list of names is on your desk."

"Thanks."

I took my rain jacket off the hall tree and went down the stairs.

The rain had eased into a steady drizzle, but it wasn't going away any time soon. I yanked at the jacket collar, stuffed my hands into the pockets and headed up Lake Street.

The drizzle discouraged all but a few brave people who roamed the sidewalks, staring into store windows. There were so few cars moving on the streets, I didn't wait for the light at Lake and Howard. It was one of the small pleasures of the off season. Most of the stores in the busy Gaslight District operated all year, but even they cut their hours as early fall eased its way into November, a brief respite between summer and the Christmas holidays.

The offices for Emmet County, the Court House, the Sheriff's Office and jail in the Bodzick wing, occupied a half-block on Division between Lake and Bay streets.

I entered the building through the Lake Street doors and wound my way around to the prosecutor's office.

"Hello, Sherry," I said. Officially, Sherry Merkel was Assistant to the

Prosecutor. She'd been with Don Hendricks since he was first elected to office. Unofficially, she stood guard to the inner office. She kept the irrelevant and the annoying away from her boss.

"That's Ms. Merkel to you, *Sam Spade*."

I smiled. "You say the sweetest things."

I thought I saw a small grin on her face. Probably not.

"He's expecting me."

"I know," she said, dragging out the second word. She pointed at the door behind her like I'd never been here before.

I knocked once and opened the door.

Hendricks was on the phone. He pointed at the metal chairs in front of his desk. Like the walls, the carpet and everything else in the office, the chairs were some shade of faded green. I knew from experience they weren't particularly comfortable. I chose the closest one.

Donald Hendricks was a big man, better than six-two, with thinning brown hair and a soft face. Too much good food and too little exercise had taken their toll and gave him a rumpled look all the time.

"All right," Hendricks said into the phone and put the receiver down.

He tugged at his already-loosened tie and pushed his shirt sleeves back above the elbows. He took a deep breath, let it out slowly and looked at me.

"Russo," he said. In the no-nonsense world of the prosecutor, that passed for a friendly greeting.

"Thanks for the time, Don."

"You're welcome. What do you need?"

"Do I have to need something? Maybe I stopped by for a friendly chat."

"Russo," he said, and looked at his watch. "I have to drive up to Mackinaw City for a meeting I don't want to go to. Don't make my day worse."

I nodded. "Fair enough."

"So what can I do for you?"

"You remember Conrad North?"

"Hard man to forget."

"That he is," I said. "The man got away with murder."

"Don't remind me." Failing to prove Conrad guilty of killing Camille North never sat well with Hendricks. He started to say something else, but paused and waited for me.

"I might have something," I said.

Hendricks leaned forward, his elbows on the desk. "What does 'have something' mean?" His eyes focused, laser-tight, on me. "What do you know?"

"Remember Annie North?"

Hendricks tilted his head.

"Conrad's first wife?"

I nodded.

"The one who disappeared?"

"That's her," I said. "Remember the case?"

Hendricks shook his head. "Enlighten me."

I offered the condensed version.

He nodded slowly. "Did you take the Geary case to find a missing woman or get Conrad North?"

Hendricks was good at his job. He didn't miss much.

"Both," I said, so easily it surprised me.

"What do you want from me?"

"Two things," I said.

"What do I get in return?"

"Another shot at Conrad North."

Hendricks considered that for a moment. I bet he liked the idea as much as I did.

"I'm listening."

"Your office keeps track of Conrad, right?"

Hendricks shook his head.

"Anybody on the case?"

"There is no case, Russo. No active case anyway."

"How about the police?"

Hendricks shrugged. "I doubt it. Petoskey, the Sheriff's Office, I would've heard if they had something new."

"How about Fleener?"

Martin Fleener was captain of the Michigan State Police based in Petoskey. He was a smart, savvy homicide detective and a good man. His specialty was interrogation — and choosing elegant three-piece suits and handmade ties. We'd occasionally worked the same case.

"Haven't talked to him," Hendricks said, "but I doubt it."

"And no one from your office is on Conrad?"

"Already said no. Got plenty to do without hanging onto that arrogant prick."

"Can't say as I blame you. Any idea where he is?"

Hendricks laughed. "You're the PI, Russo. Expect us to do your job?" He laughed again, louder this time.

Guess I had that coming. I let it pass.

"You know Vincente Diaz? He's Traverse City Police."

"Know who he is," Hendricks said, "don't really know the man. Why?"

"Annie North is his case. He wasn't all that happy I asked him about it."

"I'm not surprised."

"Would it surprise you to learn Detective Diaz gave a heavily edited copy of the case file to Patricia Geary?"

"The Annie North file?"

I nodded.

"That's not standard procedure," he said, and picked up a pencil. He began tapping it, drummer style, on the desk. "What's 'heavily edited' mean?"

I told him.

Hendricks shook his head. "A series of memos? A case file turned into useless memos?"

"Yep."

"But he gave you the real file?"

I nodded.

"That's not standard procedure either."

"Nope."

"I hope you gave it back to him."

"Sandy put in registered mail herself."

Hendricks smiled. "I suspect the good detective was trying to ditch the Geary woman. Maybe you, too."

"Be my guess, for both of us," I said. "You have any contacts down there?"

Hendricks didn't hesitate.

"How about the Grand Traverse DA's office? That good enough?"

I nodded.

"Erica Todd. One of the assistants. She worked here for a year or two. Know her pretty well."

"Well enough to reach out to about Annie North?"

"You mean do an end run on Diaz?"

"Not that," I said. "But I'd like to know if the prosecutors have anything Diaz doesn't have."

"Or doesn't want to share. You pissed him off."

"All I did was ask questions."

"You questioned how well he did his job, Russo."

"Then why hold back? Wouldn't he want me to think he was on top of the case?"

"Maybe," Hendricks said. His pencil resumed drumming.

"What if the DA learned something, but thought Diaz was just playing out his string to retirement?"

Hendricks sat back in his chair and ran a hand over the top of his head like he had enough hair to smooth out.

"Okay," Hendricks said, "I'll give her a call. But it's a long shot any way you look at it."

"All I have are long shots, Don. The case is cold, the leads are dry, the cop in charge cares more about football and the chief suspect has disappeared."

"And you've been hired to fix all that."

"Uh-huh."

"Let's get one thing clear, Russo."

"Yeah?"

"They tell me something I can give you, I do it. They tell me there's nothing there, you get that too."

"Fair enough."

Hendricks leaned in and pointed a finger in my direction. "But if they tell me it's none of my business, well, that's what I do, mind my own business. Understood?"

"Understood."

"I have a good working relationship with the folks down there. I don't want to fuck it up. You hear me?"

I nodded. "I hear you."

"Are we done here?" Hendricks said, looking at his watch. "Mackinaw City, remember?"

I put my hands in the air like I was about to surrender. "I remember," I said, and stood up. "I'm outta here."

Sherry Merkel gave me a half-hearted wave. I said good-bye and went toward the Lake Street door.

Annie North, Camille North. Two cold cases. Annie disappeared and was presumed dead. Camille was shot to death on the streets of Mackinaw City and was quite dead.

Camille originally hired me to keep her family's East Bluff cottage on Mackinac Island out of Conrad's hands during their bitter divorce. She didn't live long enough to find out that her cottage did, indeed, remain with the family.

I doubted the Grand Traverse prosecutors had paid more attention to a missing persons case than Don Hendricks paid to a murder case. But Conrad North was linked to both cases, so it was worth a look.

6

I left the County Building and headed down Lake Street. The drizzle hadn't gone away, so I yanked the jacket zipper all the way up. My phone buzzed before I had walked a block. The screen read: "you talk?"

I tapped AJ's name and waited.

"Hey," she said, "where are you?"

"On my way to the office. What's up?"

"I'll be done at work in an hour or so," she said. "How about dinner?"

I stopped for traffic at Howard. "Love to, sweetheart, but duty calls." I told her about reading the Diaz file.

"Call me tonight," she said, clicking off as I headed up the stairs.

I shook my wet jacket, hung it on the hall tree and took a bottle of water from the refrigerator. Sandy had put the two files next to each other on my desk. On top of each was a list of names, one marked "Diaz" and the other "Geary." One name, Roland Crosley, was circled. Sandy had put a handwritten sticky note near that name: "call me first."

I called.

"Here's the thing," Sandy said. "A lot of information was left out of Geary's copy."

"We know that."

"But that name, Roland Crosley, the one I circled?"

"Yeah?" I said, and looked at the name again.

"It wasn't in the Diaz file or Geary's copy."

"You lost me."

"Patricia Geary emailed me her list of names," Sandy said. "People who were close to Annie North the day she disappeared. One name doesn't show up in either the cop's file or in Geary's copy, but it was on her email list. Want to guess which one?"

"Roland Crosley."

"Now you're catching on."

"I wonder why this Crosley guy wasn't mentioned in the official file of the case?"

"Good question."

"Think you might have missed him, Sandy?"

"I checked a second time."

"Well," I said, "it's been a few years. Maybe Geary's confused."

"Nonsense. Annie was her lover, the most important person in her life. She's been fueled by anger, hurt, whatever. She's not confused."

"I don't know, Sandy."

"She hired you, didn't she? She wants closure. Do you think she'd get a name wrong?"

"Maybe we should ask her who Roland Crosley is."

"I tried," Sandy said. "I didn't hear back. I'll call again in the morning."

We ended the call and I put the lists aside. I took a long drink of water and opened the Diaz file.

I wasn't sure what time it was when I heard someone on the stairs. I looked at my watch: it was after eight.

"Michael?" AJ said as she closed the door behind her and walked to my office.

"Hi," I said.

"Hi, yourself."

She put a large grocery store bag, a paper bag with handles, on the chair. "Are you at a good place to stop?"

I put a sticky note on the page, closed the Diaz file and leaned back in my chair. "Sure. I've had enough cop lingo for one day." I pointed at the bag. "What'd you bring?"

"A surprise."

"A surprise?" I said, and smiled. "You're going to put on a wildly sexy outfit and do lascivious things on the desk?"

"Maybe later," she said, reaching in the bag. She pulled out a bottle of Newton Chardonnay. "It's still cold." She reached into the pockets of her rain jacket and took out two wine glasses: each one was dark green, with a single trillium etched on the side.

"Here," she said, handing me the bottle. I opened it and filled the glasses.

"Horseradish cheese with crackers."

"Guess I forgot to eat."

"I figured," she said. "Have at it." She raised her glass and drank some wine.

I bit into a chunk of cheese. I was hungry. I picked up a second piece.

"What made you think I'd still be here?"

AJ smiled. "You're very predictable, darling. I knew you'd just keep at it. How's it going?"

"Okay. I'm almost done."

"Have you learned anything useful?"

I shrugged. "Depends." I recapped the details for AJ and added some wine to our glasses.

"That's not much to go on," she said.

"It certainly is not."

"But I think you're right. I think Geary's confused about that Crosley guy."

AJ cut off a small piece of cheese.

"When I used to write follow-up stories," she said, "so many people remembered things wrong. But I had the luxury of the original story. I could always double-check. People remember what they want to remember."

"Sandy's gonna call Geary in the morning, see what she has to say."

AJ nodded. "Can't hurt."

I rubbed my eyes and stood up. The wet leaf-plastered streets glistened in the drizzle. Even the parking lot out back looked appealing.

"Are you sure you want to be involved with these people again, Michael?"

I turned around. "Do we need to go there, AJ? I thought we settled that."

"A little touchy, are we?"

"It's not that," I said. "It's just — it's just I don't want to talk about it."

"That's not like you, Michael. Usually I can't shut you up."

"Thanks a lot."

"Don't give me that shit. You know what I mean." AJ stood and faced me. We were across the desk from each other.

"Let's get something straight," she said. "I hope you hang Conrad's ass from the barnyard door. He deserves it. But goddamn it, Michael, do it for the right reasons."

"Meaning?"

"You feel guilty Conrad's on the loose. Nothing's going to help with that. Go after him because he murdered Camille. Annie, too, for all we know. Get him for murder, not because you feel guilty."

"It's not about feeling guilty, AJ."

"It's not?"

"It's about justice for Camille. That's all it's about."

"That's true for Hendricks. Marty Fleener, too. But it's too personal for you, Michael."

"You're wrong, AJ."

She shook her head. "You have to stay detached or you won't make good decisions. You know that."

We stood quietly for a minute, on opposite sides of the desk.

"Michael?"

"I know." I reached for her hand.

She leaned across the desk, and we kissed. "Sometimes, you know, it's hard. I worry about you."

"I know. Enough for now?"

AJ nodded. "Yeah, okay. What's next?"

"I finish the Diaz file. Not much left, but I want to get it over with."

"Tomorrow?" she said, wrapping up the rest of the cheese and putting it in the bag.

"Tomorrow I start with Doreen Masie, at her house. Tail her a few days."

"Where does she live?"

"Just north of town. On Shaw Road, off 31. I'll park down the road from her house and wait."

I paused before I asked. I knew how AJ would react.

"Can I use your truck tomorrow?" I said.

"Can it, will you?" she said. "Save the SUV-is-a-truck nonsense for somebody else. I'm tired of it."

"It's a deal," I said. "So, can I use your SUV tomorrow?"

"Sure, but why?"

"My BMW will stick out like a sore thumb parked on the side of the street. It might work in Chicago or Detroit ..."

"Take my car," she said, "you'll blend in just fine."

"Do you want my car?"

"Of course I want your car," she said, and smiled. "Might have to race a Porsche to work."

I let that go and changed the subject.

"With a little luck, Doreen will lead me to Wolfgang."

"Who will lead you to Conrad."

"Sure hope so," I said. "Unless Henri finds him first."

"My money's on Henri," AJ said.

"Mine too, but we might stumble on something else."

"Well, Mr. PI, I think it's time for me to go home. I'm not leaving this with you," she said, adding the wine bottle to the bag.

"Good thing. I want to finish the file, go home and take a shower."

"Come here," AJ said.

I moved closer and wrapped my arms around her waist. She pulled me in and kissed me. We held each other.

"I'm sorry," she said. "I didn't mean to pick a fight."

"I know. It wasn't much of a fight anyway."

"No."

"I'm too stubborn sometimes," I said. AJ leaned back and looked at me. "Sometimes?"

"All right, smart-ass, go home and let me get back to work."

She kissed me lightly on the cheek. "Yes, darling."

AJ put on her jacket and picked up the bag. "Talk tomorrow, my love," she said and left the office.

I sat down and reopened the Diaz file at the marker. So far nothing except Roland Crosley, and Sandy already caught that one.

Little more than an hour later I closed the file, put my notes away and wheeled my chair around. The wet street still glistened, but I think the drizzle had finally stopped. One lone boat, lights fore and aft, moved slowly across the bay far out in the darkness.

"You're out there somewhere, Conrad," I said. "You can't hide forever. You'll make a mistake. Sooner or later, you'll make a mistake."

7

I put on wind pants and a light jacket. The sky had cleared overnight, but a brisk October chill came along for the ride. The morning sun shot jagged spikes through the tree branches as I started my run and headed around the corner for Bay View's quiet streets.

Even though most of Bay View's cottages were shuttered for winter, construction and repair crews continued working at a feverish pace. That was always the case as Halloween closed in. Frigid temperatures and an unexpected layer of snow could show up any day.

By the time I turned on Arlington, my legs felt loose and strong. Morning runs often produced a small insight, a sliver of an idea that helped move a case along. Creative energy was often released by vigorous exercise. It was more than an interesting theory. During a long run on Mackinac Island a few years ago, I had my first inkling about the ugly side of Cherokee Point Resort. The scenic Lake Michigan setting, the beautifully ornate cottages ultimately couldn't disguise murder and blackmail.

My watch read sixty-five minutes when I punched it off and eased into a walk three blocks from home. I discovered no such helpful notions on this run, but it was still a good idea to watch Doreen Masie for a while and see what turned up.

I went behind the Perry Hotel into the parking lot at my building. My BMW was gone and in its place was AJ's idea of a car, a big, white Ford Explorer. There was a folded piece of paper stuck under the driver's windshield wiper. I pulled it out. "Enjoy the ride," it read. Very funny.

I put coffee on to brew and headed for the shower. Thirty-five minutes later, I'd dressed in jeans, a green MSU hoodie, and a pair of beat-up Brooks running shoes. The recommended outfit for a private eye on stakeout.

I was enjoying scrambled eggs and a toasted English muffin at the kitchen table when my phone buzzed.

"Morning, Sandy. You're at it bright and early."

"It's nine-thirty, boss," she said with a groan. "Are you coming to the office this morning?"

"Hadn't thought about it one way or the other, why?"

"I pulled two pictures of Doreen Masie's off her Facebook page."

"Send them to me."

"Will do," she said. "Did you learn anything from the Diaz file?"

"Nope, not a thing," I said, "except Roland Crosley's name. And you found that one."

"Yeah, well, I'll ask Geary about him," Sandy said, clicking off.

When the photos arrived, I poured the last of the coffee in my mug and took a look. The first depicted three men and one woman in business attire lined up at some professional event. The second was a head shot of the same woman. It was difficult to tell how old she was, in her fifties maybe, with flat hair and a sad face. She looked older than Wolfgang, but it was unclear by how much.

I took two cold water bottles from the refrigerator and put a fresh bagel in a plastic bag. I was ready for, well, long hours of waiting.

I climbed, and I do mean climbed, into the driver's chair of AJ's Explorer and fired up what passed for its motor. I hoped somebody would revoke my driver's license if I ever thought of this thing as a car.

I went over to Kalamazoo and north on Mitchell. Traffic on 31 was light, even for October. I passed Pickerel Lake Road, slowed and turned onto Shaw Road.

I watched the street numbers on houses and mailboxes, eventually finding Doreen Masie's small house just shy of Hiawatha Road. It was a story-and-a-half with an attached garage and two large windows on either side of the front door. Doreen was certain to be at work, since it was almost noon. I was tempted to look for an unlocked window or door, but there'd be time for that later. The house seemed quite ordinary, like others in the area, except it needed a fresh coat of paint and a new roof. I turned around and went up to 31. According to my GPS, Bristol Garden and Yard was a quarter-mile up the road, just behind Oleson's Market.

Bristol occupied a huge chunk of land surrounded by a high fence with a wide gate. I pulled in the lot and parked off to the side of the main building. The far end of the yard was littered with outdoor furniture, some wood, some colorful resin. Cement statuary of all sizes and descriptions filled the rest of the space.

I assumed Doreen worked normal hours, but decided to find out. I tapped Bristol's number and waited.

When the answer came, I said, "How late are you open?"

"Five o'clock every day," said the voice on the other end.

Since I had time to kill, I drove back downtown for a late lunch. I found an empty meter in the lot behind Lake Street and went in the back door at Roast & Toast. After a Caesar salad and a glass of iced tea, I went next door to McLean & Eakin and wandered through the fiction section.

A little after four, I made my way back to Bristol's parking lot and set my car for a clear view of the door. I turned on Interlochen Public Radio, sat back and listened to *All Things Considered*.

When the news came on at five, people began moving out of the building to find their cars in the lot. I didn't have to wait long for Doreen. She came through the door wearing a long beige coat buttoned to the neck and dirty white running shoes. Her shoulders slumped forward, and she stared at the ground as she walked. I checked the photo just to be sure. No mistake, it was Doreen.

She made her way to a dark blue Chevy Cruze two parking spots over. She paid me no attention at all. When she pulled out, I entered her plate number on a memo on my phone.

It was easy following someone who didn't suspect she was being followed. I no more than got moving when Doreen pulled into the Oleson's lot. I did, too, and waited. Twenty minutes later, she came out with two plastic shopping bags.

I figured she'd head home with the groceries, and I was right. She left the car in the driveway and went inside. I slowed to a crawl. It was dark enough that Doreen switched on several lights. All the rooms across the front of the house lit up brightly, almost like a jack-o-lantern's grin. A kitchen was on the left, the living room on the other side of the front door. Bedrooms had to be at the back of the house.

I flipped around and found a spot across the street with a clear view of Doreen's, especially the front door and garage. I waited, but nothing happened.

I watched her every day that week, and still nothing happened. Each day was the same: to work, leave work for Oleson's, then go home.

"She's got to have a life," Sandy said. We sat in the office. It was Friday afternoon.

"You'd think so, wouldn't you?"

"Wouldn't you have seen it by now," Sandy said, "if she had a life?"

"Yep."

"But you haven't seen it."

"Nope."

"How long you going to keep this up, boss?"

I shrugged. "Well, it's Friday, so the weekend is on deck. I'll bet office staff at Bristol is off until Monday."

"Are you going to pick her up in the morning?"

"If nothing happens tonight," I said, "I'll be at her house bright and early. Let's see what she does on weekends."

I looked at my watch. "Okay, time to go."

"You're not getting much work done sitting in your car. How about calling Henri to split the shifts?"

"I'd rather have him looking for Conrad. Give it another week, then we'll decide."

By four-thirty, I'd resumed my favorite position in the Bristol Garden and Yard lot. At ten minutes before five, Doreen emerged from the build-ing. A break in the pattern. A small one, but still a break. I tailed her to Oleson's.

I knew I'd have twenty minutes, so I tapped AJ's number.

"How about I meet you for dinner?" I said.

"Don't you want to see what she does first?"

"Sure. If she goes straight home again I'll wait an hour, but that's it."

"Okay," AJ said, "call me when ..."

"Hold on," I said.

"What?"

"How about that."

"What?" AJ said. "Tell me."

"Good ole Doreen's carrying a handful of fresh flowers with her gro-ceries."

"You don't say."

"Uh-huh. She hasn't done that before. Of course, it might be nothing."

"There's only one reason why the woman wants flowers on Friday night," AJ said.

"A romantic evening home?"

"Only one way to find out, Sherlock."

"Okay," I said, "stay on the line."

Doreen turned her car toward home, so I kept her just in sight. When she slowed for the house, I backed off. Fortunately, no cars turned down Shaw behind me. As I cruised by Doreen was climbing out of her car, but lights were already on in the house. Another break in the pattern. I found my usual spot on the shoulder and shut off the motor.

Someone else was in the house.

Two people moved around each other in the kitchen as if preparing food or drinks. Doreen's car sat alone in the driveway. I glanced up and down the street. No other cars were parked anywhere near her house except mine. Could be another car in the garage, or maybe Doreen's guest walked.

"Looks like I might be here a while," I said to AJ.

"I told you romance was in the air. Can you tell if it's a man or a woman?"

"Whoever it is moves like a guy moves."

"It's Wolfgang," AJ said.

"Doreen could be romantically involved with other people, AJ."

"After the boring life you've watched? You want to bet on that?"

"No."

"Cancel dinner tonight?" AJ said.

"Afraid so, darling."

"That means I don't get to play with your body either?"

"AJ."

She laughed. "'Night, darling."

I opened a bottle of water and put it in a cup holder. I unwrapped the bagel and took a bite. Not exactly a baguette from Crooked Tree, but life on stakeout was tough.

I had no idea what might happen. If they went out for the evening, I'd have a chance to see Doreen's friend and follow them. That's the best I could hope for. So I settled in and waited.

8

Thud. Thud.

"What the hell?"

Thud. Thud. A beefy fist hit the driver's side window.

"Put your hands where I can see them," a harsh voice said.

I glanced over my shoulder. A cop, behind me and to the left. He was taller than me, thick in the torso without being soft. I slowly placed my hands on top of the steering wheel. I looked right. Another cop, shorter and much thinner, stood off the passenger side of the SUV, his hand on his gun. Only in small town America would an SUV parked on the street seem out of place.

"The window," the voice said.

"Electric," I said, and the officer nodded.

I switched on the ignition (but did not hit the start button) and put down the driver's side window.

"License and registration."

"In my pocket," I said.

He nodded again. I took out my wallet and handed him my driver's license in slow, deliberate movements. Done this before.

"Registration's in the glove box," I said, pointing vaguely in that direction.

"Okay," the officer said. As I leaned over, the second officer moved forward to get a better look. I snapped the box open, reached in slowly, and took out the registration.

The officer handed both documents to his partner, who had moved to my side. I took a quick look at Doreen's house. No lights. I glanced at the digital clock. Two forty-six — Fell asleep at the wrong time. Her car was still in the drive. They could be in there or not.

"Step out of the car, please," the officer said. The other cop had put himself at the rear of the SUV.

"Why do you want me out?"

"Out of the car, sir."

I slowly opened the door and got out.

"Assume the position."

"You have a reason for this?" I said.

"Turn around, put your hands on the roof."

"No," I said. "You tell me why."

The cop tipped his hat slightly back and grinned. "Hey, Ernie, guy says he wants to know why."

"I'm a licensed private investigator working a case."

The officer stepped back.

"I'm not armed," I said.

"In the car?"

"No gun," I said. "There's no law against falling asleep on stakeout."

"Stakeout," the officer said, drawing out the word.

"License in my wallet."

"Show me. Easy."

I took out my wallet again, pulled out the card and handed it to him. He considered my PI license as Officer Ernie handed him back the other documents.

"You want to tell me why the registration," he nodded at the SUV, "doesn't match?"

"It's not my car."

"Says it's not his car, Ernie." The cop looked at the registration again. "You know the name for the car?"

"AJ Lester," I said. I shook my head. "Audrey Jean Lester, Bay Street, Petoskey."

Doreen's house was still dark. I hoped all this nocturnal activity didn't rouse them out of bed.

"All right," the cop moved his light to my license, "Mr. Russo, we're going to take a little ride down to the station. We'll call to get the car towed."

"Call AJ Lester first. She'll back me up. I'll follow you in."

"How 'bout this guy, Ernie?"

Officer Ernie moved closer, but stayed a careful distance away. "We'll be filling out paperwork the rest of the night, Jake, we do this. Got the woman's number off the printout."

Officer Jake took a deep breath and let it out slowly. "Call her," he said. Officer Ernie returned to the patrol car.

Officer Jake and I stood a few feet apart. He'd relaxed some, but his professional instincts were still alert. When Officer Ernie got out of his car, he walked up to us. That was a good sign.

"It checks," he said. "Lady's not too happy with our PI," he said, "but she backed his story."

"I'll follow you in," I said, hoping they'd changed their minds.

Officer Jake glanced at his partner, who shrugged, then handed me back my papers. "Get out of here for tonight, understand?"

"Yes," I said. The officers returned to their patrol car and drove off.

I leaned back against the SUV and folded my arms. I wondered if Doreen's friend was still there, but I couldn't wait until dawn. I'd be too obvious on the side of the road, SUV or no SUV.

"Well, hell," I said aloud and opened the door.

9

"**S**ome private investigator you are," Sandy said. We sat in my office with coffee. It tasted good — better than usual, in fact.

I'd made my way home about three and crashed on the bed for a few hours. By the time I'd taken a shower, dressed, and walked to the office, it was after nine. The air was chilly, and a light frost coated the windows of cars parked up and down the street.

"Have you been waiting for an opportunity to say that?" I peeled back a banana skin and bit off a sizable chunk.

"How could you fall asleep?"

"How does anyone fall asleep, Sandy? I dozed off, what can I say?"

"Easy, boss. You're getting a little touchy."

"I'm just pissed," I said, and drank some coffee. "I had my chance to see if it was Wolfgang. I screwed up."

I took another bite of banana. My phone buzzed. I glanced at the screen.

"Henri's on his way," I said, putting the phone down. "AJ thinks it was Wolfgang in the house."

Sandy nodded. "I'm with AJ on this one."

"We've got nothing to go on."

"We've plenty to go on," she said.

"You say. How can you be so sure?"

"We went to woman school, boss. We studied how men are jerks."

"Think I missed that lecture."

"Maybe so, but Wolfgang and Doreen are a case study."

I put my hands up. "All right," I said. "Is it okay with you if I reserve judgment?"

"Reserve anything you want, but I'll bet you a week's pay AJ and I are right."

"You can't afford a week's pay."

"Okay, I'll bet my overtime for being here on Saturday morning."

I shook my head and laughed. "You're impossible, you know that?"

"Thank you."

Sandy started to say something else, but paused when Henri came through the door.

"Good morning Sandy, good morning Michael."

"You're in a cheerful mood today," Sandy said.

"Yes, I am."

Henri hung his Carhartt jacket on the hall tree. He unsnapped his shoulder holster, slipped it off and put it on another hook. He poured a mug of coffee and took the chair next to Sandy.

"I thought you were on the island?" I said.

"Had dinner with Margo last night."

"That explains why you're in such a good mood," Sandy said. "How I love a good romance."

"I'll head back to the island this morning."

"Any luck finding Conrad?"

Henri shook his head. "Nothing. It's like he vanished. Pisses me off, I can't find him."

Sandy laughed. "Saturdays. I should've stayed home. What was I thinking?"

"I asked you to come in," I said.

"So here I am, stuck with two pissed-off men. Lucky me."

Henri looked at both of us, then said, "You lost me."

I raised my hand. "I'll do it."

It took the next several minutes (and one mug of coffee) to fill in the gaps for Henri.

He turned to Sandy. "He fell asleep?"

Sandy shrugged. "Don't look at me. I just work here."

I decided to ignore all remarks made at my expense.

"Speaking of work," Henri said. "Am I getting paid for playing spy-versus-spy?

"Patricia Geary gave me … us … a generous retainer," I said.

Sandy slapped both hands down on top of her knees. "Geez, with all this witty repartee I forgot. Be right back."

Sandy went to her desk and returned with a yellow legal pad. She flipped through several pages.

"I talked to Patricia Geary," she said. "She told me about Mr. Roland Crosley."

"That the name of the man who wasn't in the Diaz file?" Henri said.

"That's him," Sandy said. "He helped Annie when she was trying to split from Conrad. Apparently she had a hard time making it stick. Staying away. Crosley hid her out."

"Why would Crosley help Annie?" Henri said. "Did you ask Geary?"

"She didn't say it in so many words, but I'd bet it's the gay community. You know, for moral support, helping out when a relationship ends."

"Geary say where Crosley lived?" I said.

Sandy nodded. "Downtown Traverse." She flipped to another page. "Here it is. Washington Street, just down from the courthouse."

Sandy wrote the information on a sticky note and handed it to me.

"Think I'll have a talk with Mr. Crosley," I said.

"You can't just bang on the man's door and expect him to talk to you," Henri said. "Not if he protected Annie."

"Don't worry," Sandy said. "I already took care of that."

Henri and I looked at her and waited.

"I told Geary you'd want to talk to Crosley sooner or later. She said she'd tell him you're safe. That's the word she used, boss, 'safe.' You'd be 'safe.'"

"Sounds like a pretty tight-knit community," Henri said. "I'll bet Annie's not the first person he's protected."

"I'll give Mr. Crosley a call, see what he has to say. You have anything on Wolfgang's brother yet?" I said to Sandy.

She shook her head slowly. "Nothing on brother Wilhelm."

"And you can't find Conrad," I said to Henri, who shrugged.

"Fine lot of crime busters we are," I said. "How do three adults just vanish?"

"They haven't exactly vanished, boss."

"Well, I don't know what you'd call it then. Nothing on Wilhelm, and we only think we have a lead on Wolfgang. As for the man himself — not a trace."

"It's only a matter of time," Henri said. "Let me tag along behind good old Doreen for a while."

"I thought you were headed back to Mackinac this afternoon," Sandy said.

"I can take care of things, come back down Monday morning. I'll pick Doreen up at work."

"You'll keep on Conrad, too?" I said.

Henri nodded.

Sandy put the yellow pad on the desk. "I'll turn up something on Wilhelm. When are you going to call Crosley?"

I leaned forward and put my elbows on the desk.

"Right after I take care of an important matter."

Sandy's face twisted in a quizzical look. "What matter?"

"Getting my car back from AJ," I said. "Can't stand that truck of hers one more day."

Sandy rolled her eyes. "And you think I'm impossible?"

10

I gathered up my bag and coat, said good-bye to Sandy and Henri and went downstairs to the parking lot.

I rumbled my way up Bay Street. It was the weekend, people were out in force busy with fall cleanup. I pulled into AJ's driveway and put her SUV back by the garage. My 335 was parked at the curb. AJ was raking leaves into three neat piles near the street. She had on a delightfully snug pair of jeans, and a green MSU sweatshirt.

I came around from the back of the house, said hello and kissed her lightly on the mouth.

"Nice jeans."

She glared at me for a moment, then put both hands on top of the rake handle.

"Go green," I said pointing at her sweatshirt, trying to be cheerful. It was, after all, a college football Saturday.

"You fell asleep? On stakeout?"

I shrugged.

"Shrug all you want, Russo, but I'm the one the cops woke up in the middle of the night."

Sarcasm? Annoyance? Not sure which.

"Sorry about that," I said.

"No, you're not. You told them to call me, didn't you?"

AJ dropped the rake on the leaf pile. "Come on," she said, "let's sit down."

We sat on the front porch steps, and AJ put her arm around my shoulder.

"Too bad you gave up your day job to be a private eye."

"Enough already," I said. "First Sandy, now you. I screwed up."

"You want to tell me what happened?"

I did.

"Everyone makes mistakes, Michael, even you. But you were on stake-out. That's what really scared me. You made a mistake like that on stake-out."

I turned toward her. "Scared?"

"Yeah. Wolfgang could have put a bullet in your head while you were out there snoozing."

AJ hesitated, leaned in and kissed me on the cheek.

"Yeah," I said. We sat quietly for a few minutes, holding hands.

"What's next," she said, "this Crosley guy?"

I nodded. "I'll call him, see when I can drive down for a chat."

"Do you think he knows anything about Annie's disappearance?"

"I have no idea, but we know he helped Annie and the cops missed him."

"That seems odd, if you ask me."

Two squirrels chased each other across the yard and up the tall, almost-leafless maple tree at the curb.

"Do you think nobody told the cops about Crosley?"

"Could be. The question is, why not? He was obviously involved with the case."

"Could be they were protecting him. From the cops, I mean."

"Because he hid Annie?"

"Maybe she's not the only one," AJ said. "You should ask him."

"Funny, same thing occurred to me."

AJ nudged me in the ribs. "That looks like a cop car to me," she said, pointing at a black four-door sedan coming our way.

"In your neighborhood?"

AJ gently slapped the back of my head. "Maybe the cops are still after you, darling. You'd better run."

"You can be really annoying, you know that?"

"Glad to hear it," she said. "Oh look, darling, the cop car's turning into my driveway."

The black sedan came to a halt and out climbed a familiar figure, State Police Captain Martin Fleener. He was dressed in a tailored gunmetal gray suit over a white shirt and a black-and-red striped tie. On Saturday.

"Hello, AJ," he said, "Michael."

"Do you ever take a day off?" I said.

"Maybe next week," he said. "Mind if I join you?"

We slid over and Fleener sat next to AJ.

"Do you have a reason for cruising my neighborhood on a pleasant college football Saturday?" AJ said.

"I was checking the overnight reports this morning," Fleener said. "It's routine. Do it almost every day. Guess what I found?"

"I can only imagine," AJ said, grinning with anticipation.

"Now, I could've called the deputies who filed the report, but what fun would that be?"

"What fun, indeed," AJ said, still grinning.

Fleener leaned forward, looked past AJ and said, "Why did you steal AJ's car, Michael?"

"Marty…"

"Suspect, that's what they called you, a 'suspect.' The suspect was asleep in the vehicle, the report said. The vehicle belonged to someone else, the report said. The suspect, that's you, Russo, told the deputies he was on a stakeout. That's what the report said, a stakeout."

"What's your point, Marty?"

"My point?" he said. "Who the hell were you staking out?"

"Woman named Doreen Masie. I'm working a case."

"Happy you're employed," he said. "What's the case?"

I hesitated, and AJ gave me a gentle shot to the ribs.

"Tell the man, Michael. He'll figure it out anyway."

I took a deep breath and let it out slowly. "Remember Annie North?"

"Traverse woman who disappeared?"

"Uh-huh. I've been hired to find her, alive or dead."

Fleener nodded slowly, but didn't say anything.

"So that means," I started to say, but he cut me off.

"That means Conrad North," Fleener said.

"You remember him, I take it?"

"Damn right I remember him. I don't forget murderers. He put two bullets in Camille North's chest, and I couldn't get him for it. She was my case, too."

"Michael thinks he's the one who blew the case," AJ said.

"Don't flatter yourself, Russo," Fleener said. "We blew it, Hendricks and me. North's a smart man. That's all." He paused, then said, "You going after him?"

"Yeah."

"Know where he is?"

"Thought I'd ask you."

"Don't know, but I could ask around. See what turns up."

"Appreciate that, Marty."

"I'll help in any way I can," Fleener said.

I nodded. "Good. North won't be easy."

"He wasn't last time. No reason to think he'll fuck up this time either."

"We might have to, you know, move in the shadows a little," I said.

Fleener shook his head. "I have to play this one by the book, Russo. All the way. No screw-ups. We arrest North, I want it to stick."

"Fair enough," I said. "What if it gets dicey?"

"That's what you got Henri LaCroix for, isn't it?"

I needed a minute for that remark to sink in.

"Time to go." Fleener lifted himself off the step and walked toward the black sedan. "I'll let you know, I find out anything," he said without turning around.

The squirrels continued their romp around AJ's yard, darting from tree to tree. The autumn sun was up high now, and the air was warmer. From our spot on Bay Street, all seemed right with the world. If the world were only life on Bay Street.

"Man's got a point, Michael," AJ said as Fleener drove away to wherever he played cop on Saturdays.

"Which point is that?"

AJ reached over and took my hand in hers. "Fleener has to play it straight, Michael. He doesn't want to miss another shot at Conrad any more than you do."

I nodded. "He made that clear."

"But it seems to me he gave you a green light to do what you need to do."

"His comment about Henri, you mean?"

AJ nodded. "Marty's an officer of the court just like you. He couldn't very well tell you to violate the law, especially with a witness sitting here."

"I was surprised he brought up Henri," I said. "Cops think he's trouble if he's south of the bridge."

AJ put a hand on my knee and said, "Remember, darling, you don't want to screw it up, don't want to push too hard."

"Yeah, yeah. I know."

"There's a fuzzy line between legal and illegal. I run into it all the time at the newspaper, with our sources. You and Henri …"

"We know where that line is, AJ."

She turned toward me. "What about those two guys from LA? You cornered them over in Levering."

"They boxed themselves in."

"Sounds like a rationalization to me."

"They needed killing."

"My point exactly, Michael. You can't do that this time. You guys miss North again, you'll never forgive yourselves. You and Henri can't screw it up for Fleener, either."

I put my arm around AJ's shoulder, and we inched closer together.

"Feels good," she said.

"Yes, it does."

"This is going to get ugly before it's done, isn't it?"

"Yeah."

11

By the time I passed Bay Harbor (houses, condos and manicured golf course) on my way toward Traverse City, the motor had warmed up enough to get the frost off the windshield. I moved the lever to put more heat on the floor. The nights hovered around the freezing mark, and the days had grown chillier even with the sun up high. October always teased us, cool and pleasant one day, rain highlighted by wet snow the next. Being surrounded by the waters of Lake Michigan and Lake Huron did not make for predictable weather.

I took U.S. 31, a more pleasant shoreline route through Charlevoix, Torch Lake and Elk Rapids, to avoid yet another trip through Mancelona and Kalkaska. It was a Monday morning, after all, and the road was empty for long stretches at a time. It'd be a good time to let the car run a bit, but I didn't feel like playing boy racer this morning.

It took two voicemails and two messages over the weekend before I finally talked with Roland Crosley. He was hesitant, at first, even to talk on the phone, but he finally acknowledged that Patricia Geary had given him a heads-up. After that, he agreed to see me without much resistance.

I eased over and stayed on Front Street when U.S. 31 bent toward the deep blue water of Grand Traverse Bay.

I joined other vehicles as we crawled our way past retail shops, restaurants and the State Theatre. I went left on Cass away from the bay, left again on Washington. After I passed the courthouses, new and old, Washington Street turned old-money residential with a blend of new construction and tastefully restored historic homes.

I kept a close eye on house numbers. I spotted Crosley's house past the middle of the block, just shy of Franklin. I drove by the house, flipped around in a driveway and parked across the street.

Crosley's house was a three-story Victorian, all skinny windows, spindled porch railings and gleaming white paint. The front yard was sprinkled with orange and brown leaves, a few summer flowers still decorating the beds in front of the porch. Pots of colorful mums shared the front steps with two large, uncarved pumpkins. A narrow driveway led to a garage in the backyard.

There was no doorbell that I could see, so I opened the screen door and rapped on one of four small windowpanes. A few moments later, the door opened.

"Yes?"

"Mr. Crosley?"

"Yes."

Crosley had to be near seventy. He was stocky, probably five-eight with a full head of silver hair. His face was round with oval eyes and a neatly trimmed salt-and-pepper mustache. He wore gray linen slacks, a black silk T-shirt and cordovan penny loafers.

"I'm Michael Russo. We spoke on the phone."

He stepped aside and gestured me in with a slow wave of his arm.

The foyer had twelve-foot ceilings, dark wood floors and Oriental rugs. An ornate stairway led to the next floor.

"This way," he said, and I followed him into a parlor. Its décor matched the foyer. The room was large and square with tall windows on two sides, floor-to-ceiling bookshelves on the other two sides. Each bookshelf supported one of those tall ladders that glide along the floor on wheels.

"Sit down, please," Crosley said.

We faced each other from twin loveseats on opposite sides of a low coffee table.

"You said you talked with Patricia Geary?" I said.

"Yes."

"And she explained why I wanted to see you?"

"She hired your services, yes."

"She explain why she hired me?"

"I'd prefer to hear it from you."

Off to a snail's pace, we were. But I'd intruded on his world, after all, so I cut the guy some slack.

"Mr. Crosley, Patricia Geary trusted you with her partner's safety. She is trusting me to find out if Annie disappeared or was killed. She wants closure, Mr. Crosley."

Crosley nodded ever so slightly.

"She told me that Annie stayed with you for a while."

"Yes."

"After she split from Conrad."

"Yes."

"Why?" I said.

Crosley scratched the side of his face. "Why what?"

"Why you, Mr. Crosley? Lots of people live in Traverse. Why did Annie pick you to stay with?"

Crosley cleared his throat, twice, but did not respond.

I leaned forward, elbows on my knees. "You help people, Mr. Crosley, and I bet Annie wasn't the first one. You've helped other people, haven't you?"

Crosley stiffened, his shoulders moved back.

"I'm not sure what you mean, Mr. Russo."

"Mr. Crosley, I ask questions. That's how I do my job. That's how I learn stuff."

Crosley nodded again. Slowly again.

"Annie didn't get to this house by chance, did she? You've protected others. She knew where to go for help, or Patricia Geary did. None of it was by accident, was it? This is what you do, you've created a safe house."

Crosley sighed and a faint smile appeared.

"I try to help people, Mr. Russo," he said.

"How long have you been doing this?"

"About ten years, I think, maybe longer."

"How does somebody ... how did you start?"

Crosley's smile broadened. "Quite by accident, I assure you. A friend, a dear friend from college, who lived downtown needed a place stay for a few days. She was in the middle of a messy divorce, didn't feel safe at home." Crosley shrugged. "I gave her a safe place to stay until she made other arrangements."

"Do many other people need a hideaway?"

"More than you'd imagine," he said.

"But Traverse is a small town when you get down to it."

"Word gets out," Crosley said. "Not just around here."

"I take it you're not connected to local social service agencies."

He shook his head. "This way works just fine. And to answer your next question, I pay all the bills."

"All on your own? Ten years?"

"Let's just say I can afford it, so I expect nothing."

"That's quite generous," I said, eyebrows raising.

"I understand your skepticism, but that's not how I look at it. Everyone has a friend, a friend who's scared, Mr. Russo, like my friend was. A few days here might make all the difference."

"What can you tell me about Annie North?"

"Mr. Russo, I'm comfortable saying this." He cleared his throat. "Annie North stayed here."

"Had you known her before that?"

"I knew who she was, but we weren't friends, if that's what you mean."

"Did Geary make contact," I said, "put you and Annie together?"

Crosley nodded. "The first time, sure."

"What? I'm sorry, Mr. Crosley. The first time?"

Crosley nodded. "Yes, the first time."

"She stayed here more than once?"

Crosley held up two fingers in a V and said, "Twice, yes."

"Geary didn't mention that." I thought for a minute. "When was the first time?"

"Right after she left Conrad."

"Did Geary make the arrangements with you?"

"Well, Patricia told her to call me, but I made all the arrangements."

"You have this down to a routine, don't you?"

Crosley shrugged. "Something like that."

"How long was she here, the first time?"

"A week, maybe ten days."

"Is that normal? If you're hiding someone?"

"It's not all that normal, Mr. Russo. We needed a little additional time to find Annie a place to live."

"You found a place?"

Crosley nodded. "Over near Meijer, off 31. It was quite basic really. Not the kind of place Conrad would ever think to look for his estranged wife."

"Did you see her again? I mean, before she returned here."

"Here and there. A bar, a restaurant."

"You talk to her at all?"

"Nothing more than a greeting."

"When did she come back?"

"After their divorce. It was awhile, seven or eight years ago."

"Did Patricia Geary call you the second time, too?"

Crosley shook his head. "Annie just showed up on my doorstep one morning. She was terrified."

"Had something happened?"

"Of course something had happened, Mr. Russo. He came after her. Threatened her."

"Conrad?"

"Of course, Conrad." He sounded like I was asking dumb questions.

"Did she explain it to you?"

"More or less. She was terrified. Conrad threatened to kill her, she said. He wanted to get even, those were her words, 'get even,' for the divorce, the humiliation she'd caused him."

"She say anything else?"

"Something about the Mackinac cottage, I think. Conrad was married to Camille by then. You know he was married two times?"

I nodded. "Yes."

"Well, Annie thought maybe he'd forgotten their divorce, or let it go. When he showed up, she ran here. She was desperate."

"How long was she here?"

"Two or three days. I forget exactly."

"But there were no arrangements."

Crosley shook his head. "No. She just up and left. She thought he'd find out about my house sooner or later, so she ran. She ran for her life, Mr. Russo. That was the last time I saw her."

"Do you know Conrad's two sons, Wolfgang and Wilhelm?"

"I know who they are. Annie talked about them, and not approvingly."

I sat back on the loveseat and thought for a minute.

"I haven't been much help," Crosley said. "Is there anything else?"

"Do you know a Detective Diaz, Vincente Diaz, Traverse City police?"

"No, should I?"

"Diaz handled Annie's case. Your name wasn't in his file. You were one of the last people to see her alive, but the cops didn't know you. Wonder why that is?"

Crosley shrugged.

"But you're not unhappy the city cops never heard of you?"

He shrugged again.

"No one mentioned your name because they were protecting you, weren't they?"

Crosley didn't bother to shrug this time. He stared off across the room somewhere. That was all the answer I needed.

"Do you know where Conrad is these days?"

"I assume the Grand Traverse area."

"How about his sons?"

"Can't say for sure, but they wouldn't be far from their father."

"Grand Traverse again."

"My best guess," Crosley said, "but it's an educated guess."

"I'm sure it is."

"Now, Mr. Russo, I don't want to appear rude, but is there anything else?"

I shook my head and said, "No, I appreciate your time." I took out a business card and handed it over. "You'll call if you think of something else?"

"Yes, yes," he said, and started for the door.

12

"**B**ig assumption," Henri said, "that everyone thinks Conrad's in Traverse." We sat in the front office by the Lake Street windows. Sandy was at her desk.

"I'm not so sure," Sandy said. "The woman was scared, Henri."

"She might have exaggerated the threat."

"I don't think so," Sandy said. "Crosley believed her, he took her in twice."

"Conrad threatened her, Henri," I said. "Seems logical he lived in the area. Or he harassed her whenever he was in town."

"Maybe."

"You have anything interesting to report, Mr. LaCroix?"

"As a matter of fact I do."

"Did you learn anything about our Mr. Crosley?"

"Not hard to do," Henri said. "Man's not trying to hide, after all."

Henri went to his jacket and retrieved a small notebook. When he returned to his chair, he flipped through a few pages.

"Crosley was born in Traverse City in 1951. He was raised in a small, year-round house on Spider Lake, south of town. Traverse schools, Indiana University, earned a Masters degree in math. Taught at Illinois State and Bradley before he took a job at Northwestern Michigan College. Retired in 2016."

"That's all bio stuff," I said.

Henri stood and looked out the window. "Got two sources, both solid, confirming the man's run a safe house for more than a decade."

"But not a registered safe house," Sandy said.

Henri nodded. "A below-the-radar safe house."

"Protecting whom?"

"Abused spouses ..."

"Which means women," Sandy said.

Henri nodded. "Mostly women, yeah, running away from some type of violence."

"Or the threat of it, as in the case of Annie North," Sandy said. "So Crosley is savvy in the ways of violence and how to hide from it."

"Or escape from it," I said. "Does anyone but me wonder how the cops don't know this man?"

"I bet the cops do know Crosley," Henri said, "but his friends weren't talking, so the cops never knew. Probably don't trust some people, with or without badges."

"Wouldn't be surprised," I said. "You had two things to report. Care to enlighten us again?"

"Not sure how enlightening it is, but did you ever follow Doreen Masie in the morning?"

I shook my head. "No, why?"

"Well, it seems that Doreen is an exercise maven in the mornings. The Bear Creek Health and Fitness Center."

"Over by Bannister College?"

"That's the place. Followed her twice. She went to the center both mornings to work out."

"Glad to hear it," I said. "We need to know this because?"

Henri smiled. "I can think of more attractive women I'd enjoy watching work out."

"Careful, Henri," Sandy said.

"He means the lovely, gorgeous Margo Harris," I said.

"I do mean Margo," Henri said.

"Of course you do," Sandy said with a touch of sarcasm.

"Back to the story, if you don't mind," I said.

Henri nodded. "Went inside to have a look. There are a lot of women ought to rethink spandex."

"Don't go there, Henri," Sandy said. "I'm getting annoyed."

Henri put his hands in the air, a mock surrender. "Okay, okay," he said. "A woman at the counter was very helpful."

"You just waltzed right in and asked about Doreen?"

"Didn't have to," Henri said. "Convinced Lucille, that was her name, that I needed a good health club to stay in shape. Asked her if her club could do that. She pointed at Doreen two machines over and told me how much they'd helped her get into shape." Henri smiled. "Keeping me in shape would be easy, she told me. Then Lucille pointed to a man, a man who knows Doreen. Thinks Doreen's so cute he shows up most mornings just to watch her workout. Between sets, Doreen played lovey-dovey with him."

"He work out, too?" I said.

"Not so you'd notice. Sat on a recumbent bike watching Doreen and peddling with all the enthusiasm of a man waiting for a root canal."

"Know the man?"

Henri grinned. "He's under six feet easy, more round than stocky, dark complexion with a puffy face, the kind of puffy that comes from too much booze."

"Sounds like Wolfgang to me, " I said.

Henri nodded. "But I only saw him that night a couple of years ago when we rousted him and his brother and father. I went back the next day, smiled a lot and filled out a membership application while Doreen did her thing."

"The boyfriend there?"

Henri nodded. "Figured good ole Doreen was headed to work after a shower, so I followed the boyfriend."

"And?"

"He made a few stops in town, post office, car wash, that kind of thing. Then he went home — pretty sure it's home anyway."

"Where?" I said.

"Bay Harbor." Bay Harbor was an upscale community of homes,

condos, shopping and a hotel on the shores of Lake Michigan five miles south of Petoskey.

"You mean the old cement plant," Sandy said.

"A condo, closer to the highway than the water."

"Is the foundation sinking?" Sandy said, grinning.

"Sandy," I said, "do you always have to make fun of Bay Harbor?"

"You bet I do, boss. I hate to miss a juicy opportunity."

"Did you see where he went," I said, "which condo?"

Henri nodded. "Got the building, not the unit. Took a picture of the names on the door buzzers." He pulled out his phone, tapped a few times and handed it over. "Nobody named 'North.' Recognize another name?"

I enlarged the photo. "'Hoffmann.' It has to be Hoffmann. Sandy, wasn't that one of the names Conrad's family used?"

"Yeah," she said, nodding. "Conrad's family took Hoffmann when they moved to the States from Germany, long before he arrived."

"That's our boy," Henri said.

"I think so too, Henri, but we have to be sure."

"Be easy enough to check out," Henri said. "We'll sit on him. Give you a good look."

"I have a question," Sandy said. "Just tossing it out there, you understand."

"And that is?" I said.

"For the sake of argument, let's say the guy is Wolfgang, okay?"

Henri and I nodded.

"What's dumpy Wolfgang doing with Doreen? The man has a ton of money, so where's the trophy wife, you know, the tall twenty-something with big boobs? Why hang out with frumpy Doreen?"

"Hold on a second, Sandy," Henri said. "A minute ago you got irked at me when I talked about women in spandex. Now you're talking a trophy wife with big boobs?"

"This is different," Sandy said, and leaned forward on her desk. "It's a serious question, Henri. When men reach middle-age with lots of money, they go after young, beautiful women. Doesn't matter how dumpy the men are, that's what they do."

"She has a point, Henri," I said.

"Thank you, boss. Either of you gentlemen like to speculate on my question?"

"I'm not sure it matters," I said. "If the guy's Wolfgang, it's a step closer to Conrad. That's what counts."

"Maybe Wolfgang doesn't feel confident enough to chase younger women," Henri said.

"Men never lack confidence in that department, Henri," Sandy said.

Henri smiled. "Point made."

"All right," I said. "We have to check out our dumpy guy, make sure it's Wolfgang. We'll sit on the condo."

Henri shook his head. "If the man sticks to his schedule, he'll be at the health club bright and early watching Doreen."

"Then we'll pick him up when he leaves," I said.

"How 'bout we roust him instead?"

I shook my head.

"Be more fun."

"Of course it would," I said. "But we roust the son, it tips the father he's got trouble. Better we stick with our plan, follow Wolfgang for a while and see what we can find out."

"Okay. I'll swing by, pick you up in the morning," Henri said.

"Don't want Conrad calling in gunslingers any sooner than necessary."

"You say."

13

"**W**hat's in the bag?" I asked as I climbed into the passenger seat and put my travel mug of coffee into a holder. Henri's SUV was warm on a frosty morning. It was still dark out, not even a hint of sunlight in the eastern sky.

"Small buttermilk," he said, referring to Johan's donuts. "Two each."

I opened the bag. "Only two here."

"Ate mine already," he said, grinning.

Henri took Howard to Mitchell and turned east. Traffic was light in town, and we moved along easily. Once we crossed Division, the Bannister College campus crept into view. I gave it a sideways glance as we drove past the iron and fieldstone gate.

"Fond memories?" Henri said.

"Hardly."

"Still think it's a rat hole of sex and violence?"

"Sure hope not," I said. "Lot of good people work there."

"Including Margo," Henri said.

"Especially Margo," I said. "Speaking of which … how is the esteemed Professor of Literature? Still beautiful and charming?"

Henri nodded. "Not to mention smart and savvy. Arguing with that woman is always a challenge."

"You don't have to argue with her, Henri."

"Yeah, I do," he said. "I learn things, lots of things. Books, politics, movies. Lots of things."

"There," I said, "on the right."

The Bear Creek Health Club was a two-story yellow brick building a quarter-mile past the Bannister campus. It sat back from the road with a large parking lot in front. An arched brick canopy shielded the main doors from the elements.

The sun had crept above the trees, offering just enough light to scan the parking lot. Henri drove slowly to the far end of the building and parked.

"There," he said, pointing to a small steel door. "Locker rooms are just inside. The boyfriend will walk out here or the front door. We'll see him either way. His car's the third one down. The dark gray Mercedes."

"Not just a Mercedes, Henri. That's a Mercedes-AMG."

"Am I supposed to be impressed?"

"You ought to be," I said. "150 K of pure hot rod. Super-fast luxury. The man knows his cars."

"Good for him."

I pulled a donut from the bag and took a large bite.

Henri looked over. "You going to eat 'em both?"

"Dumb question."

Henri shrugged, then said, "Front door."

I looked up.

"There's our boy," Henri said.

"Good morning, Wolfgang North," I said. "That's him. No doubt about it."

Wolfgang was all round and pudgy, a fact made obvious by an awkwardly fitted black sweat suit, too tight in the waist, too tight in the thighs, too short at the ankles. He moved sluggishly across the tarmac.

"Striking figure of a man, don't you think?" Henri said.

"You can be anything you want, you have money and power behind you."

"Not to mention firearms and men who know how to use them."

"That, too," I said.

Wolfgang tossed his briefcase into the AMG and plopped into the driver's seat. He drove off and headed downtown. Henri waited a few moments, then moved out of the lot.

"Giving him a long lead, don't you think?"

"Not to worry," Henri said. "Man's an amateur. He'll probably go into town or cut over to the Charlevoix Road and go home. My bet is downtown. Don't worry, we got him."

We didn't have to wait long to find out. Wolfgang slowed for the stoplight at Division and turned right.

"You just lost the bet," I said.

"So it seems. Let's see what he's up to."

Wolfgang's Mercedes motored its way down the hill and turned north on U.S. 31.

"Where the hell's he going, Mac City?"

"I have no idea," Henri said, "but we're sticking around long enough to find out."

In less than three minutes Wolfgang's right turn signal snapped to life. Henri eased off the gas.

"Oleson's?" I said when Wolfgang turned off 31. "He's going grocery shopping?"

"Nah," Henri said. "I think it's time for breakfast at The Bistro." The small breakfast-lunch restaurant was tucked away in a tiny strip mall next to the grocery store. Big windows stretched across the front of the restaurant on either side of the front door.

Wolfgang parked beside a flashy red Corvette Z-06.

Henri eased his SUV behind a pickup truck thirty feet away as a man climbed out of the red Corvette.

"Recognize him?"

"Brother Wilhelm," I said, smiling. "We got ourselves a twofer, my man. Some days, it just pays to be lucky."

"He younger than Wolfgang?" Henri said.

"By a year or two, I think."

"The brothers North aren't in the habit of working out."

Like Wolfgang, Wilhelm was under six feet and more than a little chunky through the middle.

"His clothes fit better," Henri said. "If a long brown cardigan sweater's your thing."

I laughed. "Might as well relax. I guess we'll be here awhile."

"Yep," Henri said, and punched up the Interlochen Center for the Arts' news radio station. We settled back into the tall chair-like seats of the SUV and listened to *Morning Edition*.

"How long's it been?" Henri said.

I glanced at my watch. "Forty minutes. You in a hurry?"

"I'm tired of following people around. Why don't we roust them after breakfast? Have some fun."

"No, we'll stay with our goddamn plan."

"You're a little crabby this morning," Henri said.

"You sound like Sandy."

"You miss your run?"

"Of course I missed my run, dumb-ass, I've been with you since before the sun came up."

"I'd suggest more coffee, but our wait is over. Look." Henri pointed out the windshield.

The brothers came out of The Bistro. Each man played with a tooth-pick as they walked toward the cars.

"Can't follow both of them."

"Nope," I said. "What d'ya think?"

"Well, we know where Wolfgang lives. We can always pick him up there, or the health club," I said. "Let's stick with the red Corvette."

"Wilhelm it is."

The two men talked for a few minutes, then climbed into their cars. Wolfgang left first. After a long wait for traffic to clear, Wilhelm pulled out and headed toward downtown. Henri slipped into traffic, three cars back.

Wilhelm skirted downtown Petoskey and went south on U.S. 31.

"Where's he going?"

"Man's going home, Russo."

"Yeah? How do you know?"

"They're brothers, Russo. Brothers stick together, maybe they live together."

The red Corvette slowed and turned into Bay Harbor. It wound its way through the narrow streets. Henri followed at more than a discreet distance.

"These guys live in an expensive neighborhood," I said. "Wonder if they live in the same building?"

"Well look who's waiting for brother Wilhelm."

Wolfgang North leaned against his Mercedes.

Wilhelm parked next to his brother's sports car.

Henri slowed to a stop at the curb, fifty feet away.

"Still have that picture you took of the mailbox names?" I said.

Henri took his iPhone out and handed it over. I tapped the screen and brought up the photo.

"We assume Hoffmann is Wolfgang's alias, but that's the only one that caught my eye."

"Maybe they do live in the same condo," Henri said.

The brothers talked for a minute, then ambled up the sidewalk. Wilhelm took out a ring of keys and opened the door.

"At least it's the same building."

"It's a place to start," I said.

Henri switched off the motor.

"They have to know where their father is," I said. "My money says he's around here someplace."

Henri looked my way. "If it were up to me, I'd scare it out of them, shake it out their ass." Henri put his hands in the air. "I know, I know. Don't say it again."

I didn't.

"We'll keep an eye on Wilhelm, too," I said, "see what we learn."

"Did that with Wolfgang," Henri said. "Not much to show for it."

"You have a better idea?"

Henri shook his head. "But you can take Wilhelm."

14

"That's all you got?" AJ said.

I shrugged.

We sat comfortably at the far end of the bar at City Park Grill. It was a bit after five-thirty. People were leaving work and the bar was filling up faster than the tables. AJ drank a Chardonnay while I sipped an Oban. We shared an order of fried zucchini with horseradish sauce.

"You and Henri'd make terrible reporters," she said. "If I were your editor, I'd tell you to knock on doors, ask questions, turn over rocks. You're not digging."

"We know the brothers live together, AJ."

"Uh-huh," she said, and dipped a piece of zucchini.

"Didn't think anyone could lead a life as dull as Wolfgang, but Wilhelm's the man. Except for warming the same barstool at the Side Door several times a week, he has no social life, no romance, no friends, nothing."

"Do these guys work?"

"Not that I can tell," I said. "You know, when I first ran into these two..."

"Before Camille was killed?"

"Yeah. All they did for a living in those days was hang out with good ole dad like they were ten years old. They'd show up at the family business once in a while, but I'd hardly call it real work."

"Any luck finding Conrad's friends?"

I shook my head.

"Man didn't have friends, AJ. People on Mackinac didn't like him, didn't care about him. That was plain when I talked to people who knew him. He didn't spend time in Petoskey, Gaylord, anywhere in the northern tip. He sold the Lake Forest house more than a year ago."

I sipped some Oban and put the glass down. "Maybe I shouldn't assume Conrad's still in northern Michigan."

"But the brothers are here, Michael. If they've never strayed far from their father before, no reason to think they have now."

"I doubt the man lives in Petoskey," I said. "We'd spot him sooner or later. He'd have to go out in public once in a while."

"Where then?" AJ said. "Traverse?"

"Easier to keep a low profile."

My phone buzzed. "It's Henri. Be right back," I said, and walked out to the sidewalk. The wind had kicked up and carried a light rain with it. I stayed close to the building, away from the door.

"What's up?"

"Tailing the North brothers, they're in the same car."

"So?"

"I think something's up."

"Why?"

"Gut feeling, Russo."

"Okay, where are you?"

"South on 131. They're not going to Traverse City."

"Think they're going to I-75?"

"Could be," he said. "Don't think it's long distance. They didn't have bags."

"But you think they're up to something?"

"Stay tuned," he said, and clicked off.

I went back to my nice warm barstool and sat down. I pushed my scotch away and waved off the bartender just in case I had some unexpected nighttime driving ahead of me.

AJ put her arm around my shoulder.

"So?"

I told her what Henri had to say.

"The man's instincts are spot-on most of the time, Michael."

"Yeah, I know, AJ, but riding in the same car isn't much of a clue."

"You said yourself, they're boring men."

"Uh-huh."

"So this is something different. What's Henri got to lose?"

We sat quietly, watching the bar traffic slowly fill the tables around the restaurant.

"Since we're waiting for Henri to call," AJ said, "how's about some food?"

"Good idea."

AJ ordered the chicken breast, grilled, me the Mediterranean bow-tie pasta with a garlic-wine sauce.

We were enjoying our dinners, chatting about buying tickets for a musical at the Interlochen Center for the Arts, when my phone buzzed.

I read the screen. "Henri's on 32 East."

"They're going to Gaylord?"

"The nightlife could be hot, darling."

"In Gaylord? When's the last time anything wicked happened in Gaylord?"

I shrugged. "Beats me."

We had decided to go to the Interlochen musical, passed on dessert, and asked for the tab. As AJ put down her credit card, my phone buzzed.

"It's Henri," I said. "Meet you out front."

I left the bar and returned to the sidewalk.

"What?" I said.

"Bennethum's," he said. "You know it?"

"On Old 27? Across from Otsego Lake."

"Yeah. I'm at the bar."

"The brothers there?"

"Yep. Guess who was waiting for them?"

"Are you serious?"

"You bet your ass, Russo. It's papa Conrad, in the flesh, with a big glass of red wine."

"They see you?"

"Nah, bar's crowded. Lots of people moving around."

I looked at my watch as AJ came up next to me.

"I can be there in forty-five," I said. "Should I?"

"The brothers just sat down. Haven't even ordered a drink. Do it," he said, and clicked off the line.

I told AJ.

"Drop me at my car?"

"Let's go," she said. Her SUV was parked across the street. "I want to go with you."

"Not this time," I said. "I'd rather you stay here."

We climbed in and AJ started the motor. She drove down Lake and turned toward my apartment building.

"What you really mean is that you want me here in case you get thrown in jail for reckless driving, isn't it?"

"Something like that, yeah."

AJ pulled up next to my car, and I got out. I walked around to her side and kissed her through the open window.

"Be careful, Michael. I want you in one piece, Conrad or no Conrad."

15

I tossed my jacket on the floor behind the driver's seat, climbed in and hit the start button. As AJ drove away, I opened the glove box, took out a small battery-powered radar detector and stuck it to the windshield. Couldn't hurt, might help.

There wasn't much traffic in town, but these are not streets to hurry. I swung around past the hospital and drove straight onto 131 South. Once I passed Intertown Road, I was in rural Emmet County: few people, few houses, fewer cars.

I flipped the Xenons on bright, settled into my seat and eased the throttle down. There were moments when I loved high performance cars. This was one of those moments. The car ran effortlessly at the century mark and my concentration was honed into each mile. I loved every minute of the drive. I had to ease off the throttle only twice. Although traffic picked up as I got closer to Gaylord, I made good time. I avoided the congestion at the strip malls near I-75 by taking a couple of twisty back roads to Old U.S. 27 as it ran the length of Otsego Lake.

Forty-four minutes after I left AJ, I pulled into the parking lot at Bennethum's. It was jammed with cars and trucks. No surprise. I motored slowly past the front door. On the far side of the restaurant, lights flashed on an SUV. Henri lowered the window so I could see him. I parked the BMW and walked over to Henri.

"How long you been out here?" I said as I climbed into the passenger seat.

"Five minutes, no more," Henri said. "I walked out when the tab was dropped on Conrad's table."

"They never saw you?"

"You annoy me, you know that?"

"Sorry to question your stealth capability, Henri."

"You should be," he said. "Wolfgang's Mercedes is over there." Henri pointed to the next row of cars. "Don't know Conrad's car. He was already here when the boys arrived."

I started to say something, but Henri interrupted, "There. The front door."

Three men came our way. Conrad was a step ahead of his sons. Even in the weak lights of the parking lot, I recognized that same angular frame I'd chased before. At six-six and a trim 185, Conrad North was hard to miss even in a rain jacket and baseball cap. He was light on his feet, moving two steps ahead of the boys with the ease of a man half his seventy-four years.

They walked through two rows of cars and stopped at a Ford Focus.

"Must be Conrad's," I said.

"Not up to his usual extravagant standards."

"Man's flying under the radar, Henri. Wants to keep a low profile. Look at that cheesy jacket he's got on instead of a Burberry trench coat."

The sons said good-bye to their father and walked away to Wolfgang's Mercedes.

"You up for a mystery drive?" Henri said.

"Yep, no point following the boys."

Conrad pulled out of his parking spot and went south on Old 27.

"Doesn't look like the man's taking the freeway," Henri said.

"Traverse City?"

"Be my guess. Bet he's headed to 131."

"You lost your last bet on this family, Henri."

I pulled out my phone and tapped a message.

"That for AJ?"

"Yeah, let her know what's happening."

"She worried you want to get even?"

"Is it that obvious?"

"Yes."

"Conrad goes down for murder this time, Henri. AJ's worried I might kill him if I get the chance."

"Rather than calling the cops?"

"Cops fucked it up last time."

"They certainly did."

There were almost no cars on the road this late October evening. The rain had quit, finally, but the clouds hung around, so the moon was nowhere to be seen. Henri kept pace with Conrad's Focus, about one hundred yards back. It's easy to tail somebody, even on an empty rural road, who doesn't expect to be followed.

"Brake lights," Henri said. "He's turning on the Mancelona Road."

"Traverse is looking better and better."

When Conrad went west on M-72 at Kalkaska, that cinched it.

"I should buy a lottery ticket," Henri said.

"You should pay attention to Conrad."

"Relax, will you."

We followed the Focus along the bottom of East Bay. Traffic was heavier the closer we got to downtown Traverse. Henri closed in on Conrad's car, not that it mattered.

"Think he'll go up the peninsula?" I said.

"No," Henri said, "man lives in town someplace."

Conrad moved along smartly and went south on Division. Henri kept him in sight only a few cars ahead. When Conrad turned on Eleventh Street, we knew he was home.

"Man's got himself a condo," Henri said. The Village at Grand Traverse Commons, usually called "the Commons." An interesting blend of preservation and redevelopment, the Commons is a high-end community of specialty shops, trendy restaurants and luxury condos renovated from the decayed remnants of the old Traverse City State Hospital. The collection of ornate three-story structures looked taller because of an abundance of tall, thin windows and several spires that jutted into the air.

"I think he's going to Building 50," Henri said, referring to the old administration building.

And so he did. Conrad turned on Cottageview and parked in the lot at Building 50. Henri pulled in across from the Pleasanton Bakery and switched off the headlights.

"You see his car?" I said.

"Yep. Two rows over, by the grass."

"I'm tempted to take a run at him right now."

"Bad idea, Russo."

"Yeah, I know. First time I've been this close to the prick in a long time."

Conrad left his car and walked toward the back of Building 50 with the arrogant stride of a man unfamiliar with defeat.

"Hold on a minute," Henri said, and climbed out of the SUV. He walked a few yards down the sidewalk, then moved away from me at a pretty good clip. I couldn't see where he went. Five minutes later, he returned to the SUV.

"Where the hell did you go?"

Henri settled in behind the wheel. "Followed him inside."

"Inside? He see you?"

"Of course he didn't see me. He took the elevator to the third floor. I couldn't get up there quick enough to see which unit, but he lives on three."

"Wouldn't it have been easier to look on the door buzzer for names?"

"It would if the place had names and buzzers."

"The Commons is so exclusive no one can find you? Got to hand it to the person thought up that one. Bet the guy wears tan cords with little green ducks on them."

"Look on the bright side, Russo, we have his car and his condo. That's more than we had yesterday."

"Think he uses an alias, like his sons?" I said.

Henri nodded. "I bet he picked Hoffmann just like his stupid sons."

"Makes our job easier if you're right."

"Well, we caught one break when we stuck with Wolfgang."

"We certainly did," I said. "How do you want to play this?"

Henri leaned back on the headrest. "We should follow Conrad."

"It's gonna be tougher down here, we'll have to tag-team him."

"Might have a better idea."

"I'm listening."

"I'll tail Conrad," Henri said.

"You can't do it alone. We've had this discussion before. One person can't run a twenty-four-hour tail."

"I'm not so sure, Russo." Henri turned sideways in his seat facing me. "Try this. Conrad doesn't know we're watching. He won't catch on, unless something bizarre happens. Shouldn't take long to pick up his habits, places he goes, who he sees, the usual stuff."

"You still can't do it alone."

"I have a friend lives in Traverse … Roger Beaufort … I ever mention him?"

"Don't think so."

"Lived on the island most of his life, but his heart went bad, so he moved here four, maybe five, years ago. He has a small condo not far from here, off S. Airport Road."

"You can stay with him?"

Henri shook his head. "He's gone for the winter. He has another condo in Florida. Lakeland, I think. I'd have the place all to myself."

"We could still tag-team from your friend's condo."

"Waste of time right now. I can do it for a couple of weeks, see how it goes. I'll babysit his car to start. Figure out which unit he owns."

"Okay," I said. "Two weeks. You get nothing, we do something different. Agreed?"

Henri nodded and grinned.

"Either way, Herr Hoffmann, we got your ass now."

16

"**D**o you remember Nicole Sanderson?" Sandy said from the doorway. We sat waiting for Henri to arrive from Traverse City. He'd been on Conrad North for a little more than two weeks: it was time to decide what to do next, based on the info he'd gathered.

"Of course I do, why?"

"She's on the phone."

"Right now?"

Sandy nodded. "She expected to leave a message, but I told her I'd see if you were free to talk."

Nicole Sanderson was Camille Sanderson North's daughter. After her mother was killed, Nicole asked me to make sure the cottage remained with the Sanderson family. She hated that Conrad was her father, and despised his two sons almost as much as they despised her. Conrad North was furious when he was unceremoniously kicked out of the cottage and off the island. Nicole didn't care.

"Sure, I'll talk to her."

"Line one, boss," Sandy said when she returned to her desk.

"Hello, Nicole. It's been some time, how are you?"

"Hello, Michael. I'm doing well, thank you for asking."

"Are you still top dog in the advertising business in the Windy City?"

Nicole laughed. "That's overstating it, I think, but I'm still gainfully employed by the same agency."

"That's good to hear," I said. "What can I do for you?"

"I need your help, Michael. I'm not sure what to do. I'll make it official and hire you, of course."

"We can talk about that later. Fill me in first."

"Well, there's this couple, an older couple from Lansing. They want to buy my cottage."

"I'm surprised you're selling, Nicole."

"That's the point, Michael." She sounded frustrated. "It's not for sale."

"Then ..."

"They're a sweet old couple, they really are, but they won't take no for an answer." She paused.

"Sounds like you've talked to them more than once."

"Several times. It began when they knocked on my door one day."

"At the cottage?"

"Uh-huh, they just showed up not long after you forced Conrad out. They said owning a bluff cottage was a life-long dream. They researched all the bluff cottages, and they wanted mine. Michael, they knew more about the history of my house than I did."

"You've told them it wasn't for sale?"

"Every time. When I spent the summer months working from the cottage, I'd run into them downtown. At Doud's, restaurants, the post office. They would call me during the winter. I've even tried to be mad at them, but they're so nice, I can't ... I don't know what to do."

"Would you like me to have a talk with them?"

"Would you, Michael? Do whatever you think is best, but convince them I'm not selling my house. Please."

Nicole gave me all the contact information, and we exchanged a few pleasantries.

Then, "I'll get back to you when I have something," I said. We ended the call.

"Well, I heard your end of the conversation," Sandy said. I filled in the details and handed over the contact information.

"Okemos, huh. Go green."

"That's East Lansing, Sandy."

"Close enough for a Spartan cheer. Emily and Drew Freeland on Hamilton Road. Want me to call them?"

"Yeah, but see what you can find out about them first. I want to know why they're so persistent."

"People can be pretty screwy when it comes to 'living the dream' on Mackinac Island. It can't be the first time you've heard a story like this?"

"It's not, but check them out anyway."

"Who's the woman at Mackinac Island Realty? The one who helped you out before."

I looked up. "Her name's Irma Renner." Renner had called Mackinac home for forty years. She'd worked residential and commercial real estate for most of that time.

"Call her. Maybe she knows something."

"Good idea, Sandy."

"I occasionally have one," she said.

I picked up the phone, checked the number and called.

The woman's voice on the other end of the line was dignified, calm and professional. I told her who was calling.

"Russo," she said. "Long time. How's my favorite private eye?"

"How many private eyes do you know, Irma?"

"Only you, handsome, only you. Finally decide to bite the bullet and buy a house?"

"Sorry, Irma, not this time. I promise you'll be the first to know when the time comes."

"Good enough for me, Russo," Renner said. "So how can I help? Chasing some more bad guys, are you?"

"Not quite, Irma. But I wanted to know if you've had any questions about Nicole Sanderson's cottage?"

I heard Henri walk into the office. He waved as he passed my door.

"Well, that's funny," Renner said.

"What is?"

"Sanderson's place. That you should ask about that one."

I waited.

"We've had a lot of activity for April, people calling, making appointments, but there're no bluff houses available."

"What is it about Sanderson's then?"

"Well, there's this older couple. Name's Freeland."

"Uh-huh."

"They've been in here several times asking if the cottage is for sale. They're very sweet, and they know a lot about the cottage. They say it's the only one they want to buy. But the answer's always the same."

"They're from Lansing, Okemos, actually?"

"You know them?"

I explained why I called.

"I even left Nicole two voicemails in case she was interested in selling," Renner said. "She never called back."

"Did the Freeland folks say if they'd be back?"

"No, but they'll be back. You do this as long as I have, you can tell."

"Let me know if they show up again?"

"Be glad to, Russo," she said, and we ended the call.

17

"I'm just saying, it seems like an odd …"

"Coincidence, Sandy?" Henri said.

I sat with Sandy and Henri in the outer office.

"Be quiet, Henri LaCroix," Sandy said. "That's not a word we use loosely around here. It's just strange, that's all."

"What is?" I said.

"Nicole Sanderson calling. Just when we're chasing Conrad North again."

"You think it's not a coincidence?" Henri said.

"I don't know what it is," Sandy said. "It's just strange."

"I don't know what it is either," I said, "but we need to decide how to handle Conrad North."

"That means I'm up to bat," Henri said.

"You've filled us in while you watched him these last two weeks," I said. "Anything to add?"

Henri sat back and shook his head. "Not really. The man's a pretty dull guy."

"Except he likes to murder for a hobby," Sandy said.

We looked at Sandy but let her macabre humor pass.

"After a little more than two weeks, it was easy to figure out his routine. Breakfast out, usually the Blue Heron or Omelette Shoppe downtown. He might go shopping at the mall or on Front Street. Dinner downtown, too. Spreads his business around."

"So he's not trying to hide?" Sandy said.

"Doing a lousy job of it if he is," Henri said. "He keeps a low profile, that's all. He does the boring day-to-day things we all do."

"Still convinced he has a girlfriend?"

"Oh, yeah, the man's got a girlfriend. They're together all the time, in restaurants, on Front Street. Easy to tell."

"Know anything about her?" I asked.

Henri left his chair and retrieved a reporter's notebook from his jacket. He returned to the office and flipped a few pages.

"The lady's name is Jessica Royce, Jessie to her friends. She's thirty-six, thirty-seven ..."

"Hold on a second," Sandy said. "Isn't Conrad North the man who only screwed around with women his age?"

"That was his habit when he was married to Camille," I said.

"Apparently he developed an interest in younger women," Sandy said with a dab of sarcasm.

"Royce is from Rochester," Henri looked up, "the village of, not Rochester Hills. She married one Guy Royce, who was originally from Royal Oak ..."

"Your old stomping grounds, boss."

". . . at Shrine Church."

"Shrine of the Little Flower?" I said.

"Yeah," Henri said. "They moved to Harbor Springs eight years ago. He worked for Emmet County, the road commission, got her a job in the County Clerk's office. The good Catholic girl from Royal Oak divorced Royce three years ago."

"She still live in Harbor?"

Henri nodded. "When she's not at Conrad's place."

"She still work for the county?"

"Hard to tell," Henri said. "My money says she quit."

"Anything unusual about her, or them as a couple?" I said.

Henri shook his head. "Older man, young woman? In a resort town? Not that unusual at all. Man looks and lives the life of a retiree."

"That's not much help."

"However …"

"What?" I said.

"Never mentioned this when I called. Wasn't sure at first, now I am."

Sandy and I waited for the follow-up.

"Conrad has a bodyguard."

I glanced at Sandy, then back at Henri. "What, might I ask, does a retiree need a bodyguard for?"

"Carmine DeMio's retired," Sandy said. "He has a bodyguard, two of them, in fact."

"DeMio's a gangster," I said. "That's hardly normal anywhere, even in northern Michigan." I turned toward Henri. "You sure it's a bodyguard?"

Henri nodded. "The first week, I only picked up the kid twice."

"Kid?"

"Yeah, he can't be more than nineteen, twenty," Henri said. "After that, I watched for him. He's good. Always there but hard to spot."

"Meaning?"

"The kid never walked with Conrad. He'd be twenty paces behind or directly across the street, that kind of thing."

"Isn't it hard to protect somebody from across the street?" Sandy said.

"Only if you worry about an amateur charging up. A pro stalks the target, waits for an opening."

"So the kid sees the big picture?" Sandy said.

"Exactly," Henri said. "The kid's young but he knows what he's doing."

"Describe him."

"Like I said, can't be more than twenty. Probably six feet and skinny as a rail. Thin face, like he hasn't had a good meal in weeks. Hair's buzzed close. Wears a watch cap, black, and one of those fluffy coats, you know, the trendy ones."

"You mean a puffer jacket, the shiny fitted ones?"

"Yeah, but the kid's parka isn't fitted."

"Because you can't cover a handgun in the fitted jacket," I said.

"But you can if the puffer coat's too big."

"This kid got a name?"

"Probably, but I don't know it yet."

"Back to my question, what's a retiree in Traverse City need a body-guard for?"

"Do you think Conrad knows we're on to him?" Sandy said.

I shook my head. "How could he? Diaz doesn't care, Hendricks isn't paying attention." I put my hand on Henri's shoulder. "And he certainly didn't spot this guy."

"He certainly did not," Henri said.

"So Conrad hires himself a gunman because he expects trouble?" Sandy said. "Or, he doesn't want to take the chance."

"Any point staying on his tail, Henri?"

"None that I can see. You want to move on him?"

I stood up and went to the window. It was another cloudy, colorless fall day.

"I don't see that we have much choice," I said. "We'll put some pressure on, see what Conrad does."

"The man won't like that," Sandy said.

"No, but he's a smart guy. He'll want to know why I'm suddenly on his ass again."

"If you confront him," Sandy said, "he'll assume you're after him for killing Camille, won't he?"

"Might be a good idea if he thought that," I said, "at least for a while. He won't even be thinking about Annie. Gives me more room to maneuver."

I returned to my chair. "Henri, you're thinking something. What's on your mind?"

Henri nodded. "I see two problems. First, we have to isolate the body-guard. Don't want to kill him, not yet anyway. Just neutralize the kid."

"The other problem," I said, "is where we do this."

"Yep."

"How about his condo?"

Henri shook his head. "I don't know how the kid protects him there. I can't hang around the hallways to find out. He'd spot me."

"Has to be a public place then."

Henri nodded slowly. "We'll pick a morning when he's in town for breakfast. Be easy to see both of them that way. I'll keep the kid busy, you have a chat with Conrad. What do you think?"

"That'll work," I said. "Give us a chance to see what he does then."

"What he'll do," Sandy said with an eye-roll, "is send his bodyguard after the both of you."

18

"I'll need a few days to set it up," Henri said.

"Hard to find a good place?"

Henri shrugged. "As long as he keeps his breakfast schedule, shouldn't be too hard. Problem is the kid. I need to learn more about how he covers Conrad, from the street, from a car, that kind of thing."

My iPhone buzzed on the desk. I glanced at the screen.

"Hold on, it's Irma Renner."

"Tell her hello," Henri said.

"Irma," I said, "twice in the same day? After all this time."

"Yeah, yeah," Renner said, "save the flattery."

"Okay, what can I do for you?"

"The Freeland couple? We just talked about them?"

"Uh-huh."

"They're here," she said, "on the island."

"You talk to them?"

"No. Came out of Doud's, they were across the street in front of the Chippewa Hotel. You said you wanted to know if they showed up."

"Do me a favor?"

"Are you interested in buying a house?"

"Sorry, Irma."

"Too bad," she said. "What's the favor?"

"Set up a meeting for me. Could you do that? Tell the Freelands I'm a lawyer representing Nicole Sanderson."

"They'll think she wants to sell, if you do that."

"Let them think what they want," I said. "Just get them in a room so I can put an end to this."

"Okay, see what I can do," she said, and hung up.

Henri and Sandy had been waiting patiently.

"You forgot to say hello for me," Henri said.

"Anything else, boss, or can I get back to work now?"

Maybe not so patiently, after all.

I looked over at Sandy. "You were going to check out Freeland."

"Get right on it," she said with a half-hearted salute and left the office.

I turned my attention to Henri, but the phone buzzed again. I picked it up.

"Wow," I said. "Three times."

Irma Renner ignored my attempt at humor.

"Are you in your office?"

"Indeed, I am. Like a good private eye should be. By the way, Irma, hello from Henri LaCroix. He's here, too."

"Tell Henri I might have a tenant for him, for the apartment downtown."

"Hold on," I said, and put the phone down. "You're on speaker, tell him yourself."

She did, and followed it with, "I just got off the phone with Drew Freeland. He was very excited when I told him about you, Mr. Russo."

"That means he'll see me?"

"I'm looking at the boat schedule," Renner said. "Get a move on and you can make the two-thirty. That'll give you an hour, you leave on the five o'clock."

I glanced at my watch. "Where?"

"My office, yes or no?"

"On my way," I said, clicking off. "You hear that Sandy?"

"You don't have to shout, boss, I'm right here." Sandy had reappeared at the doorway. "Your schedule's clear the rest of the day."

I picked up my brief bag. "Drop me at my car, Henri? We can talk on the way."

"Let's go," he said, and we went for the stairway.

"Don't drive too fast," Sandy said.

"Thanks for the reminder, Mom," I said, closing the door behind me.

We cut through Roast & Toast to the parking lot. Henri's SUV was in the first row. Northern Michigan was enjoying another in a long string of gray days. The heavy clouds hung pendulous over the bay. Maybe they held rain, maybe not. After too many days, I quit worrying about the clouds.

"You'll head back to Traverse?" I said as I snapped the seat belt.

"In the morning," he said. "Staying with Margo tonight."

"Everything still good with you two?"

Henri nodded. "We're in a good place right now. Comfortable and interesting."

We made the short trip to my parking lot in less than two minutes.

"What if Conrad's girlfriend goes for breakfast?" I said.

Henri shrugged. "She's no problem. Kid's the problem, not her."

"Think she knows about the bodyguard?"

"You're a couple, you're out in public, you got a twenty-year-old male tagging along. Hard not to notice."

"But she doesn't go along all the time?"

"No, but she goes along most of the time."

"We could just pick another day."

"As long as you're not in a hurry, Russo."

"You'll let me know when you've got it worked out?"

"You'll be the first person I call."

"Thanks for the lift," I said, and went for my car as Henri drove off.

I tossed the brief bag and my jacket in the back seat and climbed in. I hit the start button and the motor growled to life. I glanced at the digital display. Unless I ran into a single-lane caravan on the Mackinac Bridge, I had plenty of time to catch the ferry out of St. Ignace.

Traffic was light all the way up U.S. 31 to Mackinaw City. Northern Michigan was in that hiatus between seasons. The bright colors of fall — red, orange and yellow — had decayed into the flat brown of leaves and grass. The sports of winter would have to wait for the arrival of snow, or weather cold enough for the ski resorts of northwest lower Michigan to make snow. Visitors stayed home until they had good reason to travel north.

The bridge was down to one lane for almost a mile near the south tower, but the cars and a few small trucks never slowed as we arrived on the St. Ignace side. I pulled into the Star Line parking lot with fifteen minutes to spare. I zipped my jacket and took a copy of Scott Fitzgerald's *This Side of Paradise* from my bag, stuffing it into the jacket pocket.

The ferry was almost empty. I had my choice of bench seats in the rear cabin of the *Huron*. I tapped a short text to Irma Renner that I'd made the ferry and settled in with my book. About the time I was trying to sort out the life of Amory Blaine, the boat's horn announced that we'd rounded the west breakwater of the island's harbor. The three other people in the back cabin watched intently as we edged our way to the dock.

I looked up and down the dock as I came off the ramp. More often than not, one of Joey DeMio's gunmen was waiting for me. DeMio had plenty of men working on the docks in Mackinaw City and St. Ignace: I'd known for a long time that I was on his short list of suspicious people, which meant I might be trouble for the family anytime I was on Mackinac. But today, no one. Not Gino Rosato, not Santino Cicci, not even that new Ivy League lawyer, Donald Harper.

I made my way up the dock to Main Street, walked past the Tourism Bureau Office and took a left on Market Street. The compact office of Mackinac Island Realty was a half-block past Astor Street, stuck between Lucky Bean coffee shop and the bank. Can't beat the location if you're in the business of selling high-priced real estate.

Mackinac Island Realty has the most popular window in town. Visitors, and an occasional local, stop to "read the window" full of photos and descriptions of houses and condos for sale. I walked into the office, a square space with a large table in the center of the floor, a smaller table with flyers and information near the door and a desk in the back of the room.

"Michael Russo, how are you?" Irma Renner said as she stood and came around the desk. I reached out to shake hands, but she smiled and gave me a big hug. Renner was five-four, almost sixty and thick in the middle, befitting her years as a beer drinker at the Mustang.

"Hi, Irma. How are you?"

Renner nodded and gestured to the couple seated at the table.

"Michael Russo, this is Emily Freeland and Drew Freeland." The couple stood, and we shook hands. Emily and Drew tested that old saw about couples looking more alike the longer they lived together. They were short, with round bodies and rounder faces. Drew wore a pair of rimless oval glasses; Emily's oval lenses featured a thin tortoiseshell frame. His steel gray three-piece suit mirrored her dark gray straight skirt and charcoal blazer.

"I'm pleased to meet you," I said. "Welcome back to Mackinac." Drew shook hands first, but Emily wasn't entirely sure what to do when I reached out. She finally took my hand, but was uncomfortable with the greeting.

"Please sit, everyone," Renner said. "Michael, the Freelands would prefer I sit in on the meeting, but it's your call."

"I'm fine with that," I said. "You're the real estate expert, in case we have questions."

Renner nodded, retrieved a yellow pad and pen from her desk and sat down.

I looked at the Freelands and said, "As you know, I represent Nicole Sanderson."

I explained that Nicole had no wish to sell her family home, and that she would prefer not to be contacted again.

"Mr. Russo," Drew Freeland said, "if I may?"

"Please," I said, and he began a long, soft-spoken, and overly detailed recitation of the couple's passionate desire to live in the Sanderson cottage. It became obvious that Drew would do all the talking: Emily was relegated to smiling adoringly at her husband as he explained the couple's quest to own the cottage.

Irma Renner stared blankly across the table as if dreaming about her first beer of the evening.

I listened politely, longer than I should have.

"Mr. Freeland," I said, "Nicole Sanderson appreciates your interest ..."

"Oh, it's more than interest, Mr. Russo. It's always been our favorite cottage." And so, he resumed the monologue.

I cut him off this time. "Please, Mr. Freeland. She doesn't want to sell. That's as clear as I can be on the matter."

"But if you were to talk with her, Mr. Russo," Drew said, "perhaps you could make her understand ..."

"Mr. Freeland, I'm on Nicole's side here. There's nothing for her to understand."

We kept up like that for a while. Finally, Emily put her hand on Drew's arm and said, "Dear." That's all she said. Mr. Freeland stopped, looked at his wife and nodded. The couple was cordial in their withdrawal from the meeting. They were as pleasant in retreat as they had been in pleading their case.

"There goes a sweet couple," Renner said. "Sweet and annoying."

"Yeah, they remind me of that cuddly aunt or uncle everyone wishes they had. Still ..."

Renner chuckled and said, "That's the first time they've walked out of here without saying 'Talk to you soon' or some such line."

"Well, I was tired of explaining it to them," I said.

Irma pushed her yellow pad toward the middle of the table. "Michael, you explained Nicole Sanderson's position just fine. It was to the point, easy to understand. But I think there's something else going on."

"Like what?"

Renner shook her head slowly. "I'm not sure," she said. "I've been doing real estate a long time. They understood every word you said. I think they accepted it."

"I don't follow."

Renner shook her head again. "It's like ... it's like it didn't matter what you said, like they were detached from the whole conversation."

"Well, this is your area of expertise." I was unsure where Irma was going with this.

"And experience, Michael. Experience with thousands of buyers and sellers over the years. It just felt like, like …"

"Think they weren't serious about buying the cottage?"

"Oh, they'd sign the papers in a heartbeat and hand me a deposit check if I'd said Nicole wanted to sell."

"What then?"

Renner tightened up her face and squinted her eyes, like she was trying hard to understand what she read in the Freelands.

"It's almost like they had no passion for the cottage they so passionately want to buy."

"Well, how about that?" I said. "Odd, don't you think?"

Renner nodded. "What can I say?"

I stood and walked to the front window. No one on the street, not on foot, not on bikes.

"Guess I might as well head home," I said. "Well Irma, you're my go-to person if I ever want to buy a house on Mackinac Island. I promise."

"Do you know anyone else in the business?" she said.

"Not really, no."

Renner had a good laugh. "I'll let you know if Drew and Emily keep asking about the Sanderson cottage."

I thanked her for arranging the meeting, and we said good-bye.

19

On the sidewalk, I looked at my watch. I had some time before the last ferry. I walked slowly down Market Street toward the park. I imagined that Irma Renner was already on her way around the corner to savor a beer at the Mustang.

The clouds were as heavy here as in Petoskey, but the air was colder. No surprise. By the time I reached Marquette Park, the south wind coming off the water in the harbor hit hard. I zipped my jacket and crossed Fort Street into the park. Except for the streetlights heading east on Main Street, Mackinac Island was quiet and dark. The off season was well underway.

I walked on the grass, past Father Marquette's statue, toward the Marquette Park Hotel. The DeMio family's legitimately owned business sat at the far end of the park, lifeless except for a hazy light or two coming from deep inside the building. Scaffolding and huge clear plastic sheets had been erected on two floors of the west end of the hotel. Winter remodeling had begun.

I walked up to the circular drive in front of the hotel. A dim light hung over the main door. The workers were gone for the day, no doubt stopping at Doud's to grab a beer or two to take with them on the last boat to the mainland.

I didn't have the same suspicious feeling about the Freelands that Renner did. That said, I understood she was relying on years of experience with buyers of every kind: it told her something was off-kilter about the Freelands and their preoccupation with Nicole Sanderson's East Bluff cottage. I had to go with her impressions.

I crossed Main Street and headed for the dock. Most of the passengers and all the freight were already loaded by the time I went aboard the *Huron*. I found a seat in the front cabin and pulled out my phone. No updates from Henri or Sandy. I tapped my contact list and sent AJ a note: "on the 5, home by 7. food?"

I pulled out my dog-eared copy of Scott Fitzgerald and settled in. I'd just finished chapter four, *Narcissus Off Duty*, when AJ got back to me.

"in mac city for work. audie's?" I wrote: "yes by 6" and returned to the adventures of young Amory Blaine.

Once the Huron's horn announced our arrival in St. Ignace, I waited for the hurried exodus of workers already clogging the lower deck.

I found my car in the lot, drove through town and across the Mackinac Bridge. The sun hung low, at the tree line, and lit up the western sky with a bright orange-red glow. We'd lose Daylight Savings Time in three weeks, forcing the sun's daily show to change again.

I left I-75 and parked next to AJ's SUV. Audie's was a low-slung building of brick and glass at the edge of the freeway. The restaurant had been serving drinks and food in Mackinaw City for as long as the bridge carried traffic over the Straits. AJ and I often stopped for breakfast or dinner as we traveled back and forth to the UP.

I went in the Chippewa Room entrance and found AJ at a table in the lounge. She waved. I walked over and kissed her.

"Hello, darling," she said. AJ had just finished work for the day, so she wore a long charcoal skirt and black wool blazer. Her face looked tired, even behind a soft smile.

"Long day?" I said.

AJ nodded. "Longer than I thought it'd be."

"What are doing up here, anyway? You said work?"

"Evening, Mr. Russo," Tanya said from behind the bar. "Nice to see you again."

"Good to see you, too. Are you managing from behind the bar tonight?"

"Manager was breakfast in the Family Room this morning, tonight's just this," she said, and smiled. "What can I get you?"

"What AJ's having."

"Another Chardonnay on the way."

I looked back at AJ. "Work?"

AJ nodded. "Yeah, Maury sent me here to get a feel for a story." Maury Weston was publisher of the *Post Dispatch* and AJ's boss.

Tanya put down a napkin and a glass of wine. I drank some.

"He wouldn't have sent you because somebody embezzled money from the flower fund."

"I wish it were that simple," she said, and glanced around the room. The lone customer was a man in an MSU sweatshirt at the far end of the bar, his attention directed at football on TV.

"There've been allegations of sexual assault and harassment."

"Where? Here?"

AJ hesitated. "Well, in the Straits area, below the bridge somewhere, but that's all I'm comfortable saying. I have to sort it out before I write the story. Can we talk about something else?"

"Okay by me," I said, opening a menu. "Let's eat."

AJ ordered a Caesar salad, I opted for a burger and fries.

"I'll put the order right in," Tanya said.

"What were you doing on the island?"

"I was just about to tell you," I said, picking up my glass.

I'd just finished recounting my phone calls from Nicole Sanderson and Irma Renner, plus meeting the Freelands, when Tanya put our dinners on the table.

"Irma thinks something's fishy. Any of that sound odd to you?"

AJ shook her head. "Don't think so."

Tanya came around the bar. "Another Chardonnay, Ms. Lester?"

"Please," AJ said, and took a bite of salad. "There's nothing odd about dreaming of a house on Mackinac. Other than the sticker shock that goes with it."

"Well, Sandy thinks it's odd that Nicole happened to call about the cottage right now, when we're hooked into Conrad North again."

AJ looked up from her salad. "You're the dude who doesn't like coincidences, what do you think?"

"I don't know, AJ, maybe this really is a coincidence."

"Stop the presses," she said, putting down her fork. "I can see the headline in tomorrow's *Post Dispatch*: 'Russo says coincidences are real.'"

"I think you're making fun of me."

"Would I do that, darling?" she said, drawing out the last word.

My phone interrupted what would have been a pithy response. I dug it out of my jacket pocket.

"Hold on a minute," I said. "It's Fleener."

I swiped the screen. "Working late, are you Marty?"

He asked me a question. "At Audie's with AJ. Why?"

I stood up and pointed to the front door. AJ nodded and returned to her salad.

I went outside, but stuck close to the restaurant wall under an overhang to stay out of the wind. "I can talk now, Marty, I'm outside."

"Listen, Russo, I thought you'd want to know. Nils Lundberg's out of jail as of three this afternoon."

Lundberg was a professional shooter from Ohio, a freelancer barely out of his teens. A bad man thought to have killed a half-dozen men the last five years. Lundberg's ass had been a guest of the Allegany County Jail in Pittsburgh. It's worth mentioning that, two years ago, I killed his younger brother when he came at me with a Beretta Nano and a fighting knife. The brother was under contract to Conrad North at the time. It was labeled self-defense after I put three .38s in his chest — labeled self-defense unless you were Nils Lundberg and the dead guy was your brother.

"You know where he is?"

"Yeah, Pittsburgh," Fleener said. "I have a couple of friends on the force. Called in a favor, they're keeping an eye on him for me."

Fleener filled in a few more details, then clicked off. I stood for a minute and leaned against the brick wall. The lights on the Mackinac Bridge cables, all green, red and blue for Christmas, sparkled in the night sky. I took a deep breath and let it out slowly.

"Well, hell."

I went back inside and sat down.

"What'd Marty want?"

"You're not gonna like it."

AJ leaned forward on the table. "It won't be the first time."

"Nils Lundberg got out of jail this afternoon."

I saw it in her face, that bolt of adrenaline that follows the arrival of fear.

"I thought he was in for longer."

I shook my head. "He served a couple years for a cheap crime, got probation for good behavior."

"Good behavior? He shoots people, Michael. Good behavior?"

I shrugged. "He's a killer, AJ, not a troublemaker."

"You've got a fucked-up sense of humor sometimes, you know that?"

"So you've told me."

She leaned forward, trying to keep our conversation private. "He wants to kill you. Be serious for a minute."

"AJ," I said, hoping not to make things worse, "I know it's serious. Fleener has some people in Pittsburgh watching him. It's the best we can do right now."

"I'm not reassured," she said, and pushed her salad away. She took a healthy drink of wine.

"What'll you do when he shows up here?"

"Call a cop. He violated his probation."

AJ glared at me.

"All right, all right. First, we don't know Lundberg'll come here …"

"Of course he'll come here, Michael. You're here."

"Man's been in jail, AJ. He hasn't worked in a year. He needs a contract more than he needs me."

"That's easy. Conrad hires him to kill you. Two birds with one stone for Lundberg."

"Conrad doesn't even know we're on him."

AJ put her elbows on the table, her face in her open hands.

"Are you sure?"

She was quiet for a moment.

"Will you call Henri?"

"Of course," I said. "He needs to know."

"That's not what I meant."

"Henri'll watch my back because that's who he is, AJ. Is that what you wanted to hear?"

She nodded. "Yeah."

"You going to finish your salad?"

She offered a small smile. "Probably."

"I know you're scared, AJ, but let's not get over our skis just yet. If he heads our way, that's a different matter. We'll deal with it at the time, okay?"

She nodded. "Yeah, it'll have to be, I guess."

Tanya came to the table. "Anything else tonight?"

"Just the check," AJ said. "Thanks."

"You headed home or to the office?"

"I have to write up my notes while they're still fresh," she said, "but I can do that at home."

I put down cash for the tab, and we went outside. AJ leaned back against the side of her SUV. The night was clear and comfortable, but colder air was not far away.

AJ pointed at the sparkling holiday lights rising up the cables on the bridge and shook her head. "It's not even Halloween yet."

20

"Nils Lundberg, huh," Henri said. We sat in my office around the desk. Sandy occupied her usual chair on the sidewall.

"And I thought this case took an odd turn when the Freelands showed up," Sandy said. "But this ... isn't just odd, it's scary." She hesitated, then glanced at Henri. "Something on your mind?"

He nodded slowly.

"We ought to deal with Lundberg before he takes a run at you, Michael."

"You mean kill him?" Sandy said.

Henri looked over at her. "Not necessarily. You got a better idea?"

"I don't even have a worse idea, but killing the guy ought to be the last idea, Henri. When we've tried everything else."

"Everything else could get your boss dead," he said, gesturing at me.

"It's too soon for that," I said.

"I just don't want to be too late for that," Henri said.

"Well, one thing," I said. "If things turn nasty, we'll know the man has arrived in our ballpark."

I sat back in my chair. "So where are we with our friend in Traverse?"

"Conrad's schedule is fairly predictable, especially early in the day." "Breakfast, you mean?"

Henri nodded. "Goes to the Omelette Shoppe downtown more than anywhere else. Late morning, usually."

"The bodyguard?"

"Always around, but he waits outside. He watches who comes and goes. There's a car lot next door and parking meters on Cass. He'll be easy to spot."

"Anything on him? Find out his name?"

Henri opened a reporter's notebook, flipped a few pages. "The kid's name is Jimmy Erwin. He's nineteen, twenty, born in South Bend."

"Notre Dame?" Sandy said.

"Not quite," Henri said. "Never graduated high school, went to street gang college."

"In South Bend?"

Henri shook his head. "Gary, then Chicago."

"That where Conrad picked him up?" I said.

"Most likely. Been with Conrad more than a year."

"Guns?" I said.

"Handgun in a shoulder holster."

"What about the girlfriend?" I said. "What's her name, Royce?"

Henri nodded. "Jessie Royce. She doesn't always have breakfast with him even if she's in town. She won't be a problem when we have a heart-to-heart with Conrad."

"Maybe we should postpone our little chat with him," I said.

"Why?"

"We can't be sure about Nils Lundberg yet," I said.

"We have no idea where he is," Henri said.

I sat forward, elbows on the desk. "Right, we don't know. But once we tip our hand to Conrad, it's a different ballgame. Conrad gets nervous, Lundberg will be his first choice for firepower."

"And Lundberg will take the job because you're here," Henri said.

"Yep," I said, "so let's give it some time."

"It isn't like us to wait for the bad guys to make the first move," Sandy said. A nervousness crept around the edge of her voice.

"We should deal with Lundberg now," Henri reiterated, putting his arms out like he was stating the obvious to a waiting audience.

"You're back to that again?" Sandy said.

"Sandy, there aren't that many alternatives."

"All right, all right, you two," I said, "lighten up, will you?"

Sandy started to say something, then passed. Henri was quiet.

"Sandy, when I said let's not tip our hand, I meant Lundberg's a wild card, at least for now. Until he shows up, *if* he shows, let's stick with what we know."

"Well," Henri said, "we know we work for Patricia Geary, and we know where Conrad is. You have anything else in mind?"

I nodded. "I do. Roland Crosley."

"That's Patricia Geary's pal, the one who runs the safe house, isn't it?" Sandy said.

I nodded. "I want to have another go at him, convince him to tell the cops what he knows about Annie North and her sudden disappearance. If he gives them a solid lead, maybe Diaz will reopen the case."

"Do you think Crosley knows more than he told you?" Sandy said.

I nodded. "Geary told him it was okay to talk with me, but he didn't know me. He had no reason to trust me past a certain point. It's worth a shot to see if he'll talk to me again, tell me more."

"When?"

"Tomorrow," I said.

"How about while you're in Traverse City," Henri said, "we get you a look at Conrad's bodyguard, up close and personal? What do you think about that?"

"I like the idea. When you headed back?"

"To Traverse? Wanted to talk to you first."

"Okay," I said, "let's do this. I'll call Crosley, set it up. Your friend's condo in Traverse have another bedroom?"

Henri shook his head. "Big couch in the living room's all yours."

"I'll take it," I said. "Want to catch AJ up on a few things before I leave. How about we meet for dinner later, in Traverse, and figure out a plan for morning?"

"Not much figuring to do. Conrad either shows up for breakfast or he doesn't. The girlfriend either shows up or she doesn't."

"But the bodyguard will show up."

"Count on it," Henri said, looking at his watch. "Time to go." He took his jacket and said, "I'll meet you at seven at Bistro Foufou. It's a few doors down from the Omelette Shoppe. I'll show you where the gunman usually watches over Conrad."

He said good-bye to Sandy and me and left the office.

"Want me to call Roland Crosley?" Sandy said.

"I've got his number on my phone," I said. "I'll do it."

I tapped the number and waited. After a few rings a soft voice said, "Hello?"

"Mr. Crosley?"

"Yes?"

"It's Michael Russo, Mr. Crosley. Patricia Geary gave me your name. Remember?"

The voice became clearer. "I remember you," he said. But that was all he said.

"I'll be in Traverse tomorrow, Mr. Crosley. I'd like to stop by and see you. It's about the Annie North case."

"Have you learned anything new?"

"Maybe," I said, stretching things a bit.

Crosley said yes, hesitantly, to a meeting, and we agreed on the arrangements.

I picked up my brief bag and stopped at Sandy's desk.

"I'm going to walk over to the paper, talk to AJ," I said. "See you tomorrow."

"Okay, boss," Sandy said. "Be careful."

I put on my jacket and went down the stairs. The wind pushed itself around Lake Street. The clouds were piled in layers of gray above the rooftops. It wasn't likely to rain, but we wouldn't see the sun any time soon. I took Howard, then cut over to State Street. The *Post Dispatch* occupied a renovated two-story house in the middle of the block. From the street it resembled other houses in the neighborhood, except for a large sign in the front yard and the single-floor addition to the back of the house that added graphic facilities and office space.

"What time are you leaving?" AJ said. We sat in her office on the second floor. It was a small square space across the hall from her boss, the publisher, Maury Weston. The floors were hardwood, covered in the middle by a softly colorful Oriental rug. Her desk was the size of a small aircraft carrier, all dingy well-used wood and nearly indestructible.

"You know," I said, "if it weren't for those two large monitors, your office has a distinctly 1940s feel. Like a theatrical set stolen from *The Front Page*."

AJ shook her head.

"What?" I said.

"What would you do if you couldn't use old black-and-white movies as a reference to something else?"

"I'd use plays, novels," I said. "I like old movies."

"No kidding," she said. "Now answer my question. When are you leaving for Traverse?"

"I'll drive down in a little while, stay overnight with Henri."

"Were you surprised Roland Crosley agreed to see you again?"

I shrugged. "A little, I guess. I'm sure he thought he was finished with me."

"I bet Patricia Geary kept him up to date on your activities."

"Think so?"

"Yeah, I do. Look, Michael, Crosley's not on the police radar, and I bet he wants to keep it that way. That means he has a vested interest in what you're up to."

AJ pushed aside a stack of manila files and a small binder.

"Besides," she said, "Crosley'd want to make sure there are no breaches in his anonymity. He'd want to protect his, what should I call it, his safe house?"

"It was certainly a safe house for Annie."

"Crosley might even have a few questions for you."

"That'd be a switch," I said. "Either way, it's worth the shot."

"Did you tell Patricia Geary you'd be in town?"

"No. If anything changes, I can always call her."

I stood and put my jacket on. "I'll text you later."

AJ smiled and came around her desk. She put her arms around my waist and we held each other for a minute.

"It'll be okay, AJ, this trip's all talk."

I felt her head move, like she was trying to say something.

"I know what you're going to say."

AJ pulled her head back. "You do?"

"Something like, 'I worry because I love you.' Words like that."

"I have a license to worry because I love you."

"Pretty close, what I said."

"You'd make a lousy reporter."

I dropped my arms. "Not sure I'm a good detective right now."

"Well then, be on your way, Mr. Detective, and see if you can change the odds a bit."

One more quick hug followed by a kiss, and twenty minutes later I was on my way, a small leather duffel bag in the rear seat with a few clothes and a copy of the latest adventures of Easy Rawlins.

I drove through town to U.S. 131 and headed south. Since Roland Crosley agreed to see me, I figured I had a decent chance of convincing him I needed his help. If Crosley would talk to Detective Diaz, tell him about Annie, well, Diaz might reopen the case. It was the best route I could think of, the best I could do.

Most of the traffic was headed away from Traverse as I was going into town. I swung off 31 onto Eighth Street and found a spot across from Bistro Foufou.

I saw Henri come from between cars as I crossed the street. "You watching somebody?"

"No, just being careful," he said. "Didn't want to find out too late Conrad picked the same place for dinner.

"Wait," Henri said as we reached the restaurant. "Look."

I turned around.

"Omelette Shoppe is a few doors down," he said, then pointed vaguely across the street. "Plenty of parking. Meters up and down the block, too.

Conrad's bodyguard usually parks in the lot over there. Better line of sight."

I nodded. "We going to stand out here all night?" I said. "I'm hungry."

Henri waved his arm, exaggerating some grand gesture. "After you."

21

"Two ways we can play this," Henri said. We sat in his SUV in the Meijer parking lot on South U.S. 31 sipping Starbucks French Roast. We'd spent the night at the empty condo of Henri's friend a couple of miles away. It was nine in the morning and the sun had already taken the chill out of the air.

"So you said last night. You sure we won't miss him?"

"Man's not had breakfast before nine-thirty, ten all the days I've followed him." He drank some coffee and put the paper mug in a holder between the seats. "So what'll it be, his condo? Or do we wait for him at the restaurant?"

"The condo."

Henri leaned forward and put his SUV in gear. "The Commons it is."

We pulled out of the parking lot and headed up Franke Road. We caught a green light and took Silver Drive to Cottageview. Henri made a slow lap around the parking lot next to Building 50.

"Over there," he said. "End of the row, Conrad's Focus."

"The girlfriend's car here?"

Henri looped the lot one more time. "Don't see it," he said.

"What else are we looking for?"

"Gunman's Honda Civic, yellow."

"Yellow?"

"Let's try over there." Henri looped around another lot, but we didn't find the Honda. He pulled into a spot opposite Pleasanton Bakery, facing Conrad's building, and shut off the motor.

"I usually wait here. Can't miss him when he drives out."

But he didn't drive out, not this morning. It was after eleven: we'd polished off two croissants from the bakery and the rest of our coffee.

"Time's up," Henri said. "No Conrad, no girlfriend, no gunman."

"You think he's still in there?"

Henri shook his head.

"We could wait a little longer."

"Morning pattern's been broken. Not worth it. We'll try again tomorrow. You up for another night on the couch?"

I shrugged. "Why not. I'll call Sandy, let her know."

"What time you go see Roland Crosley?"

"One-thirty," I said. "But I have another idea."

I pulled out my phone, scrolled through the contacts and punched the number.

"Detective Diaz, please."

Henri did a double take in my direction. "The cops? You calling the cops?"

"Michael Russo calling, Detective," I said into the phone, waving at Henri to shut up. "Detective?" The line was open, but there was no immediate response.

"Yes, Mr. Russo?"

Not exactly a civil servant's polite greeting, but at least he didn't hang up. I explained that I wanted to talk in person. It was a short call.

"Why do you want to talk to Diaz?" Henri said, staring at his empty Starbucks cup.

"Because I'm in town, because we missed Conrad, because it's Tuesday. What difference does it make? I want the soon-to-retire detective to know I haven't given up on Annie North."

"Be sure to explain it to him just that way. You know, nice and polite-like."

I glared at Henri for a moment, but let it go. "Do you want to come along, meet Diaz?"

"Meet a cop? On purpose? I'll find me another coffee and wait in the car."

"Let's go."

Henri started the motor and we left the Commons behind. He drove up Division and took Eighth to Woodmere to the offices of the Traverse City Police.

"I'll be right here when you're done with the boys in blue," Henri said, smiling.

I made my way into the building. I was greeted by the same woman who found me so annoying on my last visit. Happily, she didn't remember me, and I was buzzed through the security door quickly once she checked my name.

I spotted Diaz in his small, glass-walled office. He was on the phone, and pointed to chairs in the main room. Several cops scattered around the squad room watched me take a chair. I offered a casual wave, not that they cared.

A detective, soft and fleshy with a comb-over and a badly fitted gray suit, strolled over.

"Help you?"

"No, thanks." I motioned with a hitchhiker's thumb over my shoulder. "Waiting for Diaz."

"You mean Detective Diaz, don't you?"

See, I never really start this stuff. I was nice, polite, friendly even.

I nodded. "Detective Vincente Diaz, right." That was polite enough.

"What do you want him for?"

I smiled. "I'll wait for the detective, thanks."

"Hey, Jake," the cop said, looking over his shoulder. Another man rose from his desk and came over to join the party. His suit, black, fit better, but he was considerably thinner than Detective Gray Suit.

"We've got us a wise-ass here, Jake."

"Do we now."

"All I did was ask him nice what he wanted, and he told me to fuck off."

I never said that. You heard me. I didn't start it. I never do. Well, seldom do, but I sure didn't this time.

"All right mister, why don't you tell …"

He stopped in mid-sentence and stared at me.

"I know who you are," Detective Jake said. "You're the one helping that woman at the bank. That's you, isn't it?"

I didn't want to be nice anymore. "My business is with Diaz."

Detective Jake smiled and said, "Yep, that's him. He's the PI from up north. That case a few years ago, the missing broad. That's you, isn't it?"

I glared at the man and said, "Your mother ever wash your mouth out with soap?"

He grabbed the front of my jacket and yanked me out of the chair, which flipped over backward with a clatter-bang. Detective Jake was stronger and faster than he looked.

"Woods, Bercovicz. My office, now." The voice was loud, deep, and angry. It came from the offices. Detective Jake let go of my coat and the two men turned on their heels and walked toward the voice. A big man, tall and broad, stood in the doorway of the office opposite Diaz. He moved aside as the detectives went into the office. The big man shut the door with such force it rattled all the glass walls on his side of the room.

I saw Diaz standing at his desk. He motioned me over.

"Friendly bunch you got around here," I said.

"Some people don't know when to keep a sock in it," Diaz said. "They're about to get a hard lesson on that." He pointed in front of his desk. "Sit down."

I took a chair. "Thanks for making time to see me."

Diaz sat behind his desk and waited.

"A couple of developments in the Annie North case I thought you might be interested in."

"You don't say."

"I'm talking hypothetically. We on the same page?"

Diaz nodded. "Go ahead."

"Suppose I had a name, the last person to see Annie North alive."

"She's still alive as far as we know," Diaz said.

"Hypothetically, remember?"

Diaz shrugged.

"The person lives in town, saw Annie the day before she disappeared."

"You talk to this guy?"

"I have talked to the man, yes."

"You got a name?"

"I do, but I have to get the man's okay first. If I get it, are you interested?"

"Might be."

"That's good enough," I said.

"What else?" Diaz said.

"I found Conrad North. You interested?"

Diaz's eyes caught mine. He liked that one.

"Where?"

"Here."

"The fuck's 'here' mean?"

I paused, then said, "In town. A condo off Division."

"Sure it's him?"

"I'm sure."

I waited for Diaz to react like he did before, to resent anything I said about the Annie North case.

But he'd switched gears. He was interested.

"He using another name?" That question came from a veteran cop paying attention to his case.

"Yep," I said.

Diaz waited.

"Suppose I asked you to hold off talking to him."

"You're a funny guy, Russo, you know that? You came in here pissed I wasn't interested in the man. Now you want me to hold off?"

"Would you reopen the case?"

Diaz shook his head. "Nothing to go on, not yet anyway."

"Would you talk to Conrad?"

Diaz thought about that. "Have to admit it, Russo, you got me wondering. I might want to have a chat with the man, but I take it you'd rather I didn't do that."

"Not right now. I don't want Conrad to know we're watching."

"You've been following him?"

I nodded.

"Learn anything interesting?"

I shrugged. "Man travels with a bodyguard."

Diaz sat back and folded his arms across his chest.

"And you want to know why."

"Yeah, I do," I said. "Man's protecting himself. He's hiding something …"

"Or he plays poker, carries a lot of cash." Diaz sat forward, elbows on the desk. "Could be as simple as that, you know. It usually is."

"I'm not asking for much," I said. "Let's see if my guy will talk to you. If the answer's yes, talk to him first. Then move on Conrad."

Diaz tapped the keyboard off to his right and looked at the screen. "Ah, hell, Russo, I have too much shit on my plate. I'd have to slide your guy into my schedule as it is."

"If he agrees to see you?"

"Right," Diaz said. "It'd be three, four days before I'd have time to chase after Conrad North."

"Appreciate that," I said.

I may have sold Diaz short. There was more cop left in the detective than I thought.

Diaz pointed at the squad room. "Woods and Bercovicz," he said, and shook his head. "They're good cops. Just got some strange ideas about people, you know?"

"If you say so."

A small grin appeared on his face. "They used to pull that shit with me when I started work here. Oh, not those two, but cops just like them, a lot of years ago." Diaz paused, lost in memories. After a moment he re-focused on me. "Anything else?"

I shook my head and stood up.

"As soon as I know about my guy, I'll call."

I turned and reached for the door.

"Russo?"

I looked back. "Yeah?"

"You really think there's something to this?"

"Conrad North's a bad man, Detective. It's there. We just have to find it."

22

"Working with a cop we don't know?" Henri said. "Not a good decision, Russo." We sat in his SUV. He drank a fresh coffee. I didn't have one.

"We've worked with cops before, Henri."

"Sure, Martin Fleener, but we trust him."

"You mean, I trust him. You never trust cops."

"Probably never will either. They're more trouble than they're worth."

"They say the same thing about you, Henri. That's why they hassle you: you won't do what they tell you."

"Look who's talking?"

I turned toward Henri. "Sometimes, like now, it seemed the best choice."

"You really think Diaz will reopen the case?"

I shrugged. "Don't know, but he listened to me in there. Didn't do that before. We're going to need him on our side, we start messing with the citizens down here."

Henri drank some coffee. "Is it time to see Mr. Crosley?"

I looked at my watch. "To Washington Street."

Henri moved out of the parking lot, took Woodmere back toward downtown, and turned onto Washington.

"It's in the middle of the block," I said.

Henri slowed.

"There, the white Victorian with the long porch."

Henri parked across the street and turned off the motor. "Didn't realize I'd need more coffee. How long you going to be?"

"Move your ass, Henri, you're coming with me."

He looked over at me. "Crosley doesn't know me. He might not even talk to you."

"I want him to know we're serious. That we understand there's a risk talking to me, talking to Diaz. So, let's go."

Henri shrugged. "All right."

We crossed the street, went up the front walk and knocked on the door.

"Listen," I said. "Make sure he sees your gun, the shoulder holster. Kind of casually do it."

"You're a piece of work, you know that, Russo?"

Roland Crosley opened the door. He was (again) fashionably dressed: slacks, black T-shirt, same sweater as last time. He fixed his eyes on Henri. He didn't expect anyone else and it showed on his face.

"Mr. Crosley," I said, and explained why Henri was standing on the front porch.

"Come in, please," Crosley said with some hesitation.

We followed Crosley into the parlor. It looked as it did on my previous visit, more like a library out of the 1920s than a sitting room.

"Hello, Mr. Russo," a familiar voice said.

It was Patricia Geary. Apparently, Crosley had his own surprise.

"Ms. Geary," I said, and smiled. "Bank holiday?"

She shook her head. "No, the financial world never sleeps, I'm afraid."

I introduced Henri and we sat on one loveseat across a coffee table from Crosley and Geary on a matching loveseat.

"After Roland agreed to see you, he asked me to be here today." She smiled. "I knew you'd figure it out sooner or later, Mr. Russo."

"That you were able to keep Mr. Crosley's name away from the cops?"

Geary nodded slowly.

"Because he runs a safe house, and you'd rather the cops didn't know."

"It wouldn't be very safe if the authorities were aware of what I was doing," Crosley said. "We don't hide fugitives, Mr. Russo, but some of my guests find themselves in precarious situations with very powerful people."

"Like Conrad North."

"Precisely," he said. "Now, what brings you … the two of you … to my house today?"

"I think there's a better-than-even chance the police are about take another look at the Annie North case," I said.

Geary sat forward, her eyes wide. "I don't believe it," she said, "they'll reopen the case?"

"Well, I didn't say reopen the case, Ms. Geary."

"I didn't think so."

"But Detective Diaz is interested," I said. "I have his attention, which is more than I can say when I first met the man."

"He's 'interested' because you told him about me, didn't you?" Crosley said, edgy, annoyed.

"No, Mr. Crosley, I did not tell him about you," I said, speaking as calmly as possible. "I told him only that I knew the last person to see Annie North alive … before she disappeared. I did not tell him your name or anything about you."

"You had no right," Crosley said. "I don't like it."

"That's why I'm here," Henri said. "Two of us, Mr. Crosley."

"He doesn't get your name unless you give me the green light," I said.

Patricia Geary said, "That's why the police are interested again, isn't it? Because of Roland, because he's new to them?"

I nodded. "That, and we found Conrad North. You were right, Mr. Crosley, he lives here."

"In town, you mean?"

"Yes," I said. "The police didn't know about Conrad either. They're interested again, Mr. Crosley."

Geary reached out and put her hand on Crosley's arm. "Roland?"

The room was quiet except for the soft whirring of the ceiling fan.

Crosley took a deep breath and let it out slowly. "What would I have to do?"

"Give me permission to tell Detective Diaz who you are and how to contact you."

Crosley shook his head. "I figured that much out, Mr. Russo." He sounded annoyed, probably scared. "I meant what happens after you tell him about me?"

"He'll call you, arrange a time to talk."

"I have two conditions."

I felt like telling Crosley he didn't rate conditions, but I kept my mouth shut to see how it played out.

"First, I want Patricia with me when, what's his name again?"

"Diaz. Detective Vincente Diaz."

"Yes, I want Patricia here when the detective is here. I will only meet him here. I will not go to the police station, Mr. Russo. Is that clear?"

I wanted to say ... but I kept my mouth shut.

"It's possible he might come to your house."

"You could intercede on Roland's behalf, could you not, Mr. Russo?" Geary said.

I can only imagine what Henri was thinking.

"I'll talk to Diaz, see what I can do."

"I would appreciate that," Crosley said, and stood up.

I figured that was our signal to leave the parlor. We all shook hands and said our good-byes.

"I'll call Diaz and get back to you," I said to Crosley. "Thanks for your cooperation."

Henri and I left the house and returned to his SUV. He picked up his coffee cup and shook it gently. It was empty.

"Is this when you 'intercede' on behalf of good old Roland?"

"Give the guy a break, Henri, he's scared."

"Scared or not, he doesn't call the shots. You should have explained how these things work."

"His requests ..."

"His conditions, you mean?"

"Call them whatever you like, they're not unreasonable. Diaz will go for it. Crosley is his first new lead after all these years."

"So what are you waiting for? Call the cop house."

I took out my iPhone and tapped the number for Diaz.

When he answered, I said, "I have a verbal okay from my guy."

"Uh-huh."

"His name is Roland Crosley." I gave him Crosley's contact information.

"He has two conditions if you want to talk with him."

"I can't wait to hear this."

I explained the details.

"I don't think the Geary woman will be all that happy to see me."

"Me either, but Crosley wants her there, so she'll be there. You all right with his house?"

"Not a big deal at his house, as long as he can wait until morning. The rest of my day is packed."

"It's your decision, Detective, you and Crosley."

"I'll call the man," Diaz said, and clicked off.

"I take it Crosley's conditions were acceptable?"

"Yeah, he didn't seem to care about it one way or the other. They'll meet tomorrow morning."

"Speaking of morning," Henri said, "are we going to pick up Conrad at his condo?"

"How about we wait at the restaurant? If Conrad doesn't show, we'll have breakfast close by."

Henri laughed. "You're going to need some nourishment after another night on the couch."

23

By nine the next morning, we'd bought Starbucks at the counter in Meijer and sat in the parking lot for a few minutes absorbing the caffeine. It was another chilly morning, but the sky was blue and the sun hung just above the treetops, slowly warming the air.

"Hope they show this morning," I said. "I need a good night's sleep."

"Your idea to stay down here," Henri said. "I could've just shot him and been done with it."

I laughed. "Too soon for that, remember? Besides, I wanted to talk to Crosley, so it worked out."

Henri shifted the SUV into gear, and we drove off to the Silver Drive entrance for the Commons.

We cruised one lap around the Building 50 parking lot.

"There's Conrad's car," Henri said. "Don't see the kid's Honda."

We parked off Cottageview Drive and waited.

"See if we're luckier than yesterday," I said.

"By the way," Henri said, "the bodyguard, Jimmy Erwin? Kid's got a record."

"No surprise. What kind …"

"There, coming down the stairs," Henri interrupted. "Conrad and his woman friend."

Jessie Royce had her arm through Conrad's as they crossed the parking lot. She was about five-seven, her brown hair pulled back. She wore black jeans and a bomber jacket. Conrad, almost a foot taller than Royce, sported a blue nylon jacket and a cap with a Chicago Cubs "C" on the front.

Henri glanced at his watch. "Ten o'clock. Right on schedule."

Henri looked around, especially off to the sides, over near the Pleasanton Bakery. "Still don't see Erwin."

Conrad and Royce drove away slowly in Conrad's Focus and moved behind us. Henri pulled out and followed them. Traffic was light on Division, so he gave them plenty of room. When they turned onto Eighth Street, Henri said, "It's the Omelette Shoppe."

Conrad pulled into the parking lot next door to the restaurant and we turned into the lot on the other side of Cass from the restaurant.

"Well, well," Henri said. "See who just stepped out of the yellow Honda? Over there, at the parking meter."

"Good morning, Jimmy Erwin," I said.

Conrad's bodyguard was, indeed, tall, probably six feet, with a thin face sticking out under a black watch cap. "You described him pretty well, Henri. Sure looks silly in that big puffer coat."

"Don't let the wardrobe fool you," Henri said. "When you're skinny, hiding a holster and gun under a coat always looks silly."

Conrad and Royce stopped when Erwin called out. The three held a brief, animated conversation on the sidewalk. When they were finished, Erwin returned to his car and Conrad and Royce went inside the restaurant.

"What happens after breakfast?" I said.

Henri drank some coffee. "Depends."

"Uh-huh."

"Once they're done here, no pattern. Could be the mall or Front Street. Typical couple stuff. Most of the time, it's back home."

"How about Erwin?"

"He does what Conrad does."

"But Erwin usually meets Conrad at the condo?"

Henri nodded. "Usually."

"But not this morning. I wonder why?"

"Maybe he had a hot date last night," Henri said.

I finished the last of my coffee. "Well, I got my look at the girlfriend and the gunman."

"So plan A it is. We'll roust him after he finishes his eggs, like we would have done yesterday if he'd shown up."

"We have the edge right now," I said. "Everything changes once he knows we're on him."

"So you keep saying."

I paused. "But it's time to confront … hold on a second."

I dug the phone out of my jacket pocket. I didn't recognize the number, but I answered the call.

"Russo," I said, and listened.

It was a very brief conversation, not one I wanted to have.

"Be right there," I said, ending the call.

I pounded my fist on the dashboard, one, two, three times.

"Shit."

"What?" Henri said.

"Roland Crosley's been shot."

"Dead?"

"Yeah."

"What happened?"

"Diaz didn't say. He's at Crosley's house. Let's go."

Henri swung out of the lot, maneuvered quickly down State Street to Boardman. The residential section of Washington Street was blocked by patrol cars. Henri drove a half-block on and parked.

"Cops'll be all over the place," I said. "Sure you want to tag along?"

"Not an option this time. Crosley's part of our case."

As soon as we went around the yellow tape on Washington and started up the sidewalk, two patrol officers stopped us.

"Detective Diaz is expecting us," I said.

"Your name?" one of the officers said. I told him and he hit the talk button on his radio, spoke with someone then waved us through. The street was filled with flashing digital lights, several patrol cars, two ambulances, and two unmarked black sedans.

We were stopped again on Crosley's front porch, but not for long. "He's good," a voice said from inside the house. We walked into the foyer and another officer pointed us to the parlor, where I'd talked to Crosley yesterday.

Diaz sat on a loveseat talking to Patricia Geary. Standing off to the side was Detective Charlie Woods, the chubby cop from the station house. All three of them looked our way.

"Mr. Russo," Geary said as she stood and came over. Her face was wet with tears, her eyes puffy. I put my arms out and we hugged.

"I found him. On the floor. I thought he'd had a heart attack, a stroke, I don't know what I thought."

I looked at Diaz, but he was staring at Henri. Detective Woods, too.

"Who's your friend?" Diaz said.

"Colleague," I said, "we work …"

"Name's LaCroix," Woods said. "He's a troublemaker from up north."

It was almost imperceptible, but Henri moved a step to one side, away from Geary and me.

"This is Henri LaCroix," I said, "from Mackinac Island. He's working the case with me."

"Morning, Detective Diaz," Henri said, then turned toward Woods. "And who might you be?"

Woods took two steps in Henri's direction, "I am the po-lice," he said, stretching out both syllables. "I'd watch that smart mouth, if I were you."

"Charlie," Diaz said, "stay with Ms. Geary while I go to the kitchen with these two."

"I'll be back in a minute," I said to Geary, and we followed Diaz down a short hallway to the rear of the house. Crime scene people moved carefully around the kitchen, as well as a small porch leading to the backyard and the garage. They made notes and took pictures.

Roland Crosley lay on the tile floor in front of the refrigerator, on his right side, curled into a fetal position. A dark red stain covered the left side of his head, soaking the top of his silk pajamas and robe down to his shoulder. A half-gallon milk carton lay on its side on the floor in a pool of milk.

Diaz was the first to speak. "We're pretty sure the shooter came in the door," he said, pointing over his shoulder.

"Did you know about Roland Crosley before I called yesterday?"

"You mean had I ever heard of the man?"

"Yeah."

Diaz shook his head. "He wasn't on our radar screen."

"Did you wonder why Geary was a part of this? Why Crosley wanted her here for your meeting?"

Diaz shrugged. "We haven't gotten that far yet."

I stared at Crosley's body on the floor.

"Signs of a break-in?" I asked.

Diaz shook his head. "Door was unlocked. Everything else was tight."

"Geary found him?"

Diaz pointed vaguely in the direction of the living room. "She called it in, too. She closed the refrigerator door, but didn't touch anything else. She was pretty shaken when the patrol car arrived."

"So the shooter came through the door, walked up to Crosley and shot him? Just like that?"

"One in the temple."

"How long's it been?"

"Not even a few hours, but we'll know more after we have the report."

"Detective?" It was Henri.

"What's your name again?"

"Henri LaCroix."

Diaz nodded. "Okay, what?"

"Russo called you late yesterday, said Crosley wanted to talk."

"Uh-huh."

"You and Crosley agreed to meet this morning?"

Diaz looked at his watch. "At noon, yeah," he said, but it was still morning.

"You knew that Patricia Geary would be here?"

Diaz nodded. "What's your point?"

"Who else knew about the meeting?"

"I don't think I like that question, LaCroix."

"I don't care you like it or not, Detective," Henri said, "who else knew?"

Diaz turned toward Henri. "Look, pal, you invited yourself to this party."

Henri started to respond, but I put my hand out.

"Detective, that's Roland Crosley on the floor. He was the last person to see Annie North. He was shot to death twelve hours after he talked to you on the phone. Answer Henri's question."

"Detective Woods," Diaz said, loud enough to be heard outside the house.

Charlie Woods came into the kitchen.

"Detective, please escort these gentlemen out."

"My pleasure," Woods said, grinning.

"Out of the house and to the end of the street," Diaz said. "Just so we're clear."

"Move it," Woods barked, and waited for us to pass.

We walked up the hallway toward the front door.

"Mr. Russo?" Patricia Geary said from the parlor.

I stopped and turned.

"Keep moving," Woods said, but I ignored him. Henri, too.

Geary came into the hallway. "Are you leaving?"

"Yes," I said.

"Will you take me home, please? I walked over here this morning."

"Yes."

"You can't leave yet," Woods said as Diaz came into the hall.

"It's all right, Charlie," Diaz said. "We will need to talk again," he said to Geary, "but you can go."

Geary nodded. "You know how to find me," she said as she walked out the front door.

We followed her without further comment, but Woods kept us company all the way to the yellow tape at the end of the block.

Henri beeped the door locks and we climbed in, Geary in the back seat.

"Where to?" Henri said.

"I live on 7th," Geary said. "Just go up to the stoplight at the top of Boardman Lake and turn right."

Henri moved away slowly.

"Take Lake Street," Geary said, and we did, passing Patisserie Amie and Hagerty Insurance, underwriters for vintage cars.

I glanced at Hagerty's showroom as we went by, espying a late-60s Porsche 911. Very nice.

"You feel like talking a little?" I said to Geary.

She was silent.

I turned in my seat, but the look on her face was not anguish so much as anger.

"You okay?"

I saw her eyes move to Henri.

"Ms. Geary, Henri LaCroix knows everything I know. He's a close friend and he's working on your case. If you trust me, you can trust him."

She nodded. "It has nothing to do with you, Mr. LaCroix, it's just … it's just that I told you the cops don't care about us." Her voice was louder now, less hesitant. "I told you that, didn't I?"

"Us? You mean LGBTQ or women?" I said.

"Both," she said, "but you know what really pisses me off? Do you want to know?" She laughed, but she wasn't amused. "He was a man who wanted to help."

"He ran a safe house under the radar," I said.

"Sure. Years ago he helped women who wanted out of violent relationships, needed a place to hide, gay or straight. If you offer a safe house, word spreads. He also had friends in the community. One thing led to another, that's all."

"Second house on the right," Geary said, "with the car in the drive."

Henri slowed and stopped at the curb.

"Mind if I ask a few questions," I said, "about this morning?"

Geary shook her head. "Same things the police asked?"

"Some overlap probably."

"If you think it'll help."

"When you arrived at the house, notice anything unusual?"

She didn't hesitate. "Roland didn't answer the door, the front door. He always answered the door. That's when I went around back, saw him ... on the floor."

I asked a few more questions, but I didn't want to push. She'd been through enough.

"One last thing," I said. "Did you leave anything out when the police talked with you? Leave out intentionally, I mean."

She shook her head. "I answered all their questions, Mr. Russo. I don't trust them, but this, Roland dead ... I did the best I could."

"Do you have someone you can call? So you don't have to be alone?"

She offered a glimpse of a smile. "I already did."

Geary closed the car door and stood at my open side window. She leaned down, both hands on the door, and looked at Henri and me.

"They don't care about Annie, Mr. Russo." She shook her head. "After a few weeks, they won't care about Roland either."

"A murder gets a lot of attention," I said. "A missing person can fade away, but not a dead body."

"I'm not that naïve, Mr. Russo," she said, "I know that. It's their attitude, their arrogant assumptions. I'll miss Roland, I really will, but not half as much as the people he won't be able to protect."

24

"I thought you might have a few questions for Geary," I said to Henri. We were on our way to pick up my car. Traffic on Division was thick, moving along slowly.

"Had other things on my mind."

"Such as?"

"Conrad for one."

"Don't blame you there, but he's not going anywhere. We know where he lives, we know some of his routine, even where Wolfgang and Wilhelm live. He'll be easy enough to track."

Henri pulled into his friend's apartment complex, drove to the last building and parked next to my car.

"What else is on your mind?"

"Who killed Roland Crosley."

"I wondered about that, too, but this is a fresh case, Henri. We've just started."

"That's not what I mean."

"Yeah?"

Henri turned my way. "Think Patricia Geary's right about the cops? About Diaz and the others?"

"You asking, did they have a hand in Crosley's murder?"

Henri nodded. "For starters."

"No. I don't believe that for a second, but she's right about their attitude. Somebody ought to kick their asses into the 21st century, but that's a helluva long way from complicity in murder."

"Think they'll work the case?"

"Crosley's murder, sure. Can't have a man shot to death in his home two blocks off Front Street and ignore it. It wouldn't fly. The city fathers would raise a ruckus, the Chamber, everybody."

"But the disappearance of Annie North is a whole different matter."

"Yes, it is."

"They lost interest fast."

"That's why we're here," I said.

Henri put his hands on the steering wheel like he was about to drive away.

"I have an obvious question."

"Of course you do," I said, "let's have it."

"You think Conrad North is behind Crosley's death?"

"The thought occurred to me."

"Okay," Henri said, "let's run with that thought for a minute. Let's assume Conrad had Crosley killed. You with me?"

"So far, yeah."

"How'd Conrad know?"

"About Crosley?"

Henri nodded. "The cops didn't even have Roland Crosley's name."

"Conrad might have known about Crosley years ago, back when he had Annie killed."

"That's not what I meant. This is about right now," Henri said. "Crosley was back on somebody's radar screen. Had to be. You just talked with him. Did Conrad know you'd contacted Crosley? How'd he know?"

I sat back and thought about that for a minute.

"Not sure I like this."

"Me, either," Henri said.

"You think I was followed to Crosley's house?"

"Try this. Conrad has you watched, you visit Crosley, Conrad remembers Crosley."

"And Crosley ends up dead."

"Have you spotted a tail?"

"Haven't been looking."

"Experience, Russo. Instinct. You'd feel a tail long before you saw him."

"But we've been under the radar since this started. Conrad wasn't aware of us."

"You think Crosley getting dead is a coincidence?"

"Of course not. Be serious."

"Then you've been tailed, my friend."

"I missed it."

"Not many people could pull that off," Henri said, "but one man comes to mind."

I nodded slowly.

"Nils Lundberg."

"We know the man's out of jail," Henri said. "Is he still in Pittsburgh?"

"Last I heard."

"Time to find out."

I took out my phone and called Martin Fleener's cell. He answered after one ring.

"You must not be busy," I said.

"Guess not if I took your call. To what do I owe the pleasure?"

"Can you tell me where Nils Lundberg is?"

"Pittsburgh," he said, and paused. "Why are you asking? Something happen?"

I told him about Roland Crosley.

"Hold on," he said, "let me check."

I put the phone on speaker and set it on the dashboard. We waited.

"Russo? Still there?"

"Yeah, Marty, go ahead."

"He's in still Pittsburgh," Fleener said. "Lundberg might be good, but he can't follow you when he's in Pennsylvania and you're in Michigan."

"How fresh is the information?"

"Very. He was seen this morning at a local coffee shop."

I looked over at Henri, who shrugged.

"Appreciate the help, Marty."

"I'll get hold of you if anything changes," he said, clicking off.

"If it wasn't Lundberg," Henri said, "who was it?"

"You mean who followed me, or who shot Crosley?"

"Both," Henri said.

"Not many choices here in northern Michigan."

"Jimmy Erwin?" Henri said.

"You think so?"

Henri hesitated for a moment.

"Got a better choice?" I said.

Henri shook his head. "Not right now."

I thought for a minute. "Erwin wasn't with Conrad this morning."

"First time that's happened," Henri said. "They met at the restaurant."

"So the bodyguard left Conrad vulnerable from home to breakfast," I said, "from the Commons to downtown. The question is why?"

"What's more important than protecting your charge?"

"Killing Crosley would be more important," I said, "if Conrad ordered it."

"What'd Diaz say about the time of death, you remember?"

"Not more than a few hours. Best he could do until the ME was finished."

"Lot of moving pieces to this case, Russo."

25

"No argument from me," Sandy said. "Every time you two leave the office, this case grows more legs than an octopus." We sat in the front office. I'd arrived from Traverse first, then Henri.

As daylight faded in the western sky, the temperatures dropped. A light dusting of snow would show up any morning now. The *Old Farmer's Almanac* predicted that northwest lower Michigan would be in for an easy winter. I wondered if those farmers ever heard of lake effect snow.

"I'm with you," Sandy said. "I think Conrad ordered Erwin to kill Crosley. I bet he told Erwin to follow you, too."

"Erwin's a shooter," Henri said. "I got no problem with that. But the kid would have to be awful good to tail Michael."

"You didn't think you were being followed?" Sandy said.

"Wasn't looking, but it's the only thing that makes sense, much as I hate to admit it. I talk to Crosley, Conrad gets nervous and gives the order."

"Could be Conrad had a second guy working for him," Henri said.

"Don't worry about that right now," Sandy said, "you'll figure it out eventually. Listen to me, you two gumshoes overlooked ..."

"Gumshoes," I said, "is that what you called us? That word's so old it's got gray hair. Nobody knows that word anymore."

"I use the word, thank you very much. People who read Raymond Chandler or Dashiell Hammett know it, too."

"You mind if I interrupt lit class on detective writers?" Henri said.

Sandy started to say something, but we heard someone on the stairs.

"Probably AJ," I said. "Told her to meet me here."

AJ came through the door. Her Saturday outfit consisted of a white turtleneck, tight black jeans and a hooded parka. When she saw us staring, she stopped.

"What? Did I do something?"

Sandy spoke first. "Do you ever use the word 'gumshoe'?"

AJ looked a bit perplexed. "I call him lots of things," she said, jacking a thumb in my direction. "It sounds like I'm breaking up an important discussion." She rolled her eyes and smiled.

"Not as far as I'm concerned," Henri said. "I was trying to get these two to focus."

"How's that going?"

"Not well."

"Is this going to take long?" AJ said. "I'm hungry."

"Sandy was about to tell us how the 'gumshoe' and I messed up."

"Messed up? You?" AJ said, stretching out the last word sarcastically. "Would someone please fill me in, so I can appreciate *how* you two screwed up?"

Sandy happily reprised the last twenty-four hours.

"All right, Sandy," Henri said, "tell us what we missed."

"It so basic," she said. "I can't believe it wasn't the first thing that caught your attention."

"What is it?" I said.

"Assuming Conrad had Michael followed, why?" Sandy leaned forward on the desk and held up two fingers. "There are only two options. Conrad's been following him regularly these last couple of years."

"That doesn't seem likely," Henri said.

"Or," AJ said, "something happened, something scared Conrad."

"Thank you, *Stephanie Plum*," Sandy said. "Sure glad someone's acting like a private eye."

"Conrad could have been watching Crosley instead of Michael," AJ said.

Sandy shrugged. "It's the same problem. Michael shows up on Crosley's front porch. Once Conrad knows Michael and Crosley have talked, the man's dead."

"Think about it, Michael," AJ said. "If Sandy's right, you did something that scared Conrad."

"Like what?" I said.

"I don't know. Maybe he was afraid you were after him again, that you were going to dog him like you did before."

"But Conrad's an arrogant prick," Henri said. "He beat Russo once, he'd be convinced he could do it again, unless …"

"Unless, what?" I said.

"Unless Conrad's hiding something," Henri said, "and he's worried you've found him out."

"The man hides lots of things," I said, "how he makes his money, his occasional contacts with the mob."

"That's all old business, boss," Sandy said.

"What's that leave us with?" AJ said.

"Camille or Annie," Henri said.

That hushed the conversation. It was the realization that whenever we talked about Conrad North, the conversation eventually returned to the missing and the murdered.

"It's Annie," Sandy said. "We have nothing new on Camille's murder. I wish we did, but we don't. It has to be Annie."

"We don't have much on Annie either," I said.

"Maybe not," Sandy said, "but thanks to Patricia Geary, you reopened the Annie North case and Conrad found out."

"Hold on a minute," AJ said. "Before we get too far, how did Conrad know that? What did Michael do that got his attention?"

"How many cases you running?" Henri asked me.

I hesitated, so Sandy stepped in. "Five, four legit cases, one sort-of case."

"What's a sort-of case?" AJ said.

"Nicole Sanderson," Sandy said. "I'll get to her in a minute. Three of the cases, Stevens, Wilder, and Ray, are routine matters, nothing unusual. Patricia Geary makes four."

"What about Nicole Sanderson?" AJ said.

"She's not an official case," Sandy said, "at least I don't think so."

"Nicole's not a case," I said.

"Why not?"

"Well, for one thing," Sandy said, "we're not getting paid. The boss is doing a pro bono checking on a pesky couple trying to buy Nicole's cottage. That makes the count five cases."

Our usually talkative group fell silent, like we were trying to invent reasons why the cases were important.

"Leave the routine cases out," Henri said. "Did it occur to anyone that both Geary and Sanderson are connected to Conrad North?"

"So what?" AJ said. "The man still had to find out that Michael was nosing around again, asking questions."

"Well, it's obvious that Patricia Geary didn't call him with a heads-up." Sandy said.

"How about Diaz?" Henri said. "You talked to him at the station, maybe someone saw you and told Conrad."

"Told him what?" I said, shaking my head. "That's a long shot, if you ask me."

"Sure as hell, Nicole Sanderson didn't call her stepfather," Sandy said.

"No, she detests the man," I said, "but what do we really know about that couple ... what's the name?"

"Freeland, Drew and Emily Freeland, Hamilton Road, Okemos," Sandy said.

"Right, Freeland. Did you check them out? Talk to them?"

Sandy shook her head. "Sorry, boss. Didn't get to it with everything else going on. You think there's something screwy there?"

I shrugged. "Have no idea," I said, "but Irma Renner thought so."

"Isn't she the real estate agent on the island?" AJ said.

I nodded. "Let's make sure."

"I'll check them out," Sandy said, "first thing."

"Well, I'm not sure that helped much," AJ said.

"Yeah, it did, AJ," I said. "At least we have a lead on how Conrad knew I was on him."

"What do you think Conrad's hiding, Henri?" AJ said.

"Too early to tell," Henri said. "Only thing, I bet it's related to Annie or Camille."

"That doesn't help much either," AJ said.

"True," I said, "but one thing often leads to another. Remember, Diaz wanted nothing to do with me or Annie North until he found out the recently murdered Roland Crosley helped Annie get away from her husband."

"Think that was enough for the cops to reopen the case?" Henri said.

"Don't know," I said. "It's find out."

I picked up my cell and tapped the Traverse City police.

"Vincente Diaz, please," I said when the call was answered. "Michael Russo calling."

I set the phone to "speaker" and put it on the desk. We waited several minutes before Detective Diaz finally came on the line.

"Michael Russo calling, Detective."

"What can I do for you?" Diaz said. "Lot going on here."

"A couple of quick questions, that's all."

His squad room was noisy with loud voices, phones ringing, and a banging sound I couldn't identify.

"Make it quick," he said.

"You have the ME's report on Crosley yet?"

"Right here on my desk."

"Anything odd or unusual?"

"Not a thing," Diaz said.

"When did the man die?"

"We had it right. Two, three hours before we answered the call."

"Okay," I said. "Anything else?"

"Routine shooting, I'd say. Crime scene report ought to be here today. It won't tell us anything we don't already know."

"Appreciate the time, Detective …"

"There is one more thing," Diaz said. "I was going to call you, got too busy."

I looked up just as Henri sat up straighter and looked back at me. "Uh-huh."

"We've officially reopened the Annie North case."

Sandy silently mouthed "Yes!" as she pumped two fists in the air.

"Same status?" I said.

"It's still a missing person's case, if that's what you mean," Diaz said.

"Not a murder case?"

"I need more evidence for that."

"Like what?" I said.

"I know what you're getting at, Russo. Let's just say we're aware the two cases might be linked and let it go at that."

"Okay, okay. Thanks," I said, and hung up.

"Well," Henri said, "There's life in the old boy yet. Looks like he might not want to retire just yet."

"Crosley's murder is linked to Annie North," AJ said. "That would be too big of a coincidence, even for me."

"Never thought he'd reopen the case," I said. "I think Diaz is one piece of information away from making Annie North a murder investigation."

26

None of us had moved. We were absorbing the unexpected good news. Diaz might not be an ally in my investigation, but he was no longer an adversary.

AJ stood up. "Enough," she said. "I thought I was hungry when I walked in here. Time to be on our way, Michael."

"I could pour us some Oban," I said, pointing at the outer office.

"No. Food. My stomach's beginning to think my throat's been cut. Let's go. My treat."

"That does it," I said, and stood up. "You know where the Oban is," I said to Sandy. "Pour yourselves a drink. The lady's buying me dinner."

We grabbed our coats and headed down the stairs.

"Where we going?" I said. "Chandler's, City Park Grill?"

AJ stopped, which meant I did too.

"What?"

"You have Chardonnay at home?" AJ said.

"My apartment, you mean?"

"That's the place. Chardonnay?"

"Of course. So we're not going to Chandler's?"

AJ shook her head.

"City Park Grill?"

AJ shook her head again and smiled.

"Can I ask why not?"

"Of course you can, darling."

"Okay, I'll bite, why not?"

"How would it look if I start rubbing your leg in public?"

"Like you were rubbing my leg?"

"Let me rephrase." She pulled me close and whispered, "How would it look if I put my hand between your legs in public?"

"Like we'd be better off in my apartment."

"Now you're catching on."

"I thought you were starving?"

"I am," she said. "Roast & Toast is still open. How about we do carry-out to your living room?"

"Splendid idea," I said, and we walked into the restaurant to place an order.

Twenty-five minutes later, we closed the apartment door and put our food on the kitchen table. AJ took her coat off and handed it to me.

"Put the food in the refrigerator," she said, "pour some wine. I'll be back in a few minutes."

"Where're you going?"

"Take a quick bath."

"What about your food? Starving, and all that."

AJ ignored my comment. "I might want to screw your lights out sooner rather than later. The wine better be ready when I return," she said as she vanished down the hallway toward the bathroom.

I took a bottle of Avant Chardonnay from the refrigerator, picked up two glasses and went to the living room couch. The pipes always made an odd noise when the tub was filling with water. I poured wine in the glasses and sat back with my feet propped on the coffee table.

A few minutes later, AJ returned to the living room. She wore an old pair of my running pants and a dark gray zippered fleece with "Michigan State" lettered across the front. Her hair was pulled back tight with a hair tie.

"Pants are kind of big," AJ said, picking up her wine.

"Cheers." We touched glasses. "That tastes good."

She sat back, close to me, and put her feet up. We enjoyed being with each other, quietly.

After a while I said, "I'll get our food."

"Wait," AJ said, and put her glass on the coffee table. She turned toward me, unzipped the fleece and pulled it back. "My nipples are hard."

"I can see that."

AJ picked up my hand and kissed it. "Let's go," she said, "before I rip these pants off right here."

Some measure of pleasurable time later, AJ moved her right leg, lifted her head off my chest, and kissed my cheek. "Now I really am hungry," she said. "Making love always does that."

"I'm hungry, too."

"Give me a minute," she said.

AJ pulled the blanket and sheet back in one sweeping, theatrical gesture.

"You've been watching too many movies."

"Look who's talking," she said, and eased up on her knees. She put her hands on her hips and stared down at me. "I want you again," she said, "but I really have to eat something first."

"Okay," I said, and laughed softly.

"How about I spend the night? Do you have to be out early?"

I shook my head. "No earlier than usual. Going to run in the morning."

"Of course you are," she said, and slapped my stomach.

"Ouch."

AJ laughed. "Food now. Your body for dessert." She climbed off the bed. "Meet you in the other room."

By the time AJ arrived in the living room, I'd plated my avocado veggie sandwich, her Bleu Bay salad, put them on the coffee table and poured more wine.

"Those pants are a little big," I said.

"I tied them tight," she said. "They'll stay on, at least for a while."

I bit a large chunk out of my sandwich. AJ picked up the bowl and ate several satisfying bites of salad.

"Nice idea you had, coming back here."

"Yes." She leaned over and kissed my cheek. "Mind if I ask how you're doing?"

"About what?"

"About Conrad, about Crosley?"

I shrugged out of hesitation, not indifference. "I don't like that Crosley was killed, AJ."

"No one does, but you're not responsible, Michael."

"I know that."

"You were hired to do a job. It doesn't always go down easily."

"You're telling me," I said. "Now I'm worried about Patricia Geary."

"Because she was close to Crosley?"

I picked up my wine and took a drink. "Exactly. I don't know that she's in more danger now, but she's scared."

"After finding the body? Hell, I'd be scared and I'm way more used to this than she is."

"Good point. We need to pay more attention to her for a while."

"I think you should give her a call, run down and see her."

"Even if she says she's okay?"

"If Geary says everything's okay, it's not. Go anyway. Make up an excuse if you have to."

AJ stood and picked up the dishes.

"Hey, the pants didn't fall off," I teased.

27

"**W**hat time is it?" AJ said in a low, guttural voice. We were a tangle of legs and arms, sheets and pillows: nothing unusual, in other words.

"Clock's on your side of the bed." As if she needed a reminder.

I felt a leg move, but it wasn't mine. Then AJ rolled over. "Seven-twenty."

"You late?" I said.

She rolled back my way, put a leg across my thighs and laid her head on my chest.

"I'm okay," she said. "You're running this morning, right?"

"Uh-huh. Days are getting shorter and shorter. Don't have enough light 'till about eight o'clock."

"How about I make coffee." AJ eased herself out of bed and moved toward the door.

"You don't have any clothes on."

"I need clothes to make coffee?" She'd stopped at the bedroom door. "Is that a house rule?"

"Wouldn't want you to get cold, darling."

"Your concern for my welfare is quite charming," she said, and left the room.

A few minutes later, we sat at the small kitchen table with hot coffee. I'd put on a two-piece nylon running suit and a new pair of shoes.

"I see you found time to put your clothes on," I said.

"Have to stay warm," she replied, grinning.

"Are you going to talk to Conrad any time soon?"

I shrugged. "Sure. Roland Crosley going down got in the way."

"Of course it did, but you should do it, Michael. Conrad won't be surprised to see you."

"You're probably right."

"Of course I am," she said. "Oops, time to leave."

AJ put her mug in the sink and kissed me. "See you later."

She took her jacket from the closet and went out. I heard "Bye!" from the other side of the front door.

There was just enough morning light to run familiar streets. I clicked my watch and headed to the peaceful streets of Bay View Association. By the time I turned onto Terrace Avenue, muscles were loose and comfortable.

Few residents were left to share the community with all the construction and maintenance people. So, imagine my surprise when I spied a runner, a woman, at the far end of the street coming my way.

The gap between us closed. She was about five-seven, with a long dark pony tail that swung in pace with her stride. She wore black tights and a pale pink nylon jacket. She wasn't thin like the typical runner, but she moved with the ease and agility of one.

We waved as runners often do when they pass each other. I smiled and continued on my way. The woman must have flipped around because she was now matching my pace, stride for stride.

"Do you mind if I tag along?" she said. "I really don't know where I'm going."

"You a visitor?"

"Business trip," she said. "My first time in town. Staying at the Perry Hotel. Know it?"

"Yeah," I said. I glanced at my watch. "I live near the hotel. I'm doing forty more minutes on these streets if you want to come along."

"I'd love to," she said. We moved smoothly together the rest of the time and exchanged only a few words.

About three blocks from home, I slowed up and so did she. We walked at a brisk pace.

"I'm Bobbie Fairhaven," she said, and reached over to shake hands.

"Michael Russo." I pointed down the street. "The Perry."

"Thanks for letting me join you. I probably would have found my way back, but this was more fun. I hate to miss a run, even on the road."

"I know the feeling."

"So where are you going?" she said.

"Over there." I pointed at my apartment building. "The other side of the parking lot."

As we came around the corner of the hotel, I noticed Henri fifty feet in front of us. He was standing behind a blue Camry sedan, leaning on the windshield. His other arm was at his side, concealed by the car. Not a good sign. He glanced around the parking lot, at the hotel door, then at a row of trees to his left.

Something was up. We were twenty feet apart.

"Afternoon, Bobbie," Henri said.

She did not respond.

"Bobbie? Long time no see."

"You two know each other?" I said.

"The hell you doing here, LaCroix?" Bobbie said.

It was smooth and imperceptible, but she'd moved two steps away from me.

"Quiet neighborhood," Henri said, "friendly people."

"Bullshit."

"Bobbie, is that any way to greet an old friend?"

"I'll ask again, Henri, why are you here?"

Henri shook his head slowly. "I ask the questions around here, Bobbie."

"She said she was in town on business," I said.

"Did she now. What business would that be?"

Bobbie put her hands on her hips, like she was about to answer the question.

"Freeze, Bobbie," Henri said. His right hand, once hidden behind the Camry, held a handgun with a silencer threaded into the barrel. It was pointed at her.

"Not a move, Bobbie. Nothing. Breathe too hard, I'll put two in your forehead."

"You gonna take me here?"

"Two pops, Bobbie," Henri said. "Pop, pop. Nobody'll hear."

She remained still.

"Russo, she's got a small Beretta under the jacket, her right hip. Don't reach. Move around, come in from behind."

"Nice of you to remember, Henri," she said. "Hands on my head?"

Henri nodded. "Do it easy."

She lifted both arms in the air. I took the gun from a leather holster, stepped away and popped the clip out.

"Arms down?"

"Go ahead," Henri said.

She put her arms down.

"What're you calling yourself these days, Bobbie?" Henri said as he came from behind the car. He held his gun straight down, close to his leg.

"Said her name was Bobbie Fairhaven."

"Fairhaven?" Henri said. "She look like a Fairhaven to you? Dark skin, darker hair. Her name's Roberta Lampone — Sergeant Roberta Lampone, to be exact. Army Ranger usually on loan to the CIA as an assassin."

"U.S. Army, retired," she said, and smiled.

"You don't say? How long?"

"Eighteen months."

"Heard you were in Chicago, hanging with some of the old crew."

"For a while," Bobbie said.

"You freelancing?"

She didn't respond.

"Don't suppose you chose Petoskey for a vacation."

She shrugged.

"And here I thought you just wanted to run with a nice guy like me," I said.

"You're lucky, Russo," Henri said. "People been known to die when Bobbie shows up."

"Is that right?" I said.

"Who're you working for, Bobbie?" Henri said.

"Did I say I was working?"

"Bobbie? You told Russo you were here on business."

She kept silent.

"Come on, Bobbie, don't fuck with me."

"Fuck you, Henri. Maybe I'm on vacation."

"No, you're not, you're working," Henri said. "What is it this time, big money, big power or a big dick? Got to be one."

"Fuck you."

"You said that already. My guess is you're working for Joey."

"Joey DeMio?" I said.

"Bobbie's grandfather ran with Carmine on the South Side a lot of years ago."

"Small world," I said.

Henri nodded. "The families fought hard for a long time, then Carmine brokered a deal that ended the war."

"My father ended the war, not old man DeMio."

"Have it your way, Bobbie, but the war ended and you went to work for the DeMios."

"What could you offer the DeMios?" I said, but she ignored my question.

"Bobbie's a shooter, Russo. Army trained, wartime experience."

"Just like you, Henri," she said.

"Better than you, Bobbie," Henri said, and smiled.

"Why you working for Joey DeMio?" I said.

She turned and looked at me like she finally recognized someone else was there.

"Answer the man, Bobbie. What're you doing for DeMio?"

"Who says I work for DeMio?"

"I say so," Henri said. "What's the job?"

Bobbie shrugged. "He needed a gunman."

"He's got Cicci and Rosato for that."

"Somebody quicker, younger. Simple as that."

Henri smiled and holstered his gun.

"Give her the clip back, Russo. Put it in the left jacket pocket and pull the zipper tight."

"Still careful after all these years, eh, Henri?"

"Still alive after all these years, Bobbie. Now give her the Beretta."

I handed over the gun, and she returned it to its holster.

"You really staying at the Perry?" I said.

She looked at me again. Recognition had become disdain.

"Go on, get out of here, Bobbie," Henri said. "Back the way you came."

Sergeant Roberta Lampone, aka Bobbie Fairhaven, U.S. Army retired, backed up a few steps, turned and set into a light run up Rose Street.

"She pick you up in the middle of your run?"

"Uh-huh."

"She knew exactly what she was doing."

"I don't think she liked me much, Henri," I said as we watched Bobbie jog at a good pace toward Arlington. "Guess I'm not as charming as I used to be."

"Remember two things, Russo, you ever meet Bobbie again."

"Yeah?"

"She's an experienced killer who plays by her own rules."

I stretched my hamstrings and thought about that. But first things first.

"Henri, what are you doing here?"

"You didn't answer your phone, so I called AJ."

"She told you I went for a run?"

He nodded.

"Let's go inside," I said.

We went up the back stairs to my apartment. Henri made coffee while I took a quick shower, dressing in khakis and a navy crewneck sweater before meeting him in the kitchen. I sat down with a bottle of water and hot coffee.

"So what are you doing here?" I said.

"I've been thinking about Conrad."

"Lot of that going around," I said.

"It's time we had a talk with Mr. Conrad North," he said. "No interruptions."

"When?"

"Tomorrow."

28

Henri picked me up just after dark. I tossed a small bag in the back seat of his SUV, and he drove over to U.S. 131. The air was crisp, the sky clear. Once south of town, stars lit up the night sky. Henri moved along smoothly with the light traffic.

"Have a nice dinner with Margo?"

"Always nice," he said, "no matter the reason. What did AJ have to say?"

"A face-to-face is coming, she knew that. Only a matter of time now that Crosley's been killed. You still want to catch Conrad in town even if he's with his girlfriend?"

"As much as I'd like to clip him, get it over with," Henri said, "we'll talk to him first. Less likely to be trouble from his gunman if she's there, on the street, middle of town."

"You still sure he'll drive downtown for breakfast?" I said.

"It's a habit. Weekend's over, restaurant won't be busy. That block of Cass is good. Conrad won't be happy wherever it happens, but Jimmy Erwin won't get trigger happy out in the open like that. We can see three directions if we need to. I like it."

"So I sleep on the couch tonight?"

"Life in the big city, Russo."

"One night's my limit, then I check in at the Park Place."

"Suit yourself."

But I didn't need a hotel room. The next morning, we picked up two dark roasts from Higher Grounds Coffee around the corner from Building 50. By the time Henri swung over to the parking lot, Conrad and Jessie Royce were next to Conrad's car talking with Jimmy Erwin. Conrad left the Commons first, followed closely by Jimmy Erwin. Both cars turned onto Division for the short ride downtown.

"Think Erwin's looking for a tail?" I said.

"He hasn't yet."

Henri kept the car a discreet distance away in light traffic.

"I have an idea," he said.

"And you haven't even finished your coffee yet."

Henri waved off my attempt at morning humor. "Let's stop them after breakfast."

"You think they'll be less alert to trouble?"

"Maybe. Conrad has a nice meal, Erwin's bored. Just another morning in town."

Both cars took Front Street over to State where it became one-way. Conrad went into the parking lot next door to the Omelette Shoppe, Erwin parked on the street by the restaurant, and we pulled into the lot across the street. Henri put a row of cars between Erwin and us.

"After breakfast is okay with me," I said. "We'll sit."

Erwin left his car. He wore that familiar oversized puffer jacket to conceal a holster. He crossed Cass and waited on the sidewalk for Conrad and Jessie to enter the restaurant, then returned to his car.

Henri leaned his seat back and drank some coffee. "They won't be long," he said.

"The happy couple's not big on conversation over breakfast?"

"Or dinner," Henri said, shaking his head. "One of the first nights I tagged along, they went to Amical. I watched from the bar."

"You went inside?"

"Hell, they were gazing into each other's eyes, not looking for a tail. I lingered over a Bell's ale, thinking about a second, when they paid the tab." Henri gestured at the Omelette Shoppe. "This is eggs, not Amical."

What was left of my coffee cooled off quickly. Heavy clouds had filled the sky, and the temperature was stuck at thirty-nine according to the dashboard computer. Henri ran the motor a few times to keep the windows clear.

"Who will move first?" I said.

"Erwin," Henri said. "When he opens the car door, Conrad's alerted him they're coming out. He'll meet them on the sidewalk."

"You'll make sure it won't work that way this morning."

Henri nodded. "I'll convince Erwin no harm will come to his boss. We only want to talk, that's all. No gun play, no trouble."

"You think Erwin'll buy that?"

Henri looked over and smiled. "I'll be quite persuasive."

I'd just finished the last of the coffee, when suddenly Henri was gone. Without a word, he was out of the vehicle and moving swiftly toward Erwin's car. He closed the gap in seconds and stood next to Erwin on the street. I followed and glanced at Henri as I went by. Jimmy Erwin leaned against his car, arms folded: he didn't look happy.

I crossed Cass just as Conrad and Jessie Royce exited the restaurant. They both wore jeans and quilted parkas sized correctly, since they had no need to hide guns. Up close, Conrad seemed thinner, the lines around his mouth and eyes sharper, than the last time we'd faced each other. He saw me and stopped. Before he realized Erwin was missing, I held my arms out, palms up.

"No trouble, Conrad."

Jessie picked up that something was wrong and edged closer to Conrad. He used his arm to move her behind him.

"I just want to talk," I said.

Conrad glanced around and spotted Erwin. His shoulders sagged when he realized the setup.

"Five minutes, Conrad," I said. "Ms. Royce, good morning."

"Jessie," Conrad said. "I want to talk with Mr. Russo. Why don't you wait in the car? I'll be right along."

"But ..."

"It's all right," Conrad said. "Go on."

Jessie moved slowly away.

"How do you do it, Conrad?"

He tilted his head slightly, not understanding.

"How do you explain Jimmy over there to your girlfriend? You need a bodyguard because this is such a tough town?"

Conrad glared at me. His face was flat, expressionless. It was either boredom or contempt.

"I'd prefer not to stand here any longer than necessary, Mr. Russo. You don't have the guts to kill me right here, so what do you want?"

I smiled. If he taunted me again, I might just surprise him.

"You, Conrad, I want you. But I suspect you already know that. Otherwise, you wouldn't have killed Roland Crosley."

He stiffened and pulled his head back, just a little. I moved closer, but Conrad did not retreat.

"You didn't have to kill Crosley. He had nothing to do with this — but, what, you couldn't be sure? So you had him ruthlessly gunned down in his own home?"

"What's your point?"

"You, Conrad, you're the point. I'll get you for Crosley. And Camille."

Conrad smirked. I expected no less. He'd gotten away with killing his second wife when she was my client, had no reason to believe anything had changed.

"I know what you're thinking, but this is different. First Annie, then Camille, now Crosley. Either the cops make the case or you deal with me. One way or the other, you're going over for it."

I turned away and crossed the street to Henri and Jimmy Erwin.

"You gentlemen enjoying the morning air?" I said.

"We've been having a delightful conversation," Henri said. "Isn't that right, Jimmy?"

Erwin stared straight ahead and was silent.

"The conversation was one-sided," Henri said, "especially since I told him if he said word one, he wouldn't live to see his next birthday."

"You take his gun?"

Henri nodded. "Told him he moved even a hand, it'd be the last thing he'd ever do."

"Must have listened, he's still alive."

"You finished with his boss?"

I nodded.

"Well then Jimmy, my good man, you're free to go," Henri said. He clapped a hand on the kid's shoulder, making him jump.

Erwin looked at me, then fixed his gaze on Henri.

"I heard about you, LaCroix, heard you was a tough guy. I respect that. You cause trouble for a lot of people. I respect that, too. Don't make trouble for Mr. North. Leave him alone. Do that, and we're okay."

"Go take care of your boss," Henri said, and handed Erwin his automatic. "I'll keep the clip as a souvenir."

"See you again, LaCroix," Erwin said. "Different playing field next time." His voice was clear but thin. It didn't have enough resonance to put force behind a casual threat.

"Any playing field you want, Jimmy. Go on."

Erwin turned and walked slowly across the street to Conrad's car. Jessie sat inside, the motor running. Erwin stood with Conrad. Conrad did most of the talking, and Erwin never shifted his gaze from us.

"Let's get out of here," I said.

"You go back to the car," Henri said. "I'll hang here a minute."

"You think Erwin'll try something?"

"Probably not, but I'll wait for them to leave," Henri said, and walked slowly away from Erwin's Honda.

Conrad went to his car and left the lot. Erwin walked back to his car, opened the door: he looked back at Henri for a long moment before he got in and drove away.

Henri climbed in his SUV and started the motor. "Time to go home?"

"You in a hurry?" I said.

Henri looked over and said, "Not necessarily. What's up?"

"Omelette Shoppe's still serving breakfast."

29

Two breakfasts and plenty of fresh hot coffee later, we left Traverse City.

"Why don't you stay on 31?" I suggested.

"I can do that," Henri said, "any particular reason?"

"Haven't been through Elk Rapids or Charlevoix in a long time."

"Uh-huh."

"Two lanes all the way home," I said. "Not much traffic in late October."

"Be easier to spot a tail, too," Henri said.

"Especially a yellow Honda."

"Think Erwin's behind us?"

"Don't know," I said, "let's find out."

Henri went straight through the light at M-72. "Charlevoix, here we come."

Traffic was always lighter after the tourist season was over. We passed through Elk Rapids and Torch Lake, were still fifteen minutes out of Charlevoix.

"Nobody's following us," Henri said, "not a yellow Honda or anything else with four wheels. You can relax."

"Not sure I'm ready to relax just yet," I said.

"You expect Conrad to try something?"

"Yeah. Question is, when?"

"You push him that hard?"

"Not so hard, really, but I insulted him, made it personal. Like he wouldn't out-smart us this time."

"You could have ignored him, just kept following the clues."

"What clues?" I said. "Wolfgang? Wilhelm?"

"You wanted to poke your finger in the hornet's nest."

"It's dues time, Henri. People are dead because of him."

"The cops are working their end too, Russo. You're not the only one."

"The cops? Funny coming from you."

Henri snapped his head my way. "Look, Russo, cops have never been my favorite people, but Diaz reopened the case."

"Keep your eyes on the road, will you? Crosley's murder forced Diaz to reopen the case, Henri. I don't think he had much choice."

"Have it your way, but you put the squeeze play in motion this morning."

"First time since Camille's murder we've had any leverage to do that."

By the time we reached Bay Harbor, the sky was spitting sleet at the windshield. The wipers kept up pretty well, but ice clogged around the blades. Traffic in Petoskey was sluggish, as usual. Henri found a spot in the lot behind the office, and we went inside.

"We need to be ready for Conrad to make a move," Sandy said after we filled her in on our morning adventure.

"Does it bother you I did that?" I said.

Sandy shook her head. "Your decision, not mine. I'm just along for the ride."

Henri laughed. "Got to remember you said that. Might come in handy someday."

"Funny man," Sandy said, and picked up a yellow pad. "While you two gentlemen were busy pissing off Conrad," she held the pad in the air, "Nicole Sanderson's cottage, remember?"

"Damn, I forgot to call her," I said. "She wanted an update. Of course, I don't have anything new to tell her."

Sandy smiled and, with a touch of drama, dropped the yellow pad on her desk. "You do now."

"I do?"

Sandy nodded. "Yup. But don't call Nicole just yet."

"This ought to be good," Henri said.

Sandy pointed at the pad. "The contact information for the Freelands? It didn't work. The phone number was either old or wrong, or something. It got me nowhere."

"Did you try a reverse look-up?"

"Of course. The number doesn't exist, so …"

"It didn't work."

"Nope. So, I looked up the address, on Hamilton Road? Nothing."

"Meaning what?" I said.

"I tried a couple of sites," Sandy said, "like *Zillow*. Nothing, the address doesn't exist."

"You couldn't find a listing for the house?" Henri said.

"I couldn't find the house. It doesn't exist either."

"Seems odd," I said.

"I thought so, too," Sandy said, "so I decided to be creative, seeing as how I'm paid the big bucks."

"Now I know this'll be good," Henri said.

"It's better than that, gentlemen. I called the Meridian Township Police. They cover Okemos. Told them who I was and what I needed. They were very helpful. The house doesn't exist because the address doesn't exist. It's all trees and dirt near a golf course," Sandy looked at her notes, "called Indian Hills."

"This is probably a silly question," I said, "but did you try the name, Freeland?"

Sandy nodded. "Only one name even close, assuming we had the right spelling: an old woman who lives alone. She had no idea what I was talking about."

"Well, ain't that interesting," Henri said.

"That's the information Nicole gave me," I said. "Phone number had to work at some point because she called them."

"Did Irma Renner have the same info?"

"I assume so," I said. "She had to have something."

"Why don't you call her and ask?" Sandy said.

So I did.

"Michael Russo," Irma Renner said when she answered the phone, "how are you?"

I explained why I'd called.

"Let me look. Freeland, Freeland. Here it is," she said, and read the information.

"Same thing I've got. You heard from them?"

"Not since the day you were here."

"Any other idea how to get in touch with them?"

"I do have a note penciled in about a Mac City hotel." She gave me the name. It was just down the street from Audie's Restaurant.

"I'm not sure it'll help you find Freeland," Renner said. "I don't even remember why it's here."

I thanked Renner for her time.

"I'll look up the number," Sandy said.

"It's a stretch," Henri said.

I shrugged. "What else is new?"

"Line one, boss," Sandy said from the other room.

I gave the clerk who answered at the motel Drew Freeland's name.

I looked up at Henri. "He's ringing the room."

"How about that?" Henri said.

No answer on the room phone, so the clerk came back on the line.

"Have you seen either Mr. or Mrs. Freeland today?" I said.

"All right, thank you," I said, and clicked off.

"They haven't checked out."

"Road trip," Henri said.

30

"**T**his isn't going to be very exciting," I said. "Not sure why you wanted to tag along."

We took my BMW over to U.S. 31 and headed north. The wipers pushed aside a steady, slushy rain. Traffic was light through Alanson and Pellston but picked up the closer we came to Mackinaw City. A layer of fog choked the south tower of the Mackinac Bridge about a hundred feet above the road.

"It's been too long since I've ridden shotgun in your car. Need to recapture that special feeling."

"What feeling is that, exactly?"

"Why I like SUVs and don't like cars."

I took the Jamet Street exit and turned into the Days Inn parking lot. The place had an all-too-familiar feel of roadway motels, except for its phony stockade-like exterior.

"You want to come in?"

Henri shook his head. "Fire two shots you need my help."

"Everyone's a comedian."

I opened the car door but didn't leave just yet.

"What?" Henri said.

"Look, only three cars. Well, two and the gray van."

"So? It's a slow day in Mac City. Color season's over, snow hasn't arrived."

"Suppose one of those is Freeland's car?"

"Be helpful to know."

"You want to babysit them until we find out?"

"Had enough of that in Traverse City."

I hit the start button and moved my car around to see all three license plates. I took my phone out and tapped Marty Fleener's number. He answered on the first ring.

"In the middle of something, Russo, what do you need?"

"Need a favor."

"Of course you do. Be quick about it."

"Will you run a plate for me? Trying to ID a guy."

"I work for the Secretary of State's office now?"

"It's important, Marty, or I wouldn't ask."

"Uh-huh."

"The guy's linked to Conrad North. Be nice to know who he is."

I heard a long sigh on the other end of the line. "Give me the number."

"Three actually, three plates."

"Hurry up."

I read the plates. "We're sitting on the cars right now."

"Good for you," he said, and hung up.

"Linked to Conrad? Overstated things a bit, didn't you?" Henri said.

"Sounded more important that way."

I shut off the motor.

"You going to wait here?"

"He won't take long."

"Sure?"

I nodded. "He doesn't want me calling back." I turned on Interlochen Public Radio and took a small notebook out of the console.

Fifteen minutes later, my phone buzzed.

"Marty," I said, "what'd you find out?"

"Got a pencil?" he said.

I listened, and wrote down the information.

"You have anything new on Conrad?" Fleener said.

"Might have."

"You'll call when you know, right?" he said, and hung up before I could answer.

"Well?" Henri said.

"The black Chevy's a man from Escanaba. The other car is from Alpena."

"And the van?"

"Benton Harbor."

"Nobody's from Okemos?"

"Nope."

Henri pulled out his phone. "When all else fails," he said, "Google it. Give me the first name."

I did, and Henri tapped.

"John Chisholm is from Escanaba. He's on their planning commission. Next name?"

"Mark Bolt, Alpena."

Henri tapped, then tapped some more. "Nothing."

"Try Facebook," I said.

He tapped again. "Nothing there either."

"While you're still on *Facebook*, try Roger Bartlett."

"That the van?"

"Uh-huh."

"Got him," Henri said. "Roger Bartlett, let's see, *Actor's Equity* ..."

"Let's see the picture," I said.

Henri handed me the phone.

"Hello, Drew Freeland," I said, "and Emily Freeland."

"He's an actor?"

"Apparently they both are. Her name's Ester Blythe." I tapped the screen. "Stage credits, local theater, both of them. In Chicago mostly."

"Chicago?" Henri said. "The former home of Conrad North."

I made a few notes and handed Henri the phone. "You don't suppose, I mean, I'm guessing ..."

"Did Conrad hire two actors to pose as house buyers?" Henri said. "Is that your question?"

"Uh-huh. And the next one is: Why? Why hire actors to buy his old house back?"

"Seems obvious to me," Henri said. "He couldn't call Nicole to buy the house. She wouldn't be able to hang up fast enough."

"Isn't that what real estate agents do, sometimes anonymously?"

"Nicole would never fall for that."

"Probably not," I said. "Well, it's time to find the Freelands, or Bartlett and," I looked at my notes, "Ester Blythe."

I opened the car door. "Still want to wait here?"

"Yes."

I went through the double doors and into the motel lobby.

"Hi ya, darlin'. Come on in."

My greeter was probably in her fifties, with tanning booth color and brown hair pulled back into something resembling a bun. She wore a green cardigan and had a heavy Southern drawl.

"How are you today, Carol Ann?" I said, reading the name plate pinned to the sweater.

"Just fine, darlin', just fine. Ya'll need a room for a night?"

"Actually, no, but I could use your help." Just trying to be polite.

"What kinda help y'all need?" she said, smiling.

Felt like I'd landed in the middle of an episode of *Justified*.

"My name's Michael Russo." I took out one of my cards. "From Petoskey."

"You really a private eye, honey?" she said, looking at the card.

"Yes, ma'am," I said with a smile.

"You carryin'?" Isn't that what y'all say, carryin?"

I leaned forward just a bit and looked slowly from side to side. Her eyes followed me.

"Well, this one time," I said, and pulled back my jacket on the holster side. "Just for you."

"Oh my," she said, and stared at the gun, grinning.

It took her a moment to recover.

"What, ah, what did y'all need?"

"I'm looking for two people, a couple, in their sixties. Stocky, kind of look alike but he's bald. Name's Freeland."

My hostess smiled. "Why that'd be Drew and Emily. Nicest people you'd ever want to meet."

"Are they still here?"

She shook her head. "No."

She started to say something, then stopped and pointed a long index finger at me. "You mean, have they checked out?"

"Yes."

"They're still guests of our establishment."

"But …"

"Lunch, darlin', next door. Audie's Family Room."

"I know it," I said. "Thank you." I turned to leave.

"Y'all comin' back?" she called out from behind me, almost plaintively.

"I'll see," I said. "Bye-bye."

"Any luck?" Henri said when I was back in the car.

"Next door at Audie's having lunch."

"I'm a little hungry myself," Henri said.

"You think I need backup?"

"Don't care, I'm hungry. Let's go, or do you want to walk?"

I moved the car to a parking spot in front of the restaurant, and we went through the front door. The hostess put us in a window booth not twenty feet from the Freelands. I sat with my back to their booth on the side wall.

Henri picked up a menu. "Their food's just arrived. You have plenty of time."

"Did they notice us sit down?"

Henri shook his head. "Quit worrying, Russo. They only met you one time at the real estate office."

"Gentlemen," our waitress said. "Anything to drink?"

Henri ordered coffee, I opted for iced tea.

"Order me a club sandwich," I said. "I'll be right back."

I walked over to the other booth.

"Hello, Drew, Emily. Remember me?"

"Mr. Russo, isn't it?" Drew said, and smiled.

"That's me, Roger. I can call you Roger, can't I? And Ms. Blythe, may I call you Ester?"

Their heads turned toward each other as if on autopilot. They tried to cover it, cover their surprise, but they weren't that good.

I sat down next to Ester. "Mind if I join you? Didn't think so."

"What do you want, Mr. Russo?" Roger Bartlett said, the smile gone from his face. Ester wasn't looking too happy either.

I had no desire to continue with their play-acting and phony names.

"Who hired you to buy the Sanderson cottage?"

Roger and Ester looked at each other again, but didn't try to hide it this time.

"We do not have to tell you about our clients."

"Seriously, Roger? You claiming actor-client privilege? Is that what you're doing? I'm a lawyer, Rog, you got no privilege. Period."

Roger sat up straighter and said, "Nonetheless, I choose not to discuss the matter. Please leave or I will call the management."

I shook my head, slowly. "Roger, Roger. I know the management, Roger. Tanya's right over there. I'd be happy to call her for you." I put my elbows on the table and stared at him. "But if I do, see that gentleman in the booth by the window?" I pointed at Henri and waved. He smiled and waved back. "I will also call him over. That's Detective LaCroix, Michigan State Police homicide squad."

"Homicide?"

That was Ester.

"Dear?" Ester said, and put her hand on Roger's hand.

"All right, Mr. Russo, what do you want from us?"

"I'll make it easy for you," I said. "Did Conrad North hire you to play-act?"

"Yes," Roger said.

"To buy the Mackinac Island cottage?"

He nodded.

"Why?"

"I have no idea," Roger said.

"He ever say anything about the cottage?"

"Only that the woman who owned the cottage had swindled him out of it. That's why he needed us, to fool her."

"The woman who owns the cottage?" I said.

Roger nodded.

"She's his daughter, Roger. She inherited the house when her mother died."

"Oh, my," Ester said.

"Who created the backstory? You know, your favorite house and all that?"

"We did," Roger said, "we made it all up. We do improv all the time. Live on stage. We make things up as we go along. It's easier when you get a storyline and write it all out."

"Did you ever mention my name to Conrad North?"

Roger nodded. "After we met at the real estate office, yes, we told him about you."

"Mr. Russo," Ester said. "Can I ask you a question?"

"Sure."

"The man over there, the policeman?"

I almost forgot I'd made Henri into a cop.

"What about him?"

"You said homicide. He's a homicide detective?"

"That's right."

Ester looked at Roger, hesitated for a moment, then said, almost in a whisper, "Are we involved in murder?"

"Not yet," I said.

"Is Mr. North involved?" Roger said.

"Conrad North is the primary suspect in two murders." Okay, okay, so I bumped it up a little.

"Who did he kill?"

"The most recent death was his wife, who happened to be Nicole Sanderson's mother."

Ester pushed her plate away. Apparently she'd lost her appetite.

"You don't think we're involved in anything like that, do you?"

I shook my head. "As of right now, no."

"What should we do?" Ester said.

"If I were you, I'd pack up and head home."

"What do we tell Mr. North?"

"You said you're good at improv, get on with it. Tell him you took another job, a sick family member, but leave town. As soon as possible."

I left the thespians to think about their next act and returned to the booth by the window.

31

"**Y**ou made me a cop?" Henri said. "A cop?" I drank some iced tea and took a healthy bite out of my club sandwich. Henri had already finished his soup.

"Best I could do on short notice," I said.

"You'll ruin my reputation, this gets out."

I smiled and said, "Henri, your reputation will live on unchallenged, trust me."

The waitress poured more coffee for Henri as Roger and Ester went by. Ester glanced furtively at Henri but kept moving.

"Woman looks a little frightened, Russo, what'd you tell them? Besides that I was a cop, I mean."

"I told her you'd arrest the two of them unless they talked."

Henri shook his head. "No, you didn't. You'd turn me into a cop to scare them, but you wouldn't say that. So what *did* you say?"

I recounted my conversation with Roger and Ester.

"I assume they'll call Conrad," I said. "They're too honest to simply leave town without telling the man who hired them."

"That worry you?"

"Not sure."

"Forget it, Russo, it doesn't matter. So we discovered his little scam to buy the cottage. So what? He'll think of another way, he wants it bad enough. You can head him off at the pass, tell Nicole."

"Good idea."

"Come on, let's get out of here."

I ate the last of my club sandwich, and we paid the bill.

I took Old 31 (yes there's one of those, too) to U.S. 31 South for Petoskey. The airport parking lot was crowded at Pellston. Nice to know some things remain the same.

"At least we finally know how Conrad learned you were on his trail," Henri said.

"Yeah, that was bugging me," I said. "Never connected him to Roger and Ester's invention of Drew and Emily Freeland and Mackinac Island."

Traffic moved at a steady pace the rest of the way home. I put my car in the Lake Street lot.

"You staying in town?"

"At Margo's for a couple of days," Henri said. "Back to the island end of the week."

Henri went for his SUV and I cut through Roast & Toast to the sidewalk.

"Well, that explains several things," Sandy said after I filled her in. "Starting with why I couldn't trace, what are their real names again?"

"Roger and Ester."

"Yeah, them," Sandy said, "in Okemos, or anyplace else."

"See if you can find Nicole Sanderson for me, on the office phone."

"Will do boss," Sandy said. "Mail's on your desk and two messages, neither looks important."

"A new client?"

Sandy shook her head. "Don't think so."

I tossed out most of the mail, put the new *Runner's World* aside for later, and called back the second message. A few minutes later, Sandy appeared at the door, held up two fingers and mouthed, "Line two." I finished the call and punched a button on the desk phone.

"Hello, Nicole. Sorry, I was on the other line."

"No problem at all, Michael," she said. "I really didn't expect to hear from you so soon. Has something happened?"

I told Nicole, in some detail, about Roger and Ester and Conrad.

"Actors?"

"Yep, dues-paying members of *Actor's Equity*."

"That seems like a lot of trouble to go through."

"Same thought occurred to me."

"Why wouldn't he just hire an agent to buy my cottage? Or an attorney?"

"Good questions, Nicole."

"It seems like a pretty elaborate scheme to me."

"Uh-huh. You think of any reason why he'd do that?"

"Hah. To get even." It was not a laugh of fun. Her voice was sharp and angry. "The man's a son-of-a-bitch, Michael. He got away with murder, but we took the house back: you, me, the law. Most men would have considered themselves lucky to be out of jail, but not him. It's all or nothing."

"Assuming you're right …"

"I am right." Still sharp, still angry.

"I hear you, Nicole. I do. But is there any other reason you can think of? Anything at all?"

"That's the point, Michael. Revenge itself is a sufficient motive for that man."

"Then be alert for another try."

"Yes," she said, her voice easing up, "I will."

"If anything at all pops about the cottage, let me know. No matter how trivial — especially if it seems trivial."

"I will," she said.

We ended the call. Sandy came in a moment later and sat down.

"You heard?"

"Most of it," she said.

"I'd have expected nothing less from you."

She rolled her eyes but didn't follow up. Instead she said, "Nicole Sanderson's a pretty sharp woman. She'll be suspicious of any move now, wherever it comes from."

"You think Conrad's out for revenge?"

Sandy shrugged. "Until something better comes along, yeah. Nobody knows that man like Nicole, boss."

"Think he'll make another try?"

Sandy shifted in the chair. "The obvious answer is yes, but Conrad has to figure Nicole will be suspicious of anyone who asks about the cottage going forward."

"Makes sense," I said, "but we should assume he'll try."

Sandy looked at her watch. "Time to go home if we're done here."

"Go home."

"You meeting AJ for dinner?"

I shook my head. "She has a dinner meeting at the office. Planning special features for the holidays. I'm going home, too."

" 'Night, boss."

32

Since my car was in the lot behind Lake Street, I jumped in and headed through town to 31 North. I went left on the Harbor-Petoskey Road and drove to Crooked Tree Breadworks. Twenty minutes later, I was eating pieces of a 3 O'clock Baguette and sipping Oban while the penne pasta slowly cooked in a pan of water. I'd made a red sauce from garlic, Italian spices, crushed tomatoes and olive oil. I mixed the sauce and the penne in a proper pasta bowl and took it to the living room. I poured a little more scotch, tore off a chunk of bread and settled down to enjoy a couple of episodes of Aaron Sorkin's *The Newsroom*.

I had finished dinner when I heard a familiar buzz. The message on my iPhone read: "your office now." I'd rather have watched another episode of *The Newsroom*. But the message came from Martin Fleener.

He didn't say if it was business or personal. He didn't have to, and I didn't say no.

I grabbed a jacket and headed out the door. It was a colder evening in northern Michigan than October usually offered. A few snow flurries floated their way to the sidewalk. I walked up Howard and took a right on Lake Street.

"Russo."

I stopped and turned around. Henri LaCroix moved out of the shadows. His collar was turned up and his hands were stuffed into the jacket pockets.

"The hell you doing here?" I said.

"Text from Fleener," he said, and pointed down the street.

A Ford sedan sat at the curb in front of my building. The motor was running. Since it was dark, we walked up near the front fender, making it easier for the driver to see us. The motor went off and Marty Fleener climbed out and came around the car.

"We need to talk," he said, pointing at the stairs that led to my office.

I flipped the lights on. I put my jacket on the hall tree and opened the door of the small sideboard that was our coffee station. I took out a fifth of Oban and three glasses.

Fleener was already seated in one of the client chairs in my office. He was dressed, as always, in a tailored suit, spread collar shirt and striped tie. But it was late and the tie was loose, the collar button open. Henri took the other chair.

I went around the desk and sat down. I held up the Oban. "One finger, Marty?"

Fleener tilted his head up slightly. "Two."

Fleener wasn't easily rattled. He'd been a homicide cop too long for that, but tonight he wanted two.

"Henri?"

He nodded.

I poured Oban in the glasses and handed two of them over.

I raised my glass. "Shalom."

"Here, here," Henri said.

"All right, Marty, what's going on?" I said.

"Nils Lundberg."

"You told me he was out of jail."

"Right," Fleener said. "But that's not the problem."

I hesitated. "What then?"

"We lost him."

"Who lost him?" I said.

"Cops in Allegany County who were watching him for me."

"When did they lose him?"

"Two days ago. They wanted to make sure before they called."

"You think he's headed here?" I said.

"Of course he's headed here," Henri said, interrupting. "You killed his brother and you're here. Question is, how soon?"

"Hard to tell," Fleener said. "Soon I'd guess.

"Think he's coming after Russo on his own," Henri said, "or was he hired to do it?"

Fleener sipped some Oban and put the glass on the desk. "What're you thinking, LaCroix?"

"Conrad North," Henri said.

Fleener nodded slowly. "Could be," he said. "Conrad hires a gunman to take care of his Russo problem."

"And this gunman has his own reasons to take the job," Henri said. "Sure is a small world sometimes."

I picked up my glass and said, "Not the first time in this mess we've said that."

Fleener took another drink. "One more thing."

"Yeah?"

"He might come after AJ, too."

"Why?" I said. "Would he even know about her?"

"He's a professional," Fleener said. "It's his business to know. Besides, if Conrad hired him, he'd tell Lundberg everything he knew that might help get at you."

"What you're saying is killing her is almost as good as killing Russo," Henri said.

Fleener nodded. "What I'm saying is you have to cover her, too."

"Can you spare a cop or two?" I said. "Henri can't be in two places at once."

Fleener shook his head. "Even if I could, this is so far off the books it'd never fly."

"No cops," Henri said, "we need a pro."

"Got somebody in mind?" Fleener said.

Henri nodded. "One person for this job. Could move with AJ and never be noticed."

"Do I know him?" Fleener said.

"Her," Henri said. "Name's Bobbie Fairhaven."

"Bobbie? Sounds like she ought to be in *The Sound of Music*, not stalking killers."

Henri smiled. "That's the general idea."

"Think she'd do it?" I said.

"Would you gentlemen like to fill me in?"

"One question first," Henri said.

"Yeah?" Fleener said.

"Are we off the record, Captain?"

"We've been off the record since I walked through that door," he said. "I want to help keep AJ alive." Fleener pointed at me. "Him, too. So tell me."

"Bobbie's Army Ranger," Henri said. "We were in Iraq together."

"Seriously?" Fleener said.

Henri explained Bobbie Fairhaven. "She's a trained killer and very smart. She had my back in Iraq. I trusted her then, I'd trust her now."

"I repeat my question," I said, "will she do it?"

"Don't know," Henri said. "I'll ask her. She might do it for me."

"Marty, switching gears for a minute. Do you know a shooter, Jimmy Erwin?"

"Skinny kid from South Bend, yeah, he's on our radar screen. Why?"

"He's working for Conrad North," I said.

"That explains it," he said. "We knew he took a job, but it wasn't for the usual bad guys. So he's working for North."

"Is Erwin any good?" I said.

"Don't let his Harry-high-school looks fool you. He knows how to shoot, and he's cool under pressure. Remember Cal Hawley? Guy with an eye patch?"

"Hawley?" I said. "The Snake Plissken wannabe from Gary?"

"That's him," Fleener said. "Hawley went up against Erwin in the middle of town. Real *High Noon*. Erwin put him down, two shots. Everybody saw it, nobody could prove it in court."

"Good to know," Henri said.

Fleener took in a lot of air and let it out slowly. "If Conrad's got Nils Lundberg and Jimmy Erwin, you're going to need help."

"Marty," I said, but he held his hand up to stop me.

"We're off the record," Fleener said, "and I meant it. I'll cut you as much room as I can, but there are limits to what I can do. You shoot too many people? You're on your own."

"I understand," I said. "What about Don Hendricks?"

"Can't promise, but I'll talk to him."

Fleener looked at Henri, then me. "All right," he said, standing up. "Keep in touch."

We said good-bye and waited for Fleener to close the door on his way out.

I drank the last of my Oban, stood and went to the window. The soft glow of the streetlamps picked up light snow as it settled on parked cars. I thought I saw lights from a small boat in the bay, but it was hard to tell.

Henri put his feet on the desk and leaned back. "We have a problem."

"Only one?"

33

I sat at the kitchen table with coffee and an English muffin. I'd passed on a run this morning. The snow overnight glazed the streets, but it would be melted by afternoon. Such is life for runners in northern Michigan when the fall decides to become winter. I picked up the phone when it buzzed. I'd been waiting for Sandy to return my call.

"Morning, Sandy. You in the office yet?"

"Just parked the car. What's up?"

I offered a brief recap of Fleener's visit.

"When're you coming in?"

"Ten minutes," I said. "Henri's on his way in, too."

"Okay," Sandy said, clicking off.

I put the dishes in the dishwasher, took my coat and brief bag and headed outside. The sky was a bright blue off to the east. Once the sun came over the trees, the coating of snow would evaporate from the sidewalks and roads.

I walked up Howard. Before I arrived at the Bay Street corner, the passenger door of a black stretch limo opened and a familiar figure climbed out.

He was a trim six-one with an olive complexion and an expensive haircut. He wore a tailored charcoal suit over a white shirt and solid red tie.

Donald Harper. Lawyer to Joey DeMio.

According to Harper himself, he represented Joey's legitimate business interests. Would a graduate of Yale Law tell a lie?

"Morning, Don. The hotel's closed for the season, thought you guys would be back in Chicago for the winter."

Harper stood erect and silent.

In addition to the Marquette Park Hotel, the DeMio family owned a Victorian cottage on Mackinac Island's East Bluff. It was next door to the one owned by Nicole Sanderson. Small world ... again.

"Is the cottage still open?"

Harper ignored my question.

"Mr. DeMio would like to have a few words."

"Tell him to call, make an appointment. He knows the number."

That look on Harper's face? What was it? Derision? Maybe irritation?

"Now," Harper said as he opened the limo's rear door.

I looked inside. Joey DeMio. He was impressive even as he sat, trim, tall, with round eyes and medium complexion. His black hair was brushed straight back just like his father's. He wore gangster casual this morning. A cranberry sweater over neatly pressed black jeans.

"Get in, counselor," Joey said.

I hesitated, so he waved me in. "We need to talk. Get in or Santino will insist."

Santino Cicci, longtime muscle for the family and bodyguard to Joey, was behind the wheel.

I climbed in the back seat and sat next to Joey. Harper took the front passenger seat.

The limo was warm, almost too warm, but I suppose if you could afford to ride around in a car the size of a small living room, why not?

"Since when do you hang out in a limo?"

"Since when is none of your business," Joey said.

"You taking me for a ride? You know, like in the movies?"

Apparently not, since we were still at the curb.

"I have a problem," Joey said.

"Lousy gas mileage?"

"You don't learn, you know that?"

"So I've been told. Now, what do you want?"

"Nils Lundberg," Joey said.

Should have expected that. The Lundberg brothers, Nils and the deceased Gunner, were often hired by DeMio for their skill and experience with a variety of weapons.

"What about him?"

"Leave him alone," Joey said.

"Did you bring him up here?"

"Doesn't matter why he's here, Russo. Leave him alone."

"What's Lundberg to you, anyway? You got muscle anytime you need it. Santino's right here in the front seat, You brought in Bobbie. Why Lundberg?"

Joey was silent. That gave me a moment to think.

"You didn't, did you? Bring him here, I mean. It wasn't you."

Joey shrugged.

"It was Conrad North, wasn't it? Lundberg's working for Conrad. Did you set it up?"

"You killed his brother," Joey said.

"I had no choice, Joey, and you know it. The man came after me with a knife and a gun."

"Better watch your back, Russo."

"You warn me a guy's in town who wants to kill me, hired by another guy who wants to kill me. Why you being so nice, Joey?"

"You killed Gunner. I let it go. You try to cap Nils, I won't take it very well."

"He's a gunslinger, Joey. You can get ten of them for a phone call."

Joey took in some air and let it out slowly. "It's like this," Joey said, "Lundberg's old man, my old man ..."

"Carmine?"

Joey nodded. "Carmine was like an uncle to Oliver Lundberg. When Oliver died, Carmine watched out for Nils and Gunner while they grew up."

We were quiet.

"If he comes after me like his brother did ..."

"We'll stop you, counselor," Joey said.

"Mr. Russo." It was Harper, looking over the seatback.

"Mr. DeMio's been quite accommodating. He's been clear that the good health of Mr. Lundberg is important to him."

"Come on, Joey," I said, jacking my thumb at Harper. "Couldn't you do any better than Mr. Harvard for a mouthpiece?"

"Yale, Mr. Russo," Harper said with a sting in his voice. "I graduated from Yale, with honors."

"Bully for you, Harper," I said, and opened the door. "Nice talking to you gents. I have to go to work now."

I crossed Bay as Joey's limo edged away from the curb and motored up Howard. I went through McLean & Eakin, grabbed my *New York Times* and climbed the stairs to the office.

Sandy and Henri were in the front office when I walked in.

"That was a long ten minutes, boss."

"Had a stop to make," I said. I hung my jacket on the hall tree, poured coffee and told them about Joey DeMio.

"That confirms it," Henri said.

"Conrad hired Lundberg," I said, "not Joey."

"Uh-huh."

"Let me see if I have this straight," Sandy said as she pushed her chair back. "Conrad has two hired guns, plus his sons."

"Right," Henri said. "Not sure I'd worry about the boys in a fight."

"But Henri," Sandy said, "if you're focused on AJ and Michael, Wolfgang and Wilhelm could actually cause some trouble."

"I don't know," Henri said.

"But we shouldn't assume."

"No," Henri said. "I'll talk to Bobbie, see what she's up to."

"Want to know what I think?" Sandy said.

"Who you talking to, Henri or me?"

"She was talking to me, Russo, not you."

"You sure, Henri?"

"Aw, cut it out," Sandy said. "Don't start with the frat-boy bullshit. I'm not in the mood."

Henri and I fell silent, properly chastised.

"I understand why Fleener's worried about AJ being a target. Here's the thing, if Nils kills AJ, he won't quit. He still has to kill you."

"Because I'm the one who killed his brother."

"Revenge," Sandy said, nodding. "That's you, not AJ."

"Then we kill him before he kills you," Henri said.

"Talk to Bobbie anyway," I said.

"I'll take care of that," he said. "Be in touch." With that, Henri said good-bye and left the office.

I looked at Sandy, stared really.

"What?"

"Frat boys?"

Sandy shook her head. "Sometimes, not all the time but sometimes, you two get on a roll. It's like the rest of the people in the room aren't there. That or you don't care if they're in the room."

I put my hands up, palms out. "All right."

34

'd almost finished reading the op-ed page in the *Times* when Sandy leaned in the door.

"Patricia Geary's on the phone, boss."

"Ms. Geary. How are you?"

"Mr. Russo, I'm ... I'm not sure. Surprised, happy, I guess." Her voice mixed excitement and something else, hesitancy, caution.

"That sounds good on my end."

"You really did it. I didn't think anyone could, but you really did it."

I waited.

"Detective Diaz?" she said.

"Yes, what about him?" I wasn't sure where she was going with this.

"I talked with him. Twice. Here, in my office I mean, yesterday and again this morning on the phone. He's reopened the case."

I remembered that I forgot to tell her about that.

"That is good news," I said. "Are you more hopeful?"

"That the cops are taking Annie more seriously?"

"Yes."

"I am encouraged, Mr. Russo. I am. Apparently they consider Annie related to the murder of poor Roland."

"If she's part of a murder investigation, they are taking her more seriously. No question about that."

"I have to tell you," she said, "I am uncomfortable, maybe even a little scared. I don't know."

"About what?"

"Ever since I found Roland that morning." Her voice was breaking up, ever so slightly — it was shaky. "I never saw a dead person before. You know, a funeral parlor, but you know what I mean, don't you?"

"Most people are fortunate never to see a dead body, Ms. Geary, especially from violence."

"I guess I am scared."

"I don't blame you," I said. "He was a friend and he's suddenly gone.

"I think, I'm not sure ..."

There it was again. Being scared is reason enough to be hesitant and cautious.

"I think I'm being watched," Geary said, the words rushing out of her. "I know how foolish that must sound. You probably think I'm making it up."

"I do not believe you're making it up. I don't, Ms. Geary, I really don't."

She didn't sound foolish at all. But being scared can lead to all sorts of odd behavior.

"It feels that way. Not all the time, but it does."

"When?" I said.

"Here, downtown. I walk to work most of the time. It's not that far."

Geary lived only a few city blocks from her office at the bank. Streets filled with small houses, offices, shops. Plenty of ways to avoid detection if you knew what you were doing. She may have had something to worry about, but I didn't want to pump her fear.

"The kind of shock you've had," I said, "people worry. It's a natural response to unfamiliar trauma."

Geez, I sounded like a therapist.

"Yeah," Geary said, "I suppose you're right."

"Keep an eye out anyway," I said. "No harm in that."

"Okay, I will."

"You can call me anytime, especially if anything changes."

Patricia Geary said she would, and we ended the call.

Sandy came back to my office and sat down.

"Well?"

"Well, what? Is she being followed?"

"Uh-huh."

"The odds say no, but it's Conrad North we're dealing with here."

"So all bets are off?"

I nodded.

"How about we call the cops in Traverse City, tell them Geary's scared?"

"I'm not sure how that would help Geary."

"You never know," Sandy said. "Or call Diaz. It's his case. Two cases. He should know Geary's being followed."

"Thinks she is being followed, Sandy. Big difference."

Sandy nodded. "Of course, but the woman's still scared of her shadow, and Diaz made it an active case again. How about it?"

I shrugged. "What can it hurt?" I said, and tapped the number.

I was put through to the squad room. "Detective Woods."

It was Woods and his partner that'd screwed with me before.

"Michael Russo calling, Detective Woods, for Detective Diaz." That was polite, don't you think?

Silence from Woods, but I heard background noise, men talking, phones ringing.

"He's busy."

Polite, remember. "I'm sure he is, Detective. Tell him I'm on the line, would you please?"

"He'll be a while."

"I'll wait," I said and never called him a prick.

"He's on another line."

"Detective Woods, I'm calling about an active murder investigation. Switch me to Diaz or put me on hold."

I heard a couple of clicks.

Diaz came on the line after a few minutes.

"Michael Russo calling, Detective."

"So I heard," he said. "What do you need?"

"Patricia Geary," I said.

"Yeah?"

I told Diaz about my conversation and her fears.

"She's a civilian, Russo. This is scary stuff when you don't deal with it every day. Did you tell her that? I'm not surprised she's scared."

"Might help if you gave her a call."

"Look, Russo, I'm not a babysitter. The Geary woman wanted this, she wanted us on the case. Now she's got us. She'll get used to it."

"Being afraid or being followed?"

"There any evidence she's being followed, Russo?"

"None that I know," I said, and he clicked off the call.

"Didn't go so well, huh?" Sandy said.

I shook my head.

"It was worth the call."

"Guess so."

"I hope Patricia Geary doesn't have to pay a price because the detective doesn't want to bother with her fear."

"Me, too," I said.

"You ought to take a ride down there. Buy her lunch or something."

"I'll think about it," I said. "Okay, back to work. I have one more file to go through, then I'm texting AJ about dinner."

"Aye aye, sir," Sandy said.

35

"**I**'m not okay with that, Michael," AJ said. "I just have to tell you that."

Palette Bistro was a comfortable restaurant with an edgy, urban feel. It sat on Bay Street, an easy walk from the office. We usually left the window tables overlooking the bay for tourists in favor of two seats at the bar. Business was brisk for a mid-week evening so close to Halloween. We ordered Chardonnay and scanned the appetizer menu.

"About a bad guy trying to hurt you? I don't know anyone who would be okay with that, AJ."

"No, damn it, a bodyguard. Someone in my face all the time. How am I supposed to work? Are you sure I really need one?" She drank some wine.

I put my hand on her arm. "First of all, we don't know if she'll do it."

"She?"

"Yes, Henri's friend is a woman." I described Bobbie and how we met.

"How about an appetizer or salad?" the bartender said.

We interrupted our, ah, discussion long enough to order a Margherita pizza to share.

AJ turned my way. "Michael, did it occur to you that meeting her like that was no accident?"

I nodded. "Of course. Henri thought she set it up to meet me, too."

"Then why? Why her and not somebody we know, or one of Marty Fleener's cops?"

"There isn't anyone else," I said. "Not right now. Will you meet her if she's agreeable?"

The bartender put down silverware and the small pizza. "Enjoy," he said, and walked down the bar to greet two new customers.

We picked up a piece of pizza.

"Love the fresh mozzarella," I said.

AJ nodded and chewed at the same time.

"Michael, let me ask you something. I know you think I'm in danger ..."

"Marty does, too. And Henri."

"All right, all right, let's assume for a minute I *am* in danger. What about you? Where's your head on this?"

Not sure where this was going. "Your point is?"

"You're not responsible for me, Michael. I can take care of myself."

"Not if Lundberg comes after you, you can't."

"I'm not talking about my physical safety."

"What then?"

"I just said it, you're not responsible for me. This isn't about Nils Lundberg. It's about you, your attitude."

"The threat's very real, AJ."

"Michael, listen to me for a second. Listen to my words. I get that I need a bodyguard, but don't take responsibility for me. We don't live that way. Never have. We do well together because we don't feel responsible for each other. I appreciate the seriousness of this particular situation," she said, rapping her knuckles on the bar timed with each word. "This. Particular. Situation."

"Damn it, AJ, I get to be responsible for you because I love you."

"I know you love me."

"You've said exactly the same thing to me, same words probably."

"I know."

We were silent for a minute. AJ reached over and took my hand. We sat quietly, holding hands.

"Do you trust Henri with your life?" she said.

"Yes."

"Do you trust Bobbie what's-her-name with your life?"

I straightened up and stared at the array of colorful liquor bottles on the back shelf of the bar.

"I'm not sure."

AJ leaned in. "Then you sure as hell won't trust her with my life."

I felt like one of those colorful bottles, the tall, lanky Galliano bottle maybe, just landed on my head.

I turned toward AJ.

"You can't do your job and worry about me," she said. "If you're worried about me, it'll be harder to keep yourself alive." Her voice softened. "It just won't work. Put Henri on me or it won't work."

"Henri will do it," I said. "I'll take Bobbie with me."

"Thank you."

AJ leaned in again and kissed my cheek. "My car's parked out front, let's go."

"Where to?" I said, and put down a card for the tab.

"My house. You and me in a hot, steamy bathtub?"

I smiled. "Like last time?"

"Better than last time."

36

I pulled a pillow off my face. I thought the clock on the nightstand read 7:46, but the numbers were fuzzy. Or my eyes were fuzzy.

"Good morning, darling," AJ said. She stood at the side of the bed, most of her clothes back on, a mug of coffee in her hand.

"You going to work?"

AJ shook her head. "Home first. A quick shower and fresh clothes. What about you?"

"A short run, then the office."

AJ sat on the side of the bed. She leaned over and kissed me.

"Michael, are you awake enough for a question?"

"You mean a serious question?"

She nodded.

"Okay, if I have to."

"Nils Lundberg, is he already here?"

"Most likely. Probably Traverse City."

"Because Conrad's in Traverse?"

"That'd be my guess."

"Is he tailing you?"

"That's two questions."

AJ tilted her head. "Is he?"

"Could be."

"Have you spotted him?"

"Nope."

"If you haven't seen him, he's not here."

"Is that a reporter's educated guess, or your best hope?"

"Maybe both," she said, and kissed me again.

"You shouldn't be doing that when you're only half-dressed and about to leave."

"You'd rather I didn't kiss you?"

"Very funny. On your way, lady. I need that sexy body of yours or a cup of hot coffee. Not sure which."

"Now who's being funny?" AJ smiled, finished dressing and actually kissed me good-bye this time.

I pulled on a long-sleeved T, running pants and jacket. I drank coffee while I tied my shoes, found a light hat and gloves, and headed out the back door.

The sun was almost at the treetops. Jagged rays of light streaked the tarmac. I followed my usual route into Bay View. It occurred to me that I needed to change up my running routes until this business with Conrad was settled. I didn't want to make it any easier for Lundberg to do his job. I was moving smoothly by the time I reached Glendale near the old Terrace Inn.

I spied two runners in the distance coming from the other direction. Never thought that would happen again so soon. I didn't expect trouble, but I felt a small spike of adrenaline. The runners closed the distance between us and I recognized them: Henri and Bobbie.

Henri waved and they flipped around, pulling up next to me.

"Mind if we join you?" he said.

"Okay with me," I said. "This isn't a coincidence, is it?"

I expected Henri to answer, but it was Bobbie. "Yes and no," she said. "I wanted to talk with you anyway, so we added this loop to our run in case you were out this morning."

We moved at an easy pace, three abreast, turning onto a nearly empty Terrace Avenue.

"Do you want to walk," Bobbie said, "so we can talk?"

"I want to run," I said, "you talk."

"Told you he'd keep running," Henri said.

"Why talk here?" I said.

"Safer this early."

"Why's that?"

"The bad guys are still asleep."

We slipped into single file until we'd snaked our way around two small vans and a long trailer stacked with lumber.

"Henri told me about your friend."

"AJ Lester."

"She needs a bodyguard," Bobbie said. "You do, too."

"Should only be a few days," I said. "You in town for a while?"

"I can't do it, can't help you out."

I decided not to ask, see what she had to say.

"I wanted to tell you myself," she said, "out of respect for Henri."

"All right."

As we closed in on the end of the street near Division, I pointed and said, "That way." We swung onto Stephens and headed back.

"I already have a job," she said.

"I didn't ask."

"I can't do both jobs at the same time." She was dragging this out, and it wasn't clear why.

"Save us time," I said, "cut to the chase."

"He's like this, Bobbie. I told you," Henri said.

"I was hired by Joey DeMio," she said, "to protect his interests."

"What does that mean?"

"Joey hired me to protect Nils Lundberg, to keep him alive."

"Somebody trying to kill him?"

"You, Mr. Russo, Joey said you want to kill him."

I gave Bobbie a sideways glance.

"Joey tell you why?"

"Why doesn't matter. It's not in my job description."

"I won't kill Lundberg unless he tries to kill me."

"That doesn't matter."

"So if I defend myself, you kill me. Is that it?"

"I've been hired to protect Lundberg."

"But you'll kill me if you have to."

"Yes."

"Just so we're clear," I said.

"We're clear."

"What about Henri?" I said.

"He knows what I have to do," Bobbie said.

"That right, Henri?"

"Seems simple enough," Henri said. "Bobbie shoots you to keep Lundberg alive."

"You explain to Bobbie what happens if she does that?"

"Nah, I left that part out."

"Maybe you ought to tell her."

"Tell me what?" Bobbie said.

"You try to shoot Russo, Bobbie, I'll kill you."

She almost stumbled, but caught herself. "You'd do that, Henri?"

"Don't make me choose, Bobbie."

"We go back a long way, Henri. Afghanistan, Iraq. Remember the ambush south of Baghdad?"

"Of course I do, but Russo pays the bills."

"You could have told me that earlier."

"Would it have made a difference?" Henri said. "Would you have turned Joey down?"

"Too late now," she said. "I've got a job to do."

We were back on Terrace Avenue, keeping a good pace, working up a good sweat.

"Bobbie, why don't we head back," Henri said. "See you, Russo."

Bobbie turned with Henri and the two runners moved down the street, away from me.

I worked my way home using a familiar route. Right now, I didn't care one bit if someone watched me run. I had enough to worry about. I eased into a walk a few blocks from home. The idea of a relaxing run had faded into the realization that this case had just grown much more dangerous.

37

"I'm going to need a program if this keeps up," Sandy said. "The list of people who want to shoot you grows longer every day."

I'd walked to work after a quick shower and a light breakfast. The air was chilly. It had that real winter-weather-has-almost-arrived feel to it.

We were at the desk in my office.

"You're exaggerating a bit, don't you think?"

"I used to think running was boring," she said. "I could use some excitement in my life, maybe I should become a jogger."

"Sandy."

"Okay, boss," she said, "two things on the agenda this morning. Just so I don't forget, did you finish the Walker file like I told you?"

"Yes. What's next?"

Sandy handed me a sticky note. "I don't know if it's important or not, but Patricia Geary's called twice this morning. Agitated, nervous, couldn't tell."

"She say what it was about?"

"Not even a hint, but that woman has been businesslike every time I've talked to her. Even when she was so angry that nobody cared about Annie, she was the cool professional."

"But not today."

"Nope, not today," Sandy said. "I think you ought to call her."

I looked at the sticky note. "This number?"

Sandy nodded. "That's not her work number, is it?"

"No."

I tapped the number into my iPhone. It rang almost long enough for voicemail to take over when a voice said, "Yes?"

"Michael Russo for Patricia Geary. She gave me this number."

I heard muffled talking. I tapped "speaker" and put the phone on the desk. Sandy nodded.

"Mr. Russo, this is Patricia Geary."

"This isn't your cell, is it?"

"No."

"Where are you?"

"At the office. The phone's Makayla's. She runs commercial loans. Her office is next door."

I heard it in her voice. The short sentences, hurriedly thrown out.

"Are you all right?"

There was a moment of silence. When she began again, her voice cracked.

"I'm scared, Mr. Russo. I'm not sure what to do."

Sandy nodded. She was right.

"Did something happen?"

"The policeman, the detective who reopened Annie's case?"

"Detective Diaz?"

"He's dead."

I looked up. Sandy's mouth was open. Mine too, probably.

"Somebody killed him," Geary said. "It's all over the news."

"Pull up the *Record Eagle* and TV 7&4," I said to Sandy, and she went to her computer.

"I didn't have the news on at home," Geary said. "I heard about it when I got to work."

"Have you heard anything else?"

"No," she said. "I've been trying to work."

Sandy appeared at the door and shook her head.

"Will you be at work all day?" I said.

"All day, yes," Geary said. "I don't know what to do."

"Do you feel safe at the office?"

"Yeah, I guess so."

"You stay there. I'll come down. We'll figure it out."

"Roland, and … and now the policeman. I'm scared."

"You wait there, I'm on my way," I said, and clicked off.

I looked at Sandy.

"No details, boss. The paper, TV. All they said was Detective Diaz was found at home. The police are investigating. That's all."

"I'm going to Traverse."

"I heard you tell her."

"Get hold of Henri. Tell him to keep an eye on AJ."

I leaned over and took my .38 out of the bottom left drawer. I stood up and clipped the holster to my belt.

"I got her into this mess," I said. "Have to figure something out."

"Keep in mind that she hired you, boss."

"That seems like a meaningless distinction right now, Sandy. The woman's terrified."

38

The ride to Traverse City was quick and uneventful. I focused on my driving, of course, but I couldn't push Vincente Diaz out of my mind. The cops were always tight-lipped when one of their own was involved.

It didn't take much to convince me that his death was linked to those of Roland Crosley and Annie North. Was Conrad North stupid enough to kill a police officer? He'd never done anything to suggest stupid before. What about Nils Lundberg? Could be, but only on orders from Conrad.

Who else would take out a cop? Joey DeMio? Sure, but he knew that was bad for business, especially since he'd tried hard to appear legit. Might have to ask him anyway. Not much point asking Diaz's colleagues: they wouldn't tell me something they'd hide from the media.

I edged my way down Front Street, turned into the parking ramp. I opened the car door, then closed it again. It was worth a try.

I took out my phone, tapped contacts, then Joey DeMio's office.

Carlo Vollini answered, as expected.

"Carlo," I said. "Michael Russo calling."

"What do you want?"

I wasn't in the mood for my usual repartee with Joey's secretary, so I played it straight. "I want to talk to Joey, Carlo. Five minutes."

"He's busy."

"He's always busy, Carlo. Just five."

"What do you want to talk about?"

I'd rather duck the question, as I always did. On the other hand …

"Tell him it's about Nils Lundberg."

Not a word, but I was put on hold. Then the line cleared.

"Five minutes, Russo," Joey said. "What about Lundberg?"

"You want him to stay alive."

"Remember that, Russo."

"Remember what, Joey? You're the one put me in his sights. You loaned his brother to Conrad North."

"Get to the point."

"I might not be Lundberg's only problem."

"What's that mean?"

"Cop was killed in Traverse City."

"Diaz. What's that got to do with Lundberg?"

"Did you have Lundberg kill Diaz?"

No answer.

"Did you kill a cop, Joey?"

"You watch too many movies."

"I'm not convinced."

"Bullshit," Joey said. "We're not that stupid, asshole."

"Who is that stupid?"

"It's the work of amateurs, Russo. This is the 21st century. Only amateurs kill cops. It's a fool's move."

"Got a name for me?"

Silence.

"You know a lot of people, Joey. Give me a name."

Silence again, but he didn't hang up.

"Is Conrad North stupid enough?" I said. "Stupid enough to kill a cop?"

"That your short list?"

"That's my only list."

"Your list is long enough," Joey said, and hung up.

Well, that certainly narrowed the field of suspects.

All right, back to business. I left the car, and five minutes later was met in the bank building lobby by a man in his twenties, well dressed, holding a clipboard.

"Mr. Russo," he said. "I'm Roger Kaplan, Ms. Geary's assistant. Please follow me."

We took the elevator up and Kaplan escorted me into Patricia Geary's office.

She came around her desk as Kaplan closed the door behind me. We shook hands.

"Thank you for coming down," she said. "I'm not sure what you can do here you couldn't do from Petoskey. But I'm glad you're here."

"That's why I came down. We'll figure something out. I hoped it might ease your fear some, if I was here."

We sat down and Geary reprised what she'd told me on the phone, which wasn't much. She gestured nervously as she talked, but she seemed less frantic than earlier.

"Have you heard from the police since we talked?"

Geary shook her head. "Not a word. Do you think they'll want to talk to me?"

"I'm sure of it. They'll look at the case file. When they find out you were prominent in the Roland Crosley murder, yes, they'll call."

"What do you mean 'prominent'? I don't understand." Her voice tightened as she asked the question.

"They'll review the Crosley file, which means your name comes up. You found him that morning. Detective Diaz made Annie North part of the Crosley investigation, remember. So your name comes up again."

She paused for a moment. "Do you think the death of Detective Diaz and Roland are tied together?"

"Yes. That's another reason they'll come to see you. Are you okay with that?"

"Do I have any choice?"

"Well, not much. I suppose you could get a lawyer and refuse to talk, but I wouldn't recommend it. They'll turn over every rock to catch a cop killer."

"Could they find Roland's killer, too? At the same time, I mean."

"Can't be sure, but Crosley's murder was a Diaz case, too."

"I want to do what I can to catch Roland's killer. I'm not fond of the police, you know that, but if talking to them helps that's okay by me."

"I'm not sure you can be a help to them or not, but I hope so."

Geary hesitated, then said, "I have a bigger problem right now." Tears appeared at the corners of her eyes. She opened a desk drawer and pulled out a tissue.

"Sorry," she said.

"No apology is needed," I said. "You're entitled. This is scary stuff."

"Do you get scared, Mr. Russo?"

I smiled. "All the time."

"But you don't … pardon me if I say it, but you don't seem like you'd rattle that easily."

"They're not the same thing, not to me. I've been scared before, and it'll happen again, but I have a job to do. The job's dangerous sometimes." I could almost hear AJ laughing.

"Do you get used to being scared?"

I shook my head. "No, but I've learned how to manage it."

"I'm not used to it, Mr. Russo. Guns, people being killed, none of it." Tears slowly ran down her cheeks. She dabbed her face with the tissue.

"I'm scared to go home. I live by myself, just can't do it."

"Do you have someone you could call? To stay with for a few days?"

A glimmer of a smile. "I think I'm one step ahead of you." She picked up a cell. "The phone I called you on?"

"That's not yours?"

She shook her head. "Makayla's." Geary gestured with her thumb, hitchhiker style. "The office next door. I can stay with her. We already talked about it. She has a roomy condo a short walk from here."

Geary wrote on a notepad and tore off a sheet for me.

"Makayla's address and phone."

"Thanks." I put the paper in my pocket. "Maybe you're handling the fear better than you think."

"I hadn't thought about it like that. Of course, I have nothing to compare it to," she said, and laughed nervously.

"Let me see what I can find out from the police. I'll stay in touch."

We said good-bye, and I made my way to the lobby.

The air was crisp and clear. Days like this were why I liked the late fall in northern Michigan. I waited for the traffic to clear and jaywalked across Front Street to the parking ramp. I found my 335 and beeped the locks.

"Hold it right there," a deep voice said.

I turned around in time to see two men coming at me, one with a gun in his right hand, a badge in his left.

"I said stop. Do it."

I recognized the detectives from the station house. Charlie Woods, with the gun, and Jake Bercovicz.

"I'm carrying," I said loud enough.

"Hands in the air, now," Woods said as Bercovicz drew his pistol.

I did. Probably not a good time to argue. Be time for that later.

"Assume the position," Woods said.

I turned and leaned against the car.

One of them kicked my feet out, hard, forcing me farther away from the side of the car.

"Left hip," I said.

A hand pulled back my jacket and took the .38.

"His phone, too," Woods said, and Bercovicz found it in my jacket pocket.

"You want to tell me what this is about?" I said.

"Shut up." Woods again. "Turn around, slow."

I turned around and looked at both men. They weren't happy.

"How 'bout this guy, Jake, wants to know what this about."

"Simple question," I said.

Woods holstered his gun and took two steps towards me: only the extra pounds around his middle kept his face inches away from mine.

Bercovicz, a few steps to my left, kept his gun leveled at me.

"A cop killer, asshole."

"You talking about Diaz?" I said.

"That's Detective Diaz to you."

This was deteriorating fast.

"You think I had something to do with Diaz?"

Woods moved backward, but not far. "You were the last one to see him alive, asshole."

"The fuck you talking about?" I said. "I haven't seen him in days."

Woods shook his head. "We say different." He smiled. Not a good sign. He was playing with me.

I looked over at Bercovicz. "You want in on this?" I said. "You got anything to say?"

Bercovicz slowly lifted his gun, the barrel pushing against the skin in front of my left ear. He smirked. That was not a good sign either.

"What're we going to do with this guy, Charlie?"

"We'll take him in."

"You're arresting me?" I said. "What's the charge?"

Woods edged away from me, took three steps toward the back of my car and kicked the taillight until it cracked, scattering red plastic shards on the tarmac.

"Broken taillight, resisting an officer," he said.

"You can't be serious," I said. "That won't stick and you know it."

"It'll stick as long as we need it to," Bercovicz said.

"Turn around," Woods said, "wrists behind your back."

39

They dropped me in the back seat of their black sedan. Woods sat next to me, Bercovicz drove. He went over to Boardman, then took Woodmere for the short ride to the station.

"Pull around back, Jake, we'll go in that way."

Bercovicz turned into a lot filled with civilian cars, near the flat, uninteresting building that housed the offices of the City Police and the County Sheriff.

Bercovicz stopped the sedan next to a small door at the end of the building. Woods climbed out first, walked around and opened my door.

"Out," he said.

I slid out of the seat as best I could. Woods took hold of my arm.

"I'll wait for you in the small room, Jake," Woods said, and Bercovicz drove away.

We went through a steel door into a long, empty corridor with a wall of windows on one side, a lineup of doors on the other.

"Second door," Woods said.

I walked in first. The windowless room was only slightly larger than a walk-in closet. The walls were painted some institutional color, light green maybe, or gray. Two gray steel chairs sat on opposite sides of a dull, metal table.

Woods removed the cuffs and pointed to a chair. "Sit down."

"You really think this bullshit charge will stick?" I said.

"Sit down and shut up."

"Give me my phone, I want to make a call," I said, but Woods ignored me and left the room without a word.

I took a deep breath and exhaled slowly. This wasn't an interrogation room. There was no mirror for someone else to watch. No, this room was for waiting. And that's what I did.

I put my coat on the back of the chair and tried to avoid looking at my watch. It wasn't going to speed things up. I walked several laps around the tiny room because, well, there wasn't much else to do. I'd finished several tours of the room when the door opened and Woods returned with Bercovicz.

"Sit down," Woods said.

"I'd rather stand."

Woods glared at me. "This is how it's going to go, asshole. I tell you to do something, you do it. Or I'll make you do it. Now sit down."

I sat down.

"I want to call my lawyer."

Woods ignored me.

"Who's your client?"

"You know I'm not going to tell you that."

"Why did Detective Diaz open an old missing person's case?"

"I have a right to a lawyer, Detective."

"Who's your client?"

I shook my head.

It went on like that. They yelled at me occasionally and threatened one thing or another in between questions they shouldn't have asked. But they didn't try any rough stuff. When I figured that out, it was easier to deflect their questions or play dumb. But my patience was running thin, not that there was much I could do about that.

Their questions wandered all over the place, about people I'd never heard of, about cases that were older than Annie North's. I was giving serious thought to getting out of my chair and trying to leave the room when the door opened.

We all looked. In walked a woman in a navy two-piece business suit. She was five-six, about 115 pounds with an oval face and wide-set green eyes. Her shoulder-length auburn hair was brushed behind her ears.

"Detectives," she said.

They obviously recognized her, and Woods did not ask another inane question.

The woman stood for a moment, looked at me then back at her colleagues. She pointed to the door. "Outside," she said to them.

When the trio turned to leave, I said, "I want to call a lawyer."

"So call," she said.

"He took my phone," I said, pointing at Woods.

The woman's shoulders sagged just a bit, but I caught it.

"Give him the phone, Detective."

Woods pulled my phone out and tossed it as if he were skipping stones on the beach at Clinch Park. It bounced twice on the table and nosedived to the floor.

I glared at him, then retrieved the phone. The screen was cracked and nothing happened when I pushed the home button.

"I'll send you the bill," I said, dropping the dead phone on the table.

The woman reached into her pocket and handed me her phone. "Make your call," she said, and ushered the detectives out of the room.

When the door closed, I called Sandy at the office.

"Are you all right? Are you at the cop station?" Sandy said.

"I'm fine," I said. "I need you to ... how'd you know I was at the cop station?"

"It figured. Patricia Geary called, said the cops were giving you a hard time. 'Pushing you around,' were her exact words."

I heard raised voices, especially the woman's voice, coming from the other side of the door. Couldn't make out what they were saying, but it was not a lighthearted moment.

"How'd Geary find out?"

"Somebody that works for her saw you in the parking ramp."

"I bet it was her assistant."

"Could be," Sandy said. "Anyway, I got on the phone and called Marty Fleener. He said he'd take care of it."

I looked up when the woman came back into the room.

"Got to go, Sandy," I said. "I'll call later."

I clicked off the phone and handed it back. "Thanks."

"Michael Russo," she said, and slipped the phone into a jacket pocket. "I'm Erica Todd." We shook hands.

I tilted my head. "The name sounds familiar, but ..."

"I'm an Assistant District Attorney for Grand Traverse County," she said. "I used to work for Don Hendricks."

I knocked on the tabletop. "*That's* where I heard your name. Don reached out to you about a case."

Todd shrugged. She started to say something, but we heard two raps on the door and it opened. Martin Fleener came in.

"Erica, how are you?" he said.

"Good to see you, Marty. It's been a long time."

"Yes, it has."

"How's Don getting along?"

It was as if I weren't in the room.

"Same old Don. He'll never change."

"Good man and a better mentor," she said. "I wouldn't be a prosecutor today without him."

Fleener looked my way. "I see you're still chasing the bad guys, Erica."

"Apparently your friend, here, gave the detectives a hard time."

"That's one version of the story," I said, "but not the accurate version."

Fleener laughed. "You're a car thief," he said. "We should believe your version of the story? Erica, did you know this man stole his girlfriend's car?"

She shook her head. "Guess I missed the memo."

"I'll save the details for another time," Fleener said. "We could grab a beer, catch up."

We heard someone else rap on the door. An officer leaned in and handed Todd my holstered gun.

"Here," she said, handing it to me.

"Thanks," I said. "Mind if I ask a question?"

"I don't mind if he asks," Fleener said. "How about you, Erica?"

"Me either," she said. "What's the question?"

"Can I leave now?"

"Yes, Mr. Russo, you can leave. One condition, however."

"And that is?" I said.

"Forget today. Forget the detectives."

"Lets them off pretty easily, if you ask me."

Todd shook her head. "I'll take care of it," she said. "We have a good chief running things and a good mayor who pays attention. I'll take care of it inside. Just forget it."

I nodded. "Deal."

"What about auto theft?" Fleener said, grinning.

"Send me the bill for your new phone," Todd said.

"Thanks," I said. "Tell me where the impound lot is. I have to get my car."

"I didn't hear anything about a car," Todd said. "Hold on. I'll call them." She called. No car.

"Last time I saw it was the parking ramp downtown."

Fleener reached out and shook hands with Todd. "We good, Erica?"

"We're good," she said.

"Come on, Philip Marlowe," Fleener said, "I'll drive."

We left the room.

"Don't forget that beer, Marty," Todd said as she walked away down the hall.

The sun was up in the sky as high as we could expect this late in the fall. The morning chill had turned itself into a pleasant afternoon.

We found Fleener's sedan. He drove slowly out of the lot.

"You know where you're going?" I said.

"Relax. I know the parking ramp."

"Why did you come all the way down here? You could have made a phone call."

"You know, Russo, you have to be more careful."

"Careful about what?"

"Hassling cops," he said, "any cops, not just these guys."

Fleener went left on Front Street, then turned into the ramp.

"Second floor," I said.

"I know what you're going to say, it doesn't matter."

"They gave me a rough time, Marty, not the other way around."

"I'm sure they did, Russo, but I know you. You give as good as you get. Sometimes, just drop it and start over."

"How's that supposed to help?"

"You're a smart man. Think about the big picture."

"My car's at the end of this row," I said, and indeed it was.

"Jesus, Russo," Fleener said. "What happened?"

"I don't fucking believe it," I said as I climbed out of Fleener's sedan.

When I left my BMW, it sported a shattered taillight. I walked around the car. The other taillight was cracked, as were both headlights. The door panels were kicked in: the windshield was covered with a huge spider web of cracks. All four tires sat on their rims and the hood was smashed flat.

Fleener stood next to me. "Sorry, man, I really am," he said. "Cars are your thing. This is bullshit."

"Borrow your phone?" I said.

I called the local dealer and made arrangements for them to pick it up. I'd never prove this anything but what it appeared to be, a random act of vandalism.

"How about a ride home?" I said, and put the key under the floor mat.

Fleener nodded. We returned to his sedan and made our way out of town.

Along the Kalkaska road, just past the casino, I said, "Marty, you never answered my question."

"Which one?"

"Why'd you drive down here in the first place? I mean, you could have called ADA Todd."

"I did call her," he said, "told her to find you as fast as she could. You'd just get yourself into more trouble."

"Nice of you to worry about me, Marty," I said, somewhat facetiously.

"Don't flatter yourself, Russo. It's the case against Conrad I'm worried about."

Fleener slowed for the stoplight at U.S. 131 in Kalkaska and turned north for Petoskey.

"Look, Russo, you got a burr up your ass about this case, about Conrad North. AJ sees it, I see it, but I'm not sure you do. You have no perspective. You're laser-focused on nailing Conrad."

"And you're not?"

"Of course I am, but not the same way you are."

"Not a clear distinction, if you ask me."

"I have the larger picture in mind. I want to nail Conrad as badly as you do, but it has to be a good arrest, one that sticks. I want the son-of-a-bitch in jail this time."

Fleener slowed for traffic through Mancelona, then picked up speed, heading toward Boyne Falls.

"Is that clear enough for you?" Fleener said.

"You think I'm going to fuck up your case, is that it?"

"Not intentionally, no." He paused. "You'll be careful with Conrad himself, but the other people involved ..."

"Like the cops in Traverse City?"

Fleener nodded. "We don't need to piss off every person tied to this case. A cop, a witness, an ADA. I want all of them on our side until this is over."

Traffic picked up noticeably the closer we came to Petoskey.

"Where do you want me to drop you? Home? The office?"

I looked at my watch. "The office."

Fleener turned on Lake Street and stopped in front of my building.

"You're in the middle of the street, Marty."

"I'm a cop," he said.

I opened the door.

"Think about what I said, Russo."

40

"I'm not in that much of a hurry, boss," Sandy said. She was about to leave work early when I showed up. "Tell me."

After I finished with the details, Sandy said, "I feel bad for Patricia Geary, she must be scared to death. I'm glad she has someone to stay with."

Sandy took out a yellow pad. "Give me her contact information."

Sandy made notes.

"Are you going to rent a car while you decide what to do about yours?"

"I'll probably use AJ's."

"Her SUV?"

I nodded.

"You can't do that, boss," she said, "it won't work, for her or you. I'll rent a car. Don't argue."

"Perish the thought," I said. "I'm going to call AJ."

I wheeled my desk chair around and put my feet on the window ledge. The contrast between the nearly leafless trees across the bay in Harbor Point and the dark blue water signaled our change of seasons. Fall was about to end even if the calendar didn't catch up until December.

I tapped AJ's number as Sandy walked back in and handed me a sticky note.

"You can pick up the car before you go home," she said.

"Thanks," I said as AJ came on the line.

After a brief reprise about Traverse City, AJ said, "We ought to talk, Michael, but I can't meet you right now. I have to cover the Planning Commission meeting."

She explained why she had to be a metro reporter this evening.

"You could do your civic duty," she said, "and come with me to the meeting."

"Is that my only option?"

"Yep."

"You'll take me to pick up the rental car?"

"After the meeting," she said, and clicked off.

Sandy smiled. "You do Michael Russo Investigations proud. Being a responsible citizen, doing your patriotic duty and all."

"You're being sarcastic."

"It's nice of you to notice."

"Uh-huh. I'm leaving now," I said. "See you in the morning."

I took my coat, went downstairs for the short walk up Lake Street to the County Building. Few cars were on the streets, fewer people on the sidewalk. I went inside and made my way to the council chambers.

AJ waved when she saw me come through the door. I walked over and slid into the chair next to her. Two chairs down sat Lenny Stern, reporter's notebook in hand.

"Hi," I said to AJ, discretely squeezing her hand. She squeezed back. "Lenny, how are you tonight?"

"Evening, Russo," Stern said.

I looked around. Commission members chatted with each other (some standing, some sitting) at the front of the room.

"Mind if I ask, I'm just curious by nature, you understand, why this meeting merits an editor and northern Michigan's best reporter?"

"Do you think he's mocking us, Lenny?" AJ said.

"Russo?" Stern said. "Perish the thought."

"You guys should take your show on the road," I said. "But I'm still curious."

AJ spoke first. "There's a new planned development on the agenda. Nobody left in the office to cover. I volunteered."

"What about him?" I said with a nod at Stern, whose usual beat was crime and corruption.

Neither journalist responded. I thought for a minute, then looked at Stern.

"You're not really covering the meeting, are you?" No response. He didn't even look at me.

"You're on assignment. You're investigating someone, aren't you?"

"You'll be very happy Lenny's here," AJ said.

"Why's that?" I said.

"We can sit outside and Lenny will call me when I have to pay attention. Let's go."

AJ left her bag and notebook on the chair. We found an empty bench in the hallway near the door and sat down.

AJ took my hand. "Are you all right? I was worried about you."

"Yeah, I'm fine."

"Then what happened in Traverse City?"

"What do you mean?" I said. "Nothing happened."

AJ turned her head and moved close enough to my ear that I could feel her breath.

"Don't start with me, Michael. Two people are dead. Your client's scared she's next. You get your ass busted by the cops. Your car's a wreck And you have the balls to tell me nothing's happened? I'm tired of it, Michael."

She turned her face away from mine.

I started to say something, but AJ interrupted. "Level with me, Michael, right now."

The hallway was empty except for AJ and me on the bench. The meeting had obviously begun. The quiet was deafening.

"I don't know what happened, AJ. I can't …"

"Bullshit," she said, her hand slicing the air like a cleaver. "Just bullshit."

"AJ, I told you what happened in Traverse. That's not what I'm talking about."

"What then?" Her voice was still edgy and angry.

"It's all spinning out of control."

"You think?"

"AJ …"

"It's been out of control from the start, Michael. Ever since Patricia Geary hired you."

"I know," I said. "Two people are dead."

"It's always bad when people die," she said, "but I'm talking about you. It's you who's out of control. You're fixated on Conrad North, everything else be damned. I told you that. Do you even remember I told you that?"

I sat for a moment, only a moment.

"I remember," I said. "Funny thing is …"

"This isn't funny."

I put my hand on her arm.

"Martin Fleener," I said.

"What about him?"

I began slowly, "Funny thing is … Marty told me the same thing on the way back from Traverse. He said I'd lost perspective because I was so focused on nailing Conrad."

"Did he now."

I nodded. "That's why he went to Traverse in the first place. He could have gotten me away from the cops with a phone call. He was worried that I'd piss off too many people, people that he might need to make his case stick."

We sat quietly for a while. The tension was ebbing just a bit.

"Have I lost perspective, AJ?"

She nodded.

"Out of control."

She nodded again. "It's not like you, Michael. But this man has taken all your head space."

"Marty thinks the same thing."

"He's concerned, too, Michael. Doesn't that tell you something?"

"I just don't see it that way, I guess."

"Well, I don't know what to tell you then."

"One thing bothers me," I said.

"What's that?"

"I trust the two of you …"

"That should tell you a lot."

"… to be straight with me."

"What about Henri?" AJ said, "has he weighed in on this?"

I shook my head just as Lenny Stern opened the door. "AJ," he said, "it's time."

She looked at her watch.

"Before you go," I said, "Bobbie Fairhaven, Henri's army buddy?"

"Did you talk to her?"

I nodded. "She already has a job."

"So she can't guard either one of us."

"No."

AJ stiffened at the news. She knew Henri couldn't cover both of us. I chose not to make it worse by telling her about Bobbie Fairhaven's new job.

"Do you have an alternate plan?"

"Not yet," I said. "Let me talk to Henri. We'll come up with something."

"I'm sure you will," she said, looking at her watch. "Remember, you can't keep yourself safe if you're worried about me."

"Yeah."

"Same problem if you don't get your head straightened around. You put us both at risk. Think about that, will you please?"

I nodded. "Yes."

AJ leaned in and kissed me on the cheek. "Have to go."

41

"**Y**ou can stop laughing any time now," I said to Sandy. We sat in her office waiting for Henri.

"Sorry, boss," Sandy said, trying to stifle her amusement. "How did I know the rental car would be a brown Chevy?" She laughed again. She just couldn't help herself.

"AJ was already on her way home by the time I had the keys and found the car." I shrugged. "Too late by then."

"You'll survive," Sandy said. "I have every confidence." She didn't quite laugh.

"I sure hope that's Henri," Sandy said when we heard footsteps.

And it was.

"Morning Sandy, Michael," Henri said, hanging his coat on the hall tree.

"Would you like to hear about Michael's rental car?" Sandy said.

Henri looked as if he'd missed the memo and did not respond.

"I'll take that as a 'no,'" Sandy said. "Then would the two of you mind leaving me alone? I have work to do."

"Our pleasure," I said, and pointed to my office.

I brought Henri up to date about Geary's fears, getting busted by the Traverse City cops, Fleener to the rescue and my battered BMW.

I pushed my chair back and put my feet on the corner of the desk.

"We have to cover AJ and you," Henri said.

"AJ comes first," I said.

"No argument from me, but as long as Nils Lundberg and Jimmy Erwin work for Conrad, you and AJ are both in danger."

"Uh-huh."

"But all roads eventually lead to you."

"Because of Conrad," I said. "As long as I'm ..."

Henri nodded. "Any ideas?"

"One," I said. "Bobbie Fairhaven."

Henri frowned. "We've been down that road."

"Think she'd do you a favor if it didn't mess her up with Joey?"

Henri shrugged. "Don't know. We could ask."

"Make the call," I said. "Let's find out."

Henri took out his phone and tapped a few times.

"How's Sergeant Lampone this morning?" he said. "Same to you. Listen, Bobbie, I'm with Michael Russo. He wants to talk. I'll put us on speaker."

Henri tapped again and put the phone on the desk.

"Morning, Bobbie," I said.

"Russo," Bobbie said. "It's your dime."

Woman didn't beat around the bush. I leaned forward on the desk.

"Think I've figured out a way to protect AJ Lester."

"This involve me?"

"Yes," I said, "but not like before. You willing to listen?"

"Okay."

"You've been hired to protect Nils Lundberg — where he goes, you go. That right?"

"Something like that, yeah," Bobbie said.

I could tell from the look on Henri's face he had no idea where I was going with this.

"So, if Lundberg went after AJ, you'd be with him. Right?"

"Right."

"How about this," I said. "If Lundberg goes after AJ, send a text. To me, to Henri. That's all. Just a warning AJ's in danger."

I looked up. Henri smiled and held one thumb up.

Bobbie was silent.

"Bobbie," Henri said. "You could do that. Just a text."

"Give me a second, Henri."

He didn't.

"A favor, Bobbie. For me. What do you say?"

"No. No favors, not for you, not Russo."

Henri and I looked at each other, not sure what to say next.

"I'll do it for the woman," Bobbie said. "I'll do it for AJ Lester."

The line went dead.

"Son-of-a-bitch," Henri said.

"Yeah. I thought we'd lost her."

"Me too," Henri said. "Where the hell'd you dream that up?"

I shrugged. "Don't know. It just … I don't know."

"Well, you can stop worrying about AJ."

"Unless we get a text," I said.

Henri nodded. "You'll tell AJ?"

"As soon as I can, yeah," I said.

I sat back and put my hands up, behind my head.

"Something else on my mind. I think you'll like it."

"Let me hear it first."

"Thinking about putting more pressure on Conrad. See if we can force him to do something stupid."

"The man doesn't make many mistakes," Henri said. "Want me to rough him up a bit?"

"Not quite what I had in mind."

I stood and went to the door. "Sandy?" When she looked over I said, "Come on in." She did, taking her familiar seat by the desk.

"What's up?" she said. "You two plotting again? Heaven help me."

"Better than that," Henri said. "Dude's planning to beat up Conrad."

"Hot dog. Now you're talking."

I waited.

"If you two are all done?" They were quiet, but looked as if they'd been caught stealing cookies.

"Jessie Royce," I said.

"Isn't that Conrad's girlfriend?"

I nodded. "She lives in Harbor Springs."

"I thought she hung with Conrad in Traverse?" Sandy said.

"She does," Henri said, "but she kept her place in Harbor."

"You have any notes on her life in Harbor? Where she hangs out, friends, stuff like that?" I said.

"Hold on a minute," Henri said. He got up, went to his jacket, and returned with a reporter's notebook.

Henri flipped through the pages. "No BFF that I spotted. No one place for dinner when she eats out, which isn't often. But the woman is a regular at Turkey's for breakfast. Usually nine-thirty or ten."

"So she isn't always with Conrad?" I said.

Henri shook his head and consulted the notes.

"Most weeks, she's two days in Harbor. Usually Tuesday and Wednesday."

"What're you cooking up, boss?" Sandy said.

"Thinking about having a talk with Jessie Royce," I said.

"What're you going to tell her?" Sandy said.

I shrugged. "Haven't a clue. But she's bound to tell Conrad." I smiled.

"Who won't like it one bit," Henri said.

"I hope not."

"Okay, but you don't want to scare her," Sandy said. "Take it easy or she won't talk to you."

"You think Turkey's might work? You know, a public place. She can always scream like hell if she's afraid."

Sandy tipped her chair back against the wall. "That'd be better than showing up at her doorstep. It's still no guarantee."

"Worth a try," Henri said.

The office phone rang. Sandy stood up. "Don't you be scaring her. Find another way or forget it. That's my take on it," she said on her way out of the office.

"She's right. Better we scare Conrad," Henri said. "More fun, too."

I leaned forward on the desk. "Henri, one other thing. Something AJ told me. And Marty Fleener."

Henri nodded.

"Want to ask you, see what you think."

"Ask away," he said.

I explained their mutually held theory that I'd lost my perspective when it came to Conrad North.

"A question first," Henri said. "Do you think you're screwing up the case?"

I shrugged. "No, but I have lots of respect for both of them."

Henri's demeanor shifted. He spoke in that quiet, contemplative way he didn't very often reveal.

"I respect AJ as much as you do. Fleener, too, if I'm forced to admit it."

"You think they're on to something?"

He nodded. "I do. You have lost perspective. You're not thinking clearly on all things Conrad. I've known that for a while now."

"You never said a word."

"Didn't plan to either."

"It wasn't worth talking about?"

"I'm different from AJ," Henri said. "I don't want you to screw up the case any more than they do. But I accept that's the way you're functioning right now. I'll keep bumping you in the right direction, if I can. It's who you are, Russo. I'll work with it."

"All right. I need to think about that."

"Good idea," Henri said as Sandy returned to her favorite chair.

"Nothing urgent," she said. "Now, how about Jessie Royce? You still want to try Turkey's?"

"Best public place I can think of on short notice," I said.

"What if she doesn't show?"

I smiled. "I'll have breakfast and call it even."

42

I waited until almost ten-thirty on Tuesday. Jessie Royce didn't show. I enjoyed eggs and toast, revved up on too much coffee and watched the sky spit a rain-snow mix on downtown Harbor Springs. On Wednesday morning, I ran a couple of errands on the way and didn't walk through the front door until after nine-thirty.

Turkey's Café and Pizzeria. That name has always seemed to sell it short to me. Breakfast, lunch, and (during much of the year) dinner. And a full bar. The building has transformed itself since the 1880s when it was built. A print shop, a retail store, an ice cream parlor, then — in the late 1970s — it became Turkey's. It's a narrow space with old-fashioned wood booths along one wall, the bar on the opposite side and tile on the floor. A ragged cardboard jack-o-lantern hung at an awkward angle behind the bar.

Jessie Royce sat in a booth with her back to the door. I slipped out of my jacket and walked over. I put on my nice face, non-threatening and smiling.

"Ms. Royce?" I said in a soft voice. "Excuse me."

She looked up from her French toast.

I put down my business card and introduced myself. She glanced at the card, then back at me. Her expression was more quizzical than fearful, and she didn't yell for the management. So far, so good.

"I'd like to talk to you for a minute. Is it all right if I sit down?"

She nodded and I quickly slid into the booth.

The waitress came over, and I ordered black coffee.

"We met once, in Traverse City," I said, "but we weren't introduced."

"Uh-huh."

The waitress put down a mug of coffee. I drank some and remembered what Sandy said about taking it easy.

"I'm working on a case, and I think you might be able to help."

"Are you really a private detective?" she said, looking at my card again.

"Yes."

"I don't see how I'd be able to help you."

"If I could ask a few questions? If you can help my case, fine. If not, that's okay. I'll be on my way before you finish breakfast."

"All right," she said.

"I'm looking into the disappearance of a Traverse City woman. Her name's Annora, called Annie."

Here goes nothing … "Annie North."

"On the street that day. You were with another man. You talked to Conrad while he stayed across the street."

I nodded. "Yes."

Royce finished a bite of French toast. I couldn't tell how comfortable she was, but she still hadn't yelled for help.

"Who's the missing woman again?"

"Annie, Annie North. She was Conrad North's first wife."

Royce almost dropped her fork, but she put it on the plate instead. Her mouth was open. She looked over at the waitress who stood a safe distance away, near the back of the room.

"First wife?"

I wanted to clarify, but I didn't speak soon enough.

"Conrad's wife is dead, Mr. Russo. Camille was jogging and had a heart attack. That was two years ago."

My head was spinning. She caught me with that one. Conrad had only one wife? Camille had a heart attack? That was the yarn he'd concocted? I had to tell her.

I moved my coffee out of the way and leaned in, just a little.

"Ms. Royce, Annie was Conrad's first wife. They were married briefly a long time ago. She's the mother of Wolfgang and Wilhelm."

"I don't see how, I mean … Camille … why are you telling me this?"

"Because I need help. I'm trying to find Annie. She's been missing for a long time."

Jessie's French toast was getting cold.

"Why … why do you think I know anything?"

"I hope that you will know something, anything. I ask questions. That's how I learn stuff."

"Camille … I don't understand … Camille?"

"Camille was Conrad's second wife," I said.

"Is she dead?" It sounded as if she was no longer certain.

I nodded.

"A heart attack?" No certainty in her voice now.

I shook my head.

She stared at me and waited.

I really didn't want to do this. But here we were.

"Camille was murdered, Ms. Royce. One night in Mackinaw City. No one was ever charged."

"I don't … I can't … you'd better go, Mr. Russo."

"I wanted …"

"Now," she said. "Go away now. Please."

Enough was enough. I didn't need to pile it on. I dropped a five on the table, took my coat and left Turkey's Café and Pizzeria.

I sat behind the wheel of the brown Chevy and stared out the windshield. There were days when I didn't like my job. This was one of those days.

A few moments later, Royce exited the restaurant. She walked quickly across the street, head down, arms held tightly at her sides as if she was walking into a stiff headwind. I was afraid the headwind was Conrad North.

I left town and took the Harbor Petoskey Road back to Petoskey. The wipers swung rhythmically, back and forth, moving the water aside. I tried to push Jessie Royce out of my head. It didn't work.

I parked behind the office and went upstairs.

"I don't know what I expected," I said to Sandy after I described what had just taken place. "Still trying to sort it out."

We sat in the front office. The rain-snow mix had turned into sleet that the wind blew against the tall windows, tap-tap-tap, tap-tap-tap.

"Well, for one thing," Sandy said, "I wouldn't have expected the man to lie."

"Seriously? You wouldn't expect Conrad to lie? After all we know about him?"

"Not about this, boss. This is very personal stuff, stuff you share when it's a new relationship. That's how you get to know each other. Didn't he think it would come out sooner or later? That his ex was murdered? Like when she met his friends. They knew about Camille."

"What about skipping over Annie?" I said. "If you think the heart attack story is bad, how bad is it to delete your first wife from the conversation?"

"That sucks," she said. "The whole thing … everything Conrad North has touched, sucks. You know that?"

Sandy pushed her chair back and stood up. She walked over to the windows and stared down on Lake Street.

"He must have thought it wasn't possible to tell a new girlfriend about that. Can you imagine, 'Oh, darling, I almost forgot to tell you that both of my ex-wives died of unnatural causes.'" Sandy shook her head. "It sounds like a bad novel."

"You're doing a disservice to bad novels," I said, "not to mention giving the man too much credit. He doesn't deserve it."

Sandy went back to her desk and sat down. "The man deserves nothing, not one damn thing, as far as I'm concerned. I guess I imagined how a decent guy would deal with that."

"A decent guy? With two dead wives?"

"Good point," Sandy said. "You're certain the news took Jessie Royce by surprise?"

"No doubt about it," I said. "She was stunned. You could see it in her face. Hearing about Annie caught her, but Camille? Her demeanor changed. Her behavior. It was … it was that obvious."

"Look ahead a bit," Sandy said. "Do you think she'll tell Conrad? About you showing up. Will she ask him about what you told her?"

"Would you be able to stuff it that far down? If you were her?"

Sandy shook her head. "Any normal, healthy woman would have to be shaken to the core by news like that. I wouldn't think it possible to stuff it. But I'm not her either."

"Be happy you're not in her place."

"So, how long will it take," Sandy said, "before she tells Conrad? A day, a month, or an hour?"

"I can't answer that," I said. "I have no idea. One thing I do know, however, is Conrad will react quickly. He won't be able to stop himself."

"Because you've tossed a monkey wrench into his life?"

I nodded. "Big time. It's one thing to stop the man on the street and threaten to put him in jail. He can push that off as macho bluster. But what I said to Jessie Royce? That messes up the version of reality he foisted off on her."

"Not to mention you messed with his girlfriend."

"Yes, I did."

"How will he come at you?"

I shrugged.

"Will he do it alone?"

"That's not his pattern of behavior."

"So he'll come himself, but not alone?"

"Conrad's done that before."

"Or just send somebody," Sandy said. "Like Lundberg."

"Yeah," I said, "or Jimmy Erwin."

"Or both."

"If he sends Lundberg and Erwin together," I said, "it'll be to kill somebody."

"Not somebody, boss. You."

43

As it turned out we did not have to wait long at all. Two days later, I was on the phone with a prospective client. Sandy was at her desk.

I heard the hall door open, but paid no attention. Out of the corner of my eye I caught someone moving very quickly past my door. Almost a blur. A few moments later, the blur was back.

Nils Lundberg.

He held a 9mm automatic in his right hand, Sandy by the arm with his left. He motioned for me to put down the phone. I never took my eyes off Lundberg as I ended the call.

Lundberg was slightly taller than six feet, trim with an angular face and close-cut blonde hair spiked with gel. Up close he looked like his younger brother, except for the obvious. Nils was alive, Gunnar was dead.

"Stand up," Lundberg said. "Do it slow."

I did.

"You carrying?" Lundberg said as he put the 9mm to Sandy's head. She didn't so much as wince.

I shook my head. "No."

"Out here," he said, pulling the pistol away from Sandy as he backed up. I came around the desk and stepped into the outer office.

Over by the hall door stood Jimmy Erwin, leaning against the door jamb, arms folded across his chest. His oversized puffer coat was unzipped. His face was without expression as he watched the three of us.

Lundberg let go of Sandy's arm. "Sit," he said, "by the windows." He watched Sandy cross the room and take a chair. He looked back at me.

"You, too," he said, pointing at the windows with his gun.

I did as I was told. When I went by Lundberg he stuck out his foot, and I tumbled to the floor, face down. He kicked me in the ribs, hard.

"Roll over," he said.

I looked up at him. I was in a decidedly bad position.

"Motherfucker. I told you to sit down," he said, laughing. A bad sign.

He kicked me in the ribs again, hitting the right side this time. He bent over, stretched out his arm and put the barrel of the 9mm on my chin. His face was drawn tight, his eyes narrow.

"I ought to put you down right now like you did my brother, you son-of-a-bitch. My brother." He pressed the gun harder against my chin.

"Nils." It was Jimmy Erwin. "Easy, Nils. You'll have your chance."

"Shut up, Erwin. Not your brother we're talking about."

Erwin came off the door jamb and moved a step closer to Lundberg. If Lundberg forgot about me, even for a second … but he didn't.

"We have a job to do, Nils," Erwin said in a softer voice. He was trying to calm Lundberg down, keep the situation from exploding out of control.

It wasn't much, but I seized on a small window of hope that Sandy and I would survive the next few minutes.

"We have a job to do," Erwin said again.

"I don't need to be reminded," Lundberg said, still angry. He took the gun away from my face and straightened up. But his arm was still extended, the 9mm still pointed at me.

Erwin moved to Lundberg's side. "Nils."

After a final moment's hesitation, Lundberg put his arm down. "Get off the floor, asshole. Do it now."

I sat up carefully then got to my feet, never taking my eyes off either man. My ribs hurt, and I was unsteady, but I did my best to cover it. I had no intention of adding to the advantage they held over us.

"The chair," Lundberg said.

I sat next to Sandy.

Lundberg and Erwin moved slowly toward us. Erwin put himself far enough to Lundberg's side that I couldn't watch both men without moving my head. These guys were good. They knew what they were doing. They'd done it before.

Nils Lundberg took one last step. "We're delivering a message from Mr. North."

"No shit." It was Sandy. "Do we look that stupid?"

Lundberg looked as surprised as I probably did. He didn't know what to say.

"No, ma'am." It was Erwin, again. "We want to be clear, that's all. Who sent us, why we're here."

Lundberg shifted his feet for a moment, but he recovered.

"Mr. North wants a meet." He gestured at me with his gun hand. "You. Just you and Mr. North. He says it's time for a truce."

I nodded.

"You come alone," Lundberg said. "Understand?"

I nodded again.

"Say it, asshole. Do you understand?"

"I understand."

"Today. Six o'clock."

"Where?"

"Beech near Woodland," Lundberg said. "Know it?"

"I'll find it."

"Last house on the left. Number's 4016. Got it?"

"I got it," I said. "You done?"

"We're done when I say we're done, asshole, not before. Understand?"

"I understand."

"Mr. North wanted me to tell you one more thing." He glared at me.

I waited, but Lundberg was going to draw this part out.

"I want to make sure you understand this, Russo."

"Okay."

"You and the broad, here."

We waited.

"Want to make sure you understand what's going to happen, you don't pay attention."

Dragging it out, he was.

"Both of you."

He obviously liked this part.

"Stay away from Jessica Royce."

Finally, there it was.

"Mr. North says don't talk to her, don't follow her, don't go to her house. Understand?"

"I understand." No point arguing.

Lundberg grinned hard, like a bad impression of Jimmy Cagney doing Cody Jarrett in *White Heat*. Except I'd bet Lundberg never heard of the actor or the movie. "*Made it, Ma. Top of the world.*"

"Here's the good part," Lundberg said. "You go anywhere near Miss Royce, I kill you. Any way I want. Two shots, three, to the head. Never know what hit you."

Lundberg took a step closer. He leaned in, but the gun stayed at his side.

"No. No head shots. It'll be slow. Knees first, or a shoulder. Real slow. You're going to feel the pain. Understand?"

I was silent.

"Do you understand?" Lundberg was almost yelling. "Say it."

"I understand," I said.

Lundberg didn't move. He glared at me, but the gun remained at his side.

"Nils," Erwin said. "We're done here. Let's go."

But Lundberg was frozen in place.

"Nils. Now. Let's go."

Lundberg straightened, turned on his heels and went for the door. Without a word, Erwin followed him. They were on the steps. We heard the outside door when it slammed shut.

I took in a lot of air and let it out slowly. I turned toward Sandy.

"'Do we look that stupid?' Is that what you said? 'Do we look that stupid?' The hell were you thinking? They had guns pointed at us!"

Sandy shrugged. "It just sort of came out. What can I say?"

I shook my head. "You know where Henri is?"

"At Margo's, I think."

I went to my desk, picked up my iPhone and tapped his number. Voicemail answered.

"Call me now."

44

"Looks like we might have snow pretty soon," Sandy said. She leaned on the window frame and looked out over Lake Street. "Sky's heavy. Snow's on the way for sure."

Sandy turned away from the window.

"What happens now?"

"Before six o'clock, you mean?"

She nodded.

I sat in one of the client chairs by the window.

"We'll work something out."

"Henri and you."

"Yep."

The phone buzzed, and I looked at the screen. "Henri. You're on speaker in the office."

"What's up?" he said.

"Where are you?"

"Margo's," he said. "Why? What happened?"

"We had visitors."

"Tell me."

I did.

"Henri?" It was Sandy. "Do you think Conrad really wants a truce, you know, to settle things?"

"Doubt it," he said. "Russo?"

"Not his style," I said.

"Why meet then?" Sandy said.

I was quiet: Henri, too. It only took Sandy a second.

"Oh, shit," she said.

"Got that right," Henri said.

"Do you think it's a set-up, too?" Sandy said to me.

"Until a better alternative comes along," I said.

"I'll go take a look at the house," Henri said, and clicked off.

Sandy was back at the window, staring out.

"Sandy?"

She didn't react. "Sandy?"

"What?" she said, but did not turn around.

"You okay?"

"No."

"We've been here before. Remember the Lake Street shooters?"

"Of course I remember them. It's just that … this just hit me over the head. Give me a minute to absorb it, will you?"

"Take what time you need," I said, tapping AJ's number.

"Michael?" AJ said quietly. "Are you okay?"

"Yeah."

"I wondered. Usually you don't call."

"You busy?"

"I just stepped out of a meeting. Why?"

"I need to talk."

"Tough day here," she said. "Can it wait 'till tonight?"

"No. Sorry. Okay if I walk over?"

"Well …"

"I wouldn't ask."

"Okay. Wait in my office if I'm not there."

"On my way." I hung up. "Sandy …"

"I heard," she said. "You're going to the paper now?"

"Yeah," I said. "Back soon."

I took my coat and stuffed the phone in a pocket. Outside, I tugged at the collar to keep the wind away. The sky was myriad shades of gray, all dark: the bite of snowfall was in the air.

It didn't take me long to walk to the *Post Dispatch* offices on State Street.

I climbed the front steps and entered the building. Typical of houses of the period, a living room was left of the central hallway, a parlor to the right. A receptionist at a counter in the old parlor greeted people who came through the door.

I waved a hello to Vickie Stauton behind the counter and went upstairs. Only three rooms occupied the second floor. The office of the publisher, Maury Weston; AJ's office (directly across from his); and a conference room at the back. Both offices were empty, and the door to the conference room was closed.

I took a chair in AJ's office and picked up a hard copy of the *Post Dispatch*.

I'd just gotten to the sports page when I heard AJ coming down the short hallway.

"Hello, darling," she said as she sat behind her desk. "What's so urgent it can't wait?"

I began with my morning visitors and ended with Henri's unscheduled reconnaissance of the house.

AJ listened patiently, which isn't always the case, then said, "If it's so obviously a set-up, why take the bait?"

"First, I want to see what Henri discovers about the house."

"Will that change anything?"

"Not sure," I said.

"Do you think Conrad assumes you'll show up?"

I nodded.

"Because his goons delivered the message?"

"Yeah, and because it would never occur to him that I'd say no."

"I take it you have no plan worked out, you and Henri?"

I shook my head. "Hard to do until we know more about the house."

"You aren't thinking about going alone, are you?"

"No."

"Because Conrad won't show alone, will he?"

"Not a chance of that happening."

"I don't like this, you know."

"Me, either."

"Then why do it, Michael, why ..." AJ's shoulders sagged, just a bit. "Never mind."

"What?"

"I know why."

"You sure?"

AJ smiled. "I know you too well, Michael."

45

Henri sifted through a few pages in his notebook. We sat in the front office with Sandy. It was after three o'clock.

"The house is at the end of the street."

"A dead end?" I said.

He nodded.

"Other houses?" I said.

"Nothing close. Vacant lots across the street. Nearest house is three lots away. Not sure anyone lives there. Backyard isn't much of a yard. The ground climbs up pretty quick, a big hill for around here."

"What's up above?"

"A road."

I shook my head. "Not good."

"Why not?" Sandy said.

"Put a couple of gunmen up there with rifles, we could be dead in a hurry."

"About the road," Henri said. "It's a busy street. More traffic than you'd think. No good places to hide on top of the hill."

"Too easy to be spotted?"

"Yes," Henri said.

"Any good lines of fire?"

"Not really, too wide open."

"How about the house?"

"Small wood frame, two floors, porch in front, center door with windows on either side, middle window upstairs."

"He could put guns in the upstairs window."

"Too obvious. First place we'd look."

"Back of the house?"

"A door in, two windows main floor, one window up."

"Garage?"

"No garage. Big hill in the backyard, remember?"

I nodded.

We sat quietly for a minute.

"What do you think?" I said.

"We'll walk right up the middle of the goddamn street," Henri said.

"But, Michael, Conrad will know you didn't come alone if you do that," Sandy said.

"Doesn't matter, Sandy," Henri said. "No way Conrad walks out on the front porch by himself."

"Nils Lundberg?" Sandy said.

I nodded. "And Jimmy Erwin."

"Look, you guys, I have to ask a question," Sandy said.

"Go ahead," I said.

"Did it occur to you to say no? You, too, Henri. Did it?"

I was quiet. Henri was quiet.

"You're not answering me. Not going to the house isn't an option, is it?"

"No, Sandy," I said. "It's not an option."

"Then what about a public place? A restaurant, Pennsylvania Park? Just you and Conrad."

"It won't work," I said.

"Lundberg wouldn't shoot you in the middle of the goddamn park," Sandy said.

"That's not it."

"No?"

"Conrad knows I'll keep after him, Sandy."

"And sooner or later," Henri said, "Lundberg makes a run at Michael. It's better to end it."

"People will die."

"This needs to end," I said.

Sandy came out from behind her desk and went to the sideboard. She took out one glass and the bottle of Oban. She carefully poured two fingers and returned to her chair.

"Little early isn't it?" I said.

"Not today."

46

"It's time," Henri said, "you ready?"

We sat in my office. Sandy had long since kicked off her shoes, put her feet on the desk. I'd been paging through a *Runner's World*, although I hadn't paid much attention. Street lights around town were waiting to snap to life, but plenty of daylight was left.

"Ready," I said, and rechecked my Luger 9mm before putting it away.

"Been a long time since I've seen the Luger in your shoulder holster," Henri said.

"Not that long," I said. "Still have the .38," I pulled back my jacket, "if it makes you feel better."

Henri picked up a green nylon duffel bag. "Let's go."

We went down the stairs to the parking lot and found Henri's SUV. A few flakes of snow danced to the ground: the wind had picked up off the bay. Henri drove straight up Howard and crossed Mitchell.

"You going right to Beech Street?"

"Close," Henri said. "We'll park on Rush Street, walk down from there."

"A little obvious, don't you think?"

"The whole fucking thing's obvious, Russo. House on a dead-end street, no other houses close enough to see."

"Until they hear the gunfire."

"As long as we're still alive, I won't care."

"Somebody'll call the cops," I said.

"We should be able to cut across the empty yards and be away by the time the cops arrive."

Henri turned off Howard and moved slowly down Rush Street. He switched off the automatic running lights.

"The house is down that way," he said, pointing through the windshield. Near the end of the second block, Henri pulled over and cut the motor.

"We'll walk from here," he said.

Henri unzipped the duffel bag, pulled out a shotgun and extra shells.

"That's not your old 12 gauge."

"A Benelli M-4 Tactical."

"That so."

Henri looked over at me. "Semi-auto, built for the Marine Corps. Designed to kill people."

He tossed the bag in the back seat and we climbed out of the SUV, closing the doors as quietly as we could.

"This way," Henri said.

We went to the end of the block and over to Beech Street. We'd gone about fifty feet. "Down there," Henri said, pointing. "At the end of the road, the only house."

We walked right down the middle of the road. I put the Luger in my right hand and held it straight down. Henri carried the Benelli close against his leg.

There wasn't much to see. A broken-up tarmac road, empty lots of bare dirt and scraggly weeds. And no place to hide. Conrad knew that, and he knew we were coming.

"Don't have to be much of a private eye to guess this is a set-up," I said.

"Uh-huh," Henri said, and stopped. "There."

The house was on our left. A narrow clapboard house with a small front porch three steps off the ground. The place needed somebody to fix it up: paint on the siding, grass in the yard.

"Not the first-class accommodations I'd pick for Conrad North," I said.

"What did you expect, Russo, a jack-o-lantern for Halloween? Keep your eyes on the windows. If they're going to hit us, it won't be from the porch."

We left the street and slowly strode up what a long time ago had been a front walk to the house.

We stopped when the front door opened. Two men came out on the porch, Nils Lundberg first, followed by Jimmy Erwin. Lundberg carried a .45 in his right hand, pointed down. Erwin held a TEC-9 automatic pistol close to his side, his jacket unzipped.

They eased their way down the porch steps. When they got to the yard, they fanned out and stood about twenty feet apart, Lundberg opposite me, Erwin a few steps across from Henri. These guys were experienced professionals. They knew what they were doing, not that I needed a reminder.

"Where is he?" I said.

Neither man answered.

We waited.

"North," I said. "Conrad North."

After a few long moments, Conrad came through the door, followed by Wolfgang and Wilhelm. Didn't expect the brothers. North was dressed elegantly enough for a cocktail party. Maybe he had plans for later this evening.

Conrad and the brothers moved down the steps but remained several feet away from, and behind, Lundberg and Erwin, forming a loose triangle.

No one spoke.

Finally, Henri broke the silence. "Jimmy Erwin."

"LaCroix," Erwin said.

"Let's talk," Henri said. "You and me."

"Now? Here?"

Henri nodded. Erwin thought for a moment, then nodded.

"Half-way," Henri said, and took a step forward.

Erwin took two steps.

"Where're you going?" Conrad said, loud and sharp.

"Shut up." It was Lundberg.

Henri and Erwin moved until they were only a few feet apart. Conrad stared at the two men, but Lundberg never took his eyes off me.

Daylight continued to drain from the sky, but there was enough to see every move, every change in tactics.

"How you doing, Jimmy?" Henri said.

Erwin nodded. "What do you want?"

"I want you to drop the TEC-9 and walk away."

"Why would I do that?"

"You got no dog in this hunt, Jimmy."

"Got a job to do," Erwin said, "just like you."

"Not like me, Jimmy," Henri said.

"How's that?"

"I'll walk away from this alive."

"Guess we'll see about that."

"I got respect for you, Jimmy Erwin. I respect who you are."

Erwin moved his head ever so slightly, but I caught it. He was surprised.

"You'll be the first one I shoot, Jimmy."

"Better take Lundberg first," Erwin said, "he's better than me."

"Not that much better, Jimmy. He's not smart like you. He's fixed on killing Russo. He doesn't see the big picture, like you. Gives Russo the edge. He kills Lundberg, I kill you. All we'll have left are those three. This is bad, Jimmy. It's as good as done. Walk away."

"That's enough." It was Conrad again. "Time for us to talk, Russo. You and me. Time to call a halt to the bullshit."

"Two dead wives aren't bullshit," I said. "You're going over for them."

"Let's work out a deal, you and me."

"Nothing to work out. The cops get you and the boys. That's all."

"You forget about them?" Conrad said, gesturing at Lundberg and Erwin. "Five of us, two of you."

"Don't add up that way," I said. "We know what we're doing."

"And we don't?" Lundberg said. There was an angry edge to his voice.

"Won't matter to you, Lundberg," I said, "you'll be dead."

"That so?"

I nodded. "I kill you, Henri takes Jimmy, and I'm back where I started." I pointed at Conrad. "With them."

"Kill him," Conrad said, almost shouting at Lundberg. "Kill 'em both."

But nobody moved. Not them, not us.

It was as if sprinters were crouched on the line waiting for the starter's gun.

"LaCroix." It was Jimmy Erwin. He slowly bent over and let the TEC-9 fall to the ground. He zipped up the puffer jacket and walked past Henri toward the street.

Henri nodded.

"Get back here, you son-of-a-bitch! You took my money."

But Erwin kept walking. Lundberg watched him go down the street. He was recalculating his odds of living out the night. They didn't look good.

"Kill them, Lundberg," Conrad said. "That's what I paid you for."

Lights. Bright lights. Spotlights. On the left. On the right. Two large floodlights snapped on from the top of the hill behind the house, bathing the entire property with light.

Cars moved up the street fast and came to a halt. More lights, bars of blue-and-red lights.

"Freeze," a voice said over a speaker. "Everybody, freeze."

Tension held the air, waiting for a wrong move.

"Put your weapons on the ground," the voice said, "and move two steps back. Do it now."

We all did as we were told.

Car doors opened and men with guns emerged from behind them.

A man came around the side of the house and walked right into the middle of our early evening gathering.

It was Martin Fleener.

"There'll be no killing tonight, gentlemen."

A small troop of State Police came out of the shadows: from our left, from our right and from the cars. All of them had long guns, automatic weapons and vests. State Police Tactical would be my guess.

"Don't be the first one to do something stupid," Fleener said.

He waved his arm, and two officers moved in front of Lundberg.

"Open your jacket, nice and easy," Fleener said.

Lundberg did as he was told, and one of the officers took a handgun off his right side.

"Russo, you and LaCroix. Extra guns on the ground." But Fleener never looked our way. "No arguments. I'm not in the mood."

Conrad took a step forward and smiled. "It's lucky for us that you arrived when you did," he said. "We were being threatened by ..."

"Shut up," Fleener said. "Open your coats. The three of you. Officer, check them."

The officer looked for weapons but found none.

I noticed that another officer stood off to the side with Jimmy Erwin, his hands cuffed behind his back.

"Conrad North," Fleener said. "I have a warrant for your arrest."

"You do not," Conrad said with a touch of arrogance, but without much force. "What's the charge?"

"Assault and battery," Fleener said.

"What?" Conrad said. "I want a lawyer."

"You'll get one," Fleener said. "Officers, read these gentlemen their rights and escort them to a car."

"Why us?" Wilhelm said. "We didn't do anything."

Conrad threw him a look. "Shut up."

The officers marched the three men to a patrol SUV and drove off.

Fleener walked up to Nils Lundberg. "That leaves you, Mr. Lundberg." Fleener stared at him for a moment, then continued, "We don't like killers around here. You're under arrest."

Lundberg smiled. "Didn't kill nobody," he said.

"Maybe not, but you violated the terms of your probation." Now it was Fleener who smiled. "You left Allegheny County too soon, Mr. Lundberg."

Another officer marched Lundberg to a waiting SUV and the big lights on the hill snapped off. Now, only a few floodlights on the patrol cars lit the front yard.

The sky had grown darker in the last several minutes, and the rain-snow mix had gone away. A few people had wandered up the street to see what was going on.

But the excitement was over.

Fleener turned to Henri and me. He bent down and took the Benelli M-4. He emptied the shells.

"Nice gun," Fleener said. "Kill a lot of people with one of these."

Henri didn't respond, although I knew what he was thinking.

"You don't have a license for this one," Fleener said. "We'll add it to our collection." He called an officer over and handed him the Benelli.

"Pick up your guns," Fleener said to us.

We did.

"How the hell did you get here, Marty?" I asked.

"We've had too many people killed around here, Russo. I don't like it. Hendricks doesn't like it. Doesn't matter if it's you two," he waved his arm, "or them. No more killing."

"But how'd you know?"

"About your little soiree?"

"Yeah."

"A tip," he said, "an anonymous tip. Can you believe it?"

"I believe the tip," I said. "But you don't follow tips, especially anonymous ones."

Fleener turned up the collar on his coat and shoved his hands into the pockets. Only two patrol cars remained. The officers leaned against one of them, waiting for Fleener to wrap it up.

"Too many details," he said.

"Not sure what you mean," I said.

"Caller knew specifics, not just where and when, but knew names."

"Names?"

Fleener nodded. "Had all your names, every single one of you."

"Is that right?"

"Caller wanted to convince us the tip was good."

"Obviously worked," Henri said. "Question?"

Fleener nodded.

"Conrad North. Assault and battery?"

Fleener smiled, almost grinned. "Some days, the hits just keep coming."

"Is it legit?"

"Oh, yeah," Fleener said. "As legitimate as they come."

"Who'd he beat up?" I said.

"Woman friend," Fleener said. "Can't remember the name."

"Royce?" I said. "Jessica Royce?"

"That's her. She walked into the Sheriff's Office. He worked her over pretty good. Black eyes, broken nose. Easy warrant."

"How did you find out?"

"Someone recognized North's name and called me."

"Will it stick?" I said.

"Royce's solid. She won't change her mind."

"You going to put Conrad in the room?"

"We'll have a nice talk. I have lots of questions I think I'll ask him."

"You caught a break, Marty. It might work, for Annie, Camille."

"Yeah, it just might," he said. Fleener looked over at the officers, then back at us.

"You got a car someplace?"

"Down the street," I said. "Can we go now?"

Fleener was quiet for a moment. "This one would have been bad. Lot of dead people, we didn't have that tip. You two would have been right in the middle of it. Go on, leave."

"Jimmy Erwin, Captain?" Henri said.

"What about him?"

"He's a smart kid."

"He's a hired killer."

"Gave him a chance to walk away, he took it," Henri said. "Changed the odds in our favor."

"He did Roland Crosley in Traverse City. Pretty sure they can make the case."

Fleener started to walk away, then stopped. He stared back at Henri.

"You calculated the odds in a gunfight? Is that what you just said? A gunfight on city streets." Fleener shook his head. "Go on, get out of here."

Fleener motioned to the officers and they drove off. Fleener followed in his car.

The people I'd spotted earlier had slowly disappeared into the scenery as we walked back up the street. Didn't blame them. They didn't want to be that close to violence.

47

"It's been two days," AJ said. We sat in the kitchen with coffee. The sun was bright and warm through the side window. There'd be no snow today.

I'd spent the last two nights with AJ at her house. I actually took a day off and did chores around the yard, raked leaves, trimmed bushes. It was a nice break from the malevolent world of Conrad North and Nils Lundberg.

"You think we would've heard more by now," AJ said.

"Lundberg's gone, we know that."

"Pittsburgh's welcome to him. He'll do more time behind bars, don't you think?"

"Fled probation. Allegheny County will throw him back in jail and tack something on. Fleener said he'd see to it."

AJ smiled and put her hand on mine. "That's good to hear."

My phone buzzed on the table. The screen read: "call now."

"It's Sandy."

I tapped the office number and put it on speaker.

"Morning, boss," Sandy said.

"Good morning, Sandy," AJ said.

"Morning to you, too, AJ. Is he around?"

"Right here, Sandy."

"Your days off are over."

"That so?"

"Hendricks' office called. He wants you there at ten."

"Anything else?"

"Just that. Bye."

I looked at my watch. "Have time to go home and clean up if I get a move on."

"Want a ride?"

"Rather walk."

"Then go," AJ said. "Let me know."

I kissed her, grabbed my coat and left by the kitchen door. The temperature had yet to make it above freezing, but with no wind, the sun still felt warm.

I took a quick shower, put on the usual outfit and added a navy blazer. I walked at a good pace up Bay Street to the County Building and wound my way through the hallways to Don Hendricks' office.

"They're in the conference room, Mr. Russo," Sherry Merkel said. Merkel was executive assistant and gatekeeper for the prosecutor.

I went two doors down the hall, knocked on the door and let myself in.

The rectangular room featured a long wall of windows, fresher institutional green paint than most of the offices, and a dark wood table that fit the room. Around the table sat Martin Fleener, ADA Erica Todd, and Don Hendricks at the head of the table. I took the chair next to Fleener.

"Good morning," I said.

"You know Erica Todd, I believe," Hendricks said.

I nodded. "We've met, yes."

Neither Todd nor Fleener offered any smart remarks about our first encounter in Traverse City.

"I wanted you all here this morning," Hendricks said. "First, to bring Todd and Russo up to date on the concurrent investigations surrounding the deaths of Roland Crosley and Vincente Diaz in Traverse City, Camille Sanderson North in Mackinaw City and, last, the disappearance of Annora North of Traverse City."

That caught my attention. Didn't expect Camille or Annie to be part of the discussion. Not yet, anyway.

"We also have to make a decision on another matter."

He'd lost me. "We" didn't usually include me.

"Russo, just so you know," Hendricks said, "Erica Todd came up here to question Conrad and his sons specifically about events in Grand Traverse County. Marty talked to them as well, of course."

"You talked to the brothers, too?" I said.

"Uh-huh," Fleener said.

"How'd that go?" I said, somewhat facetiously.

Hendricks cut in, "More about the brothers in a minute." He loosened his already-loose tie.

"Now, about Lundberg and Erwin. Lundberg's back in the Allegheny County jail. The court has yet to decide on additional punishment for leaving the jurisdiction."

"Question?" I said. Hendricks nodded.

"Did you talk to Lundberg, Ms. Todd?"

"No," she said, and nodded toward Hendricks.

"Allegheny County wanted him back. Fast." Hendricks shrugged. "I didn't want to fight about it. He's not going anywhere."

"What about Jimmy Erwin?" I said.

"Oh, I talked to him," Todd said. "For a few minutes until his lawyer arrived and told him to shut up."

"A teenage gunman has a lawyer?"

"He does," Hendricks said, "if he works for the Baldini crime family."

Second surprise this morning.

"Jimmy Erwin works for Joey DeMio? Since when?"

"I have no idea," Hendricks said. "Before Erica even walked into the room, Otto Blatnic shows up."

"Lawyer for Carmine and Joey?"

"That's the man."

"Expensive representation for a gunslinger."

"That's what we thought," Hendricks said. "By the time Blatnic was finished with his big city routine, Erwin walked away, free as a bird."

Todd jumped in. "It was my fault," she said. "I didn't expect a criminal defense attorney. Won't happen again."

"You'll stay on him?" I said.

She nodded. "We'll take another run at him."

"Which brings us back to the North family," Hendricks said. "You want this Marty?"

Fleener nodded. "Truth is I didn't get any further with Conrad than Erica did with Erwin. The man's lawyer told him to shut up, too."

"Was it Oliver Kilgore?"

"Yep. All the way from the Windy City just to fuck with us."

"Thought you said it was a solid case?"

"Kilgore wasn't pushing back on the assault charge," Fleener said. "In fact, he let Conrad answer some questions about Jessica Royce I wouldn't have let him touch if he were my client."

"Why?"

"Kilgore tossed us a bone. We could play with the assault charge as much as we wanted, but he wouldn't let Conrad near anything related to Annie or Camille. Not a thing."

"Is he out on bail?"

"Guest of Emmet County," Hendricks said. "Kilgore screamed bloody murder, but the court suddenly had a backlog. We bought ourselves another day or two."

"You said there was more about the brothers?"

"This is where it gets interesting," Hendricks said. "Erica."

Todd leaned forward and opened a manila folder. "I talked to Wilhelm first. Had about twenty minutes before he asked for a lawyer."

"He have one?" I said.

"Man who works with Kilgore, named," she looked at the folder, "Harry Schell. So Schell joins the party, but that first twenty minutes alone with Wilhelm, well ... we might have gotten lucky."

"I'll jump in for a minute," Hendricks said. "We talked to Jessica Royce after she filed assault charges against Conrad. Wanted to make sure she wouldn't withdraw the complaint if we used it to get him into a room with Fleener. The woman was angry, threw us anything she thought would nail the son-of-a-bitch. A lot of it was worthless nonsense. But one piece … Royce overheard the brothers in a drunken argument one night. Wilhelm rambled on about the cottage, something like, 'You did it. You helped the old man.' And Wolfgang shot back, 'You were in the backyard, too. We both did it.' That's a decent recap from my notes."

"Did what?" I said.

"That was my first question to Wilhelm," Todd said. "I pitched it quick before he could settle down."

"And?"

"He froze. Went pale as the proverbial ghost. Tongue-tied, couldn't think of anything to say. I asked him again a different way. Same result."

"What did you make of that?" I said.

"Something happened at the Mackinac Island cottage."

I looked around the room.

"You're not serious," I said. "You're not seriously suggesting they buried a body in the backyard, are you?"

Silence.

"Hell, if I said that, Don, you'd kick me out of here for being a wise-ass."

"Yes, I would," Hendricks said.

"Then why are you pretending this is serious?" I said. "Don't you have a better theory?"

"Trust me, Russo," Fleener said, "we thought it was nuts, too, that we'd seen too many movies. But the last piece. For the hell of it, I took the official date of Annie North's disappearance, added about thirty days and talked to the freight company that services the island."

"You guys are starting to sound too much like me," I said.

"Less than a week after Annie's disappearance, Conrad shipped two well-worn steamer trunks, remember those, the big ones, like in old movies? He shipped the trunks from St. Ignace to his cottage."

"I don't fucking believe this," I said. "I really don't."

I paused. "What now?"

"That's where you come in," Hendricks said.

48

The *Huron* sounded a mournful horn as it passed the breakwater on its first trip of the day. The expected dusting of snow overnight never happened. The sky to the east was a deep blue as the sun climbed above the horizon. It would be a pleasant November day on Mackinac Island.

The exodus of workers to the lower deck had begun. I told Marty Fleener to let them all go.

"Your men will be waiting for us, right?" Fleener said.

"Everything's all set. Just got a text from the contractor."

"You pulled it all together fast, Russo. Got to hand it to you. You knew the people to call because you know the island." Fleener shook his head. "Contractors, vehicle permits, power company. We never would've … we couldn't have done it that fast."

"It's nice to be needed."

"Yeah, but just a couple hours of phone calls?"

"More like half of yesterday," I said. "It helped that I name-dropped the State Police."

The *Huron* tied up and put down the ramp. We left the ferry and made our way up the dock. We spotted a uniformed officer coming our way.

"Captain Fleener," he said, tugging at the collar of his heavy coat.

"Morning, Sergeant," Fleener said, and introduced me to Sergeant Cliff Ginther from the St. Ignace post.

"Everything all set?" Fleener said.

"Yes, sir. We rode over, Officers Piper and Brooks and me, on the freight boat with the contractors. They're waiting at the house."

We headed down Main Street toward Marquette Park.

"Okay if we stop for coffee at Doud's?" Ginther said.

"Good idea," Fleener said.

With hot coffee in our hands, we made our way up the stairs at the back of the park. From the top of the East Bluff, all seemed well with world. The bright sun put a red glow on the cottages, the trees, the rooftops of the buildings below us at street level.

"There's something you don't see very often on Mackinac Island," Fleener said.

In front of the Sanderson cottage, at the edge of the road, was a flatbed truck. Three men, dressed in thick Carhartt coats and insulated pants, sat on the empty bed facing the harbor, drinking coffee. Off to the side were two uniformed officers.

"Good morning, gentlemen," Fleener said. Introductions were made all around. "What do we do first?"

"First I recheck my survey," said Dick Allison, the crew foreman. "I ran a preliminary check yesterday. Right after I talked with you, Mr. Russo."

"What are you checking?" Fleener said.

"This whole island's rock," Allison said. He turned and pointed to the backyard about thirty feet off the road, up a shallow hill.

"The flags mark all the utilities. The wood steaks, up top there, those are mine. Best places to dig."

"More than one place?"

Allison nodded. "Three," he said. "Only three."

"Let's get to it," Fleener said.

"Ah, Captain?" Allison said. "Lot of rumors? About what we're digging for? You don't mind my asking."

"Less than twenty-four hours?" Fleener said. "Rumor spread that fast?"

"Around here? Yes, sir."

"What're the rumors saying?" I said.

Allison looked at Fleener, kicked at the dust on the tarmac, and said, "Somebody's buried up there. Anything to it?"

"It's a possibility," Fleener said.

"Ah, man," said one of the workers seated on the truck. "No shit?"

Allison took that as his signal. "All right," he said. "Let's go to work."

The men hopped off the truck, picked up shovels and walked up the gentle slope to the backyard off to the rear and side of the Sanderson cottage. A dingy yellow front-end loader sat nearby in the yard.

Sergeant Ginther and the officers followed the workmen.

Fleener and I went to a low fieldstone wall that separated the Sanderson property from the yard next door. The sun had moved far enough along in the sky to wash the wall in bright, warm light. We sat on the wall and waited.

"Still think this is a crazy idea?" Fleener said.

"Maybe crazy is a little harsh," I said. "More like desperate."

"What does that mean?" There was a sharpness to Fleener's voice.

"Take it easy, Marty. Didn't mean anything by it. It's just … well, you said I was too fixated on nailing Conrad. Isn't that what this is?"

Fleener looked up the hill. Allison moved slowly around the yard with a small device in his hand. We heard it beep every so often.

"Desperate?" Fleener shook his head. "Don't think so, Russo. We've got the steamer trunks coming to the house. The freight schedule. Hell, it evens explains the actors hired to buy the cottage. We have Wilhelm's comments. That's all worth following up, don't you think?"

"The comments of a fortyish boy of a man, comments relayed by a woman out to punish her abusive lover. The trunks? Convenient coincidences you grabbed to fit a shaky theory."

"Aren't you the guy who doesn't believe in coincidences?"

"Yeah, but this pushes my theory too far, Marty."

We heard Allison pointing and saying something to his men. They began slicing away the top layer of grass, then digging out the dirt.

"All right, so it's a long shot," Fleener said. "A long shot seems pretty good to me right now."

I started to say something, but he cut me off.

"Don't say it, Russo. Maybe I'm just as screwed up as you are."

"Don't need two of us, Marty," I said, "but we're sitting on a stone wall watching those guys dig up the backyard …"

The front-end loader fired up and lumbered its way over to the spot where the grass had been removed. We watched silently as two large scoops of dirt were put to one side. Then it backed away and was switched off. The men returned with their shovels. It was slow going.

After a while, foreman Allison walked down.

"Nothing, Captain. Went down almost four feet, hit more rock." He shrugged.

"You moving to the next spot?" Fleener said.

Allison nodded. "Get started before lunch, sure."

"You hungry, Russo?"

"No."

"Me either."

After the grass was skimmed off the second site, the men returned to the flatbed and broke for lunch.

"Let's take a walk," Fleener said. And so we did, to the far east end of the bluff. Beautiful Victorian cottages and a few less ornate, smaller houses all faced the water, looking down on the channel between Mackinac and Round Islands.

"Ever thought about living here, Russo?"

"I did one winter a long time ago. Before I bought the Lake Street building. Haven't thought about it since. I like where I am."

We wandered back to the Sanderson cottage and sat on the wall, still waiting. It went on like that. Slow, laborious work, only using the loader where there was no danger of hitting a sewer pipe or electric line.

Fleener and I sat quietly most of the time, enjoying the view of the Straits and the harbor, glancing occasionally at the activity up the hill.

Dick Allison strolled down to us. It was the early afternoon.

"This will be our last try," he said. "All the rest is rock. No room to bury a squirrel, let alone … I mean … sorry."

"Forget it," Fleener said.

"That wasn't good," Allison said. "I've never done this kind of thing."

"It's all right, really," Fleener said.

With that, Allison turned around and went back up the hill.

"Feel bad for the guy," I said.

"Jesus, Russo," Fleener said, "are we so used to this, you know, bodies in the ground that it doesn't reach us anymore?"

"I can't answer that Marty. Wish I could. Maybe I don't want to think about it too much."

The workmen stepped aside, making room for the front-end loader to move more dirt.

"I started on road patrol," Fleener said, "in Ottawa County. Bad crashes, lot of blood, mangled bodies. I thought I'd never get used to it. My partner said I'd get used to it." Fleener took in air and let it out slowly. "He was right. Homicide is worse than road patrol ever was. I pay no attention to it."

"Yes, you do, Marty. You pay close attention every time. You're a professional and you're good at what you do. The job demands the attention you give it."

The loader was moved out of the way and the workmen picked up their shovels again.

"I know, I know," Fleener said. "But I run into a man like Allison. This scares the shit out of him. Some days I wish it still scared me."

"Captain Fleener." It was Sergeant Ginther.

Fleener and I got off the wall and looked up the hill.

Two of the workmen had turned away from the site. The officers watched as Allison kept digging.

When Allison stopped, the officers moved in for a closer look.

"Captain," Ginther said. "You'll want to see this."

49

It snowed overnight. Two inches. Children loved it, drivers didn't. Most people marked the event by doing nothing different at all. They went to work or school, they shopped or sat in the dentist's office.

"Did you finally talk to Patricia Geary?" Henri said. He was drinking a Blue Moon from the bottle.

We sat at a corner four-top at the Side Door Saloon: Henri, Sandy, AJ, and me. The room was a large rectangle with a few dividers and walls filled with memorabilia. It was minutes before six and the room, especially around the bar, was busy with the local after-work crowd.

"About an hour ago," I said. "Geary's been in Grand Rapids on business most of the week."

"How'd she take the news?" AJ asked.

I sipped some scotch and put down the glass. "I wish I could have told her in person."

AJ started to say something, but I put up my hand. "I know what you're going to say."

"It was the right decision, Michael," she said.

"I wanted her to hear about Annie from me, not TV, not some reporter."

"Lenny Stern will have our story online tonight thanks to you," AJ said, and tipped her glass in my direction. "The paper tomorrow. It's a good piece."

"You're welcome," I said.

"Back to Geary for a minute," Sandy said. "Was she surprised about Annie?"

"No," I said. "She was convinced from the start Annie was dead, remember?"

"What'd she say when you told her about Conrad?"

"She was happy to hear the man's in jail, but she doesn't believe he'll go down for Annie."

"What'd you tell her?" Henri said.

"I played it straight, told her this was our best chance." I shrugged. "But I didn't want her to get her hopes up for nothing."

"That's what happened before," Sandy said. "Poor woman."

Henri got up and went to the bar, exchanging his empty for a new bottle of Blue Moon. He was about to sit down when he pointed and said, "Look who's here."

We all turned toward the door.

Martin Fleener.

He stopped at the bar, dropped a few bills on the counter and grabbed a beer. Fleener wound his way through the crowd to our table. He grabbed an empty chair from the next table, stuck it between AJ and Sandy and sat down.

"Mind if I join you?" he said, smiling.

"Don't you turn into a wise-ass, too," Sandy said. "I couldn't take it."

"How'd you know we were here?" I said.

Fleener took a long pull on the beer and set the bottle quite deliberately on the table.

"I'm a cop," he said, "I know things."

"He is a wise-ass," Sandy said, lifting her glass. "Maybe I need something stronger than iced tea."

"Ms. Jefferies," Fleener said, "why are you drinking iced tea? You're not at work."

"I have a long shopping list on the way home," she said. "I can't very well walk around Meijer drunk."

"Good point," he said. He drank some beer.

"This is off the record," Fleener said. He looked around the table. We were quiet.

"I want to hear it. I'm serious, I want to hear you say it."

"Off the record," I said.

"Me, too," Sandy said, "off the record."

Henri nodded.

"Say it."

"We are off the record," Henri said.

"And now you, Ms. Lester," Fleener said. "I especially need the word from a member of the Fourth Estate."

"Agreed," AJ said. "We're off the record."

"All right, then," Fleener said, and finished his beer. He held the bottle in the air. In fewer than thirty seconds a bartender brought him a fresh one.

"What's going on, Marty?" I said.

"We got him," Fleener said.

"What do …"

"We got the son-of-a-bitch."

AJ leaned in and almost whispered, "It's Conrad North, isn't it? You got Conrad?"

Fleener nodded slowly. "By the balls."

Henri silently stared at Fleener. Sandy's mouth was open.

"How good?" I said.

"As good as it gets," Fleener said.

"Heard that before," Henri said. "I'll believe it when I see it."

"You're a real pain in the ass, you know that?" Fleener said.

"So you've told me," Henri shot back. "But I won't …"

I put my hand on Henri's arm. "What happened, Marty?"

Fleener looked around, but no one was paying us any attention.

"It'll be a couple of days before the paperwork is done." He looked at AJ, again.

"We're off the record, Marty," she said. "But can I have Lenny Stern call you? When it's out, I mean."

"Tell him to call Hendricks. Better if it comes from the prosecutor's office."

"Okay," AJ said.

"Marty?" I said.

"We had another go at the three of them. Erica Todd came back up from Traverse. She took the boys. I took Conrad. Plan was to switch off after a while." Fleener drank some beer. "Conrad's lawyer, Kilgore?"

"From Chicago?" Sandy said.

Fleener nodded. "That's him. So I get past name-rank-and-serial-number and Kilgore won't let him answer anything else. Strategy worked before, they figured it'd work again."

"But?" AJ said.

We waited.

"It was Erica. She started with Wilhelm. Figured he'd be an easier target than the brother after she rattled him the last time."

"His lawyer there?"

"Uh-huh."

"Were you watching?"

"Yep. Had to take a break from Conrad. I watched the whole thing. Didn't take long. Erica reminded Wilhelm about the backyard: jerk tried to play it tough. So Erica said, and this is a quote, 'We found Annie. We found your mother's body.'"

"Jesus," AJ said. "Hardball."

"Yes, it was," Fleener said. "He started shaking, really shaking. Then he started talking. Told his lawyer to shut up or leave. Took him less than five minutes to turn on dear old dad. He said Conrad was there the whole time, gave directions to the brothers. Couldn't stop him from talking, but nobody was trying to."

Fleener rubbed his eyes and drank some beer.

"I went back to Conrad and his lawyer. I told them Wilhelm was giving a statement, told them I'd be glad to provide a copy. So I did, gave them each a copy."

Several people at the bar broke out in song. Someone's birthday apparently. A lot of laughing, too.

"When they finished reading the statement, Kilgore asked for the room. I waited in the hallway. A few minutes later, Kilgore stuck his head out the door and wanted to see Hendricks."

"And?"

"Game, set and match. He's going away for a long time."

"For Annie?" I said.

Fleener nodded. "Yes."

"But not Camille," I said.

"Not specifically," Fleener said, "but we know he hired Lundberg's brother to kill Camille and you killed the brother. Conrad North will never hurt anyone again. Can you live with that, Russo?"

He didn't give me a chance to answer.

"We wanted to get Conrad, and we did. The brothers, too."

"Yes we did," I said.

"Good riddance," Sandy said. "Man killed two women and beat on a third."

"It's fitting," AJ said, "that it was a woman who threw the first grenade. Thank you Jessie Royce."

Sandy raised her glass of iced tea. "There is a god in heaven."

We sat quietly for a few moments. The birthday group moved from the bar to a large table on the other side of the room. The bartender put a cupcake in the middle of the table. It had one candle stuck in it.

"Marty?" I said.

"What?"

"You ever find out who called in the anonymous tip?"

"About the shootout you two cowboys had planned at the house?"

"Yeah, that tip." I let the crack go.

Fleener shook his head. "Nope."

"We still off the record, Captain?" Henri said.

"We are."

"Bobbie Fairhaven called you. She told me the next day."

"Your army buddy?"

Henri nodded. "Joey DeMio hired her to keep Russo from killing Nils Lundberg."

"Thought it was Lundberg who wanted to kill Russo?"

"Well, yeah, but …" I said.

"So your army buddy called us in to keep Lundberg alive for Joey. That what you're telling me?"

Henri nodded, again. "She was just doing her job the easiest way she could. Simple as that."

Sandy finished her iced tea. "Time to go," she said. "Meijer then home."

"Me too," Fleener said. "I'll walk out with you."

Sandy and Martin Fleener said their good-byes and left the bar.

"I'm on my way to Margo's," Henri said. "You two ready?"

AJ and I walked out to the parking lot with Henri. We stopped at his SUV.

"Sleep well tonight, AJ. You too, Michael."

AJ gave Henri a big hug and we went to AJ's SUV as Henri drove off. We climbed in, and she started the motor.

"Before we go," she said, and turned toward me.

"What?"

"Is it over, Michael?"

"We finally got Conrad, if that's what you mean."

"Well, yeah … but how are you feeling right now?"

"Good. He won't hurt anyone else, like Marty said."

She put her hand on mine.

"But what about you?"

I was quiet for a few moments.

"You're not talking about Conrad, are you?"

"Not right this second, no."

"Is this about me losing perspective again?"

"It's about how you lost it, Michael. Letting Conrad get to you that way, he became an obsession."

I picked up AJ's hand and kissed it.

"I mean, I do feel good that, you know, Henri, Fleener, all of us finally got Conrad North. It's just that … I don't know, it feels like there should be more."

"There can't be more, Michael. Conrad North was a bad man and you finally put him away. That's a lot."

AJ put the SUV in gear.

"Come on," she said, "let's go home."

ACKNOWLEGEMENTS

Most important, I thank the authors in my writing group, Marietta Hamady, Winnie Simpson, and Aaron Stander. Our discussions and their detailed critiques helped make my writing clearer and the mystery more exciting. I treasure their friendship and support and enjoy the easy camaraderie of our sessions.

Several other folks also willingly made Michael Russo's latest adventure a better read. They include Frances Barger, Shawn Cordes-Osborne, Tanya Hartman, Wesley Maurer, Jr. and the writers around the table at the Mystery Writing Workshop at the Interlochen Center for the Arts. Three of the four scenes written and critiqued at the workshop made it into this novel. That's the third time I've been able to say that, and I still think it's pretty cool.

Heather Shaw and Scott Couturier, edited the manuscript and took it apart over and over again. Plot, characters and dialog. I often got annoyed with both of them ... then revised the writing to implement their suggestions. I'm sure they're laughing as they read this. I'll try to remember that the next time they take a proverbial red pen to my writing. Thanks to Heather and Scott, I've learned new things about my characters and the situations I've created for them.

A few words about Aaron Sorkin, a man I've never met, but whose writing has helped me improve every chapter of the Michael Russo series. Sorkin has created interesting, intelligent stories featuring crisp, dense dialog coming from smart, savvy, sometimes irritating, arrogant characters. But always characters of complexity and depth ... Toby Ziegler, Amy Gardner, Neal Sampat, or Rebecca Halliday.

And just so I don't forget, I made stuff up, all of it. The characters, events, and plot twists. Just like the first four Russo adventures, I invented everything at the kitchen table with coffee, by the fireplace with a nice single malt, or on a relaxing run on the trails on Mackinac Island.

Peter Marabell grew up in Metro Detroit, spending as much time as he could street racing on Woodward Avenue in the late 1950s and visiting the Straits of Mackinac. With a Ph.D. in History and Politics, Peter spent most of his professional career at Michigan State University. He is the author of the historical monograph, *Frederick Libby and the American Peace Movement*, soon to be published by Kendall Sheepman Company. His first novel, *More Than a Body*, was published in 2013. The first of the Michael Russo mystery series, *Murder at Cherokee Point* (2014) was followed by *Murder on Lake Street* (2015), *Devils Are Here* (2016), and *Death Lease* (2018). As a freelance writer, he worked in several professional fields including health care, politics, and the arts. In 2002, Peter moved permanently to northern Michigan with his spouse and business partner, Frances Barger, to live, write, and work at their Mackinac Island business. All things considered (Peter still says), he would rather indulge in American politics, or Spartan basketball, after a satisfying five-mile run on the hills of Mackinac Island. Find out more about the author at www.petermarabell.com.

OTHER BOOKS BY PETER MARABELL

MICHAEL RUSSO MYSTERIES

Murder at Cherokee Point

Murder on Lake Street

Devils Are Here

Death Lease

also

Frederick Libby and the American Peace Movement

More Than a Body

Made in the USA
Middletown, DE
17 June 2019